A Parcel of Fortunes

A Parcel of Fortunes

Frank Ahern

Matador
9 Priory Business Park,
Wistow Road, Kibworth Beauchamp,
Leicestershire. LE8 0RX
Tel: 0116 279 2299
Email: books@troubador.co.uk
Web: www.troubador.co.uk/matador
Twitter: @matadorbooks

ISBN 978 1788038 706

British Library Cataloguing in Publication Data.
A catalogue record for this book is available from the British Library.

Printed and bound in the UK by 4edge limited
Typeset in 11 pt Minion Pro by Troubador Publishing Ltd, Leicester, UK

Matador is an imprint of Troubador Publishing Ltd

About the Author

Frank Ahern is a graduate of Trinity College, Dublin. He has spent much of his life working in the home counties and now lives in Dorset, enjoying its rich natural world.

He is currently working on his second novel, *Ghost-lines*.

For Sue

I see men's judgments are
A parcel of their fortunes, and things outward
Do draw the inward quality after them
To suffer all alike.

– Antony and Cleopatra, Act III

PART I

VISITINGS

CHAPTER 1

He rises from his desk and walks to the window, gazing out across the river. At eye level, perched on the blanched, bone-like branches of a dead Alder tree across the river, is a cormorant, its wings outstretched in a gesture of crucifixion. They are striking, these large birds sitting in this tree, spread in heraldic posture as they dry their black, sun-flecked feathers. Matthew feels spread-eagled in his own way. But with no warming sun, only a cold creeping sense that his life is slipping beyond his control.

Who was the sinister man who'd approached him that morning, delivering what might be construed as a death threat? Or might not. Matthew Agnew is not, after all, a typical target for a would-be-assassin, or even for a would-be-assassin's messenger boy. Too old and, a mere archivist, too peripheral to be swept into the unpredictable currents and eddies of political life. And too peripheral, surely, to be of any interest to the cloak-and-dagger world of hit men and their errand boys.

The window from which he has been gazing is set high in the towered corner of the main school building. It is reached by the seventy-one steps of a narrow spiral staircase. The stone stairs have been worn in their centres by decades of footsteps; generations of grimy hands have created a patina of shiny, seamy blackness on the stone handrail spiralling down the scuffed walls.

Matthew emerges from the tower by the river, the cormorant still emblazoned in the tree. He needs someone to share the burden of the morning's bombshell. If that's what it is. He needs to tell someone about the mysterious stranger. He will explain that the warning he has received is probably a response to a letter that he had sent a fortnight earlier. A letter to a former pupil of his, asking for clarification on some matters he has been researching. The trail that has led to the writing of the letter has been a trail that has twisted and turned, a trail which perhaps has more in keeping with a detective enquiry than a piece of historical research. Or perhaps neither.

*

It should have been ordinary, the tour that morning; one of the occasional tours Matthew gave of the eighteenth- and nineteenth-century parts of the main building complex. Today's group – a local history society – contained the usual suspects, pursuing what might be called their geriatric daytime distraction: it could be walking, or touring, or eating out, or visiting places of historic interest; it didn't really matter which, so long as the outings filled some hours and occupied their minds.

Their clothing and footwear were predictable, a uniform of age, you might say, with their sensible shoes and baggy anoraks. Only today, there had been one person who had seemed somewhat out of place. Younger and differently dressed. Tall and thickset – a bit of a bruiser? – he had a large, square-shaped head with a heavy jawline and, incongruously, large blue eyes. Who did he look like?

Who?…Tommy Cooper? Yes! Tommy Cooper! Wearing a cheap-looking suit and heavy, thick-soled black shoes; tie knot hung at an angle a good two inches beneath the collar of his shirt, the top button of which was undone. Tommy Cooper, comedian and magician. But his lookalike today was giving no hint of comedy and, beyond suddenly and mysteriously appearing in this group of people, no hint of magic.

The visitors are at the heart of the school campus, a large Georgian country house, built originally because of its easy reach to the London to Bath road. Matthew has talked briefly about the school and is now introducing his guests to the Grand Hall, where he is starting his tour. 'In the 1850s, shortly after the country house became a school, the buildings were improved and extended through the endowment of a rich ironmaster. His one stipulation was that a neo-Gothic dining hall be created in the style of an Oxford college refectory.' He explains that the impressive room is too small these days to serve as the school dining hall, but is regularly used for concerts, small drama productions and the occasional formal dinner. And of course as an attraction to visitors.

He invites his guests to look upwards to the striking timber roof. Sculpted stone corbels carry the arch-braced trusses; these and the purlins and wind-braces are colourfully and ornately decorated in Burgundy red, cyan and gold. 'Many people find the roof the most impressive part of this room and they take for granted what in many ways is much more interesting, the delicately worked panelling below. I suppose it's because the eye is immediately drawn towards the colour and the scale of the roof. And then to the high-set perpendicular windows…I guess that the expanse of dark wood creates a rather gloomy atmosphere.' There is some nodding of heads; one or two of the guests look on in quizzical disagreement. 'On the other hand, perhaps one should see the rather oppressive over-timbering as entirely appropriate to a Victorian creation mimicking a medieval style.' More nodding of heads. Matthew then proceeds to discuss the panels. Created by a well-known Venetian woodcarver in Italian walnut, they are Renaissance in style, finely detailed and rich in symbolism. 'No two panels replicate each other. What I want to do is concentrate simply on one or two so that you get a sense of the close detail and of what the panel is saying to us.' He points out motifs and images, glosses the classical and literary references in the carving.

Matthew enjoys giving the tours. He likes the interaction with people, the interest they show as he explores and explains the different features of the building. But today, he is somewhat hesitant in his delivery. He is uneasy. The Tommy Cooper character is striking a wrong note. He does not seem to be paying much attention; in fact, if anything can be read on his almost expressionless face, it is the sullen indifference of a bored pupil, with just a hint of mild hostility.

As the group leaves the hall for their next stop, Matthew is approached by their leader, a small man with thick glasses and a comb-over of thin white hair, who asks him about the ill-dressed stranger.

'Oh, I thought he was one of yours.'

A look of distaste appears on the man's face. 'No. No. Certainly not.'

Reluctantly, Matthew approaches the tall man. 'I'm sorry,' he says quietly, 'I gather you're not part of the history group, and I'm afraid I don't know who you are.'

'Actually, Mr Agnew, I've come to have a chat with you. But that can wait. I'm finding this, er, most, um... instructive.'

The tour comes to its conclusion where it started, in the Grand Hall, the stragglers hobbling up to thank their host before a more formal thanks is offered by the group leader.

The Tommy Cooper lookalike hangs back as the group exits and, once they have eventually filed out, Matthew asks him if he'd like to come to the Archive Room.

'No, this will do…Mr Agnew.' A leer on his face?

In the gloom of the darkly timbered hall, Matthew notices a change in the man's voice. It sounds coarser and deeper than earlier. 'I've got a simple message for you, Mr Agnew. Stop delving. Desist. You won't want Special Branch descending on you, believe me. They can be very… unpredictable. They can…magic…people away.' He smiles and gives a dismissive laugh that once again has echoes of Tommy Cooper.

'Can you tell me who you are, please, sir?'

'Goodbye, Mr Agnew.'

The man walks past his host, bumping him roughly with his shoulder, nearly knocking him off balance. And is gone.

Leaving Matthew to think, after he has regained his composure. Is he frightened? Should he be? What is the appropriate response to this unsettling visitation?

'Desist'. Quaint choice of word. And a vague injunction, too. Desist from what? The message is cryptic. 'Stop delving'. Delving, digging. Ah yes, a little clearer. But isn't that what archivists do? Delve? Explore? Research? And isn't Matthew now a school archivist of three years standing, with a successful career of English teaching behind him? No longer delving into rich literary soils, delving instead into the lumpy and sometimes stony substratum of records, documents, ephemera and the suchlike?

No calling card from the caller. No provenance, as the archivist might say. No provenance, no name. Name not necessary. Matthew knows who it is. 'I hereby christen this man…Tommy Cooper.' Tommy Cooper, interloper, ill-dressed thug. Thug? Ah, perhaps he should be frightened.

He hazards a guess, as an archivist should, at the provenance of Tommy Cooper. And decides that he should at least be apprehensive.

*

In the evening Matthew and his wife, Rachel, were due to attend a drinks party at the Headmaster's. His house was a short walk from the Agnews' two-hundred-year-old cottage, which lay just beyond the school grounds on the edge of the arboretum.

The door of the house was open, so they walked in and were greeted in the cavernous hallway by Rosie Dogget, the Headmaster's wife. A warm, generous-spirited woman with a knack of making people feel that they mattered to her and that she was there for them if needed. Someone to turn to if Tommy Cooper proved too troublesome?

She pointed them towards the large drawing room. As they entered, Matthew could hear chatter about the Scottish Independence Referendum, taking place today, 18 September 2014: early indications were of a very high turnout. What would the morning bring? News that the United Kingdom had been fractured? A difficult result to call.

Immediately, on the far side, Matthew spotted Henry Baines, the Deputy Head. A portly man with a round puffy face, he had a large, angry-looking wart on the side of his neck just above the collar. On most days the collar would chafe the wart to the point of bleeding, leaving speckles or streaks of blood on his shirt. Henry had been

Head of History for many years before his elevation. There had been some vitality to the younger man. Now, as he approached retirement, the energy had drained; despite his position as Deputy Head, he was deemed largely irrelevant both to staff and to pupils.

Although younger than Matthew, Henry was a relic from the past. Unmarried and without any other focus for his affections, he had invested his entire emotional being in the school. If in recent years it had, on occasions, tested his steadfastness – admitting girls to the school was a big betrayal in his view – the school remained all that he had; and so he in turn remained loyal, supporting a headmaster whose vision was to the future, while his was to a traditional past long gone. They needed each other. Henry craved the position and status that only the Headmaster, Toby Dogget, could give him in his beloved institution; and the Headmaster valued Henry's daily reporting back of the tittle-tattle of the Senior Common Room, indiscrete and treacherous though it frequently was.

Rosie Dogget approached Matthew with a plate of canapés. As he was about to take one, a plump, puffy hand appeared from behind him and clumsily scooped up a couple of smoked salmon blinis.

'Thank you, Rosie.' It is Henry. He stuffs both blinis in his mouth at once and, before finishing them, splutters, 'Ah, Matthew, how did your tour go today?' A sly smile spreads across his face. 'I saw you trotting round with your admiring group of tottering geriatrics! Now, are you sure you are telling them the right things?' The sly smile is replaced by a look of irritation. 'You know, I really can't…I never could…understand why Toby didn't appoint a proper historian as archivist.' And then another smile, smug this time.

'What you mean, Henry…what you mean is that you

can't understand why Toby didn't hold the job open for you so that you could slip into a quiet semi-retirement.'

Henry harrumphs, dislodging a speckle of blini that has caught on the corner of his mouth, and stomps away.

Matthew knows how dearly Henry would have loved the archive job. Knows that Henry wasn't ready to step out of the limelight when the post came up. Knows that Henry will never forgive him for being in the right place at the right time and taking the cushy little number he wanted for himself. Poor Henry. If he'd been a little older he'd have pipped Matthew to the post. But he wasn't. And didn't. And the resentment he feels towards Matthew festers quietly away like the angry wart on his neck.

Oh God! It suddenly strikes Matthew that Henry might have seen the Tommy Cooper man. If he has, he will want to find out who the incongruous figure was, will want some telling detail about the man that he can report back to Toby Dogget. Not that Matthew has any. But if Tommy Cooper comes from where Matthew thinks he comes from, then it will be as well that Baines knows nothing at all about the visitation. Or there will be complications.

As Henry moved away, Matthew caught the eye of his wife from across the room. A quizzical look. He mouthed 'Baines by name and bane by nature,' knowing that she would read the familiar description. She nodded a smile back to him, then cast her eyes heavenwards.

*

'A proper historian,' Henry had said, perhaps because he believed that an archivist should be a historian; more likely because he believed that the archivist should be him. But what exactly was a 'proper' historian? At the age of sixty, after many years of running a successful English department, Matthew had opted to retire and had been offered the post of part-time School Archivist. Unsure of his suitability, it was to his father, a retired history lecturer, he had turned for advice.

Michael Agnew, a widower in his eighties, lived in a riverside apartment in Marlow. He was a wise man, deliberate in his thinking, slow to judge, and by habit tentative and provisional in the counsel he offered. Matthew had visited on a sunny October afternoon, some four years before Tommy Cooper's descent on the school. There was a cool breeze coming in from the river, despite which the two men had sat on the balcony of the flat, Michael with a rug over his knees. To the right loomed William Tierney Clark's 180-year-old suspension bridge, elegant country cousin to his earlier streetwise Hammersmith Bridge. Beyond lay All Saints Church and a little further downstream Marlow Lock.

There was something bracing in the cool, lemony October sunlight, and sitting out on this balcony gladdened Matthew's heart. His father had bought the flat shortly after the unexpected death of his wife, selling Hyghcliff, the rambling house in which Matthew and his siblings had grown up.

A large cruiser sailed by beneath them, the engine throatily throbbing, the water outlet whooshing gently. On the upper deck a group of people chattered and bantered, drinks in their hands. They had wrapped up well, clearly determined to drain the last dregs of summer before winterisation beckoned the craft into dock. Matthew watched the cruiser's wash moving towards the riverbank until, with hollow slaps and muffled claps, it hit first the moored boats and then the pontoon below the balcony.

When Michael Agnew had downsized to his riverside flat, he had allowed himself one great indulgence to satisfy an old ambition, the purchase of a 23-foot slipper launch,

11

Farewell, which for most of the year he kept moored to the private residential pontoons in front of the flat. The wash had given the boat some movement, and it was now straining at its mooring ropes, rising up like a tied-up dog trying to break free.

Matthew rose from his chair and said he would make some coffee for them both. In the kitchen, he looked at the familiar painting that his daughter, Daisy, had done of *Farewell* when she was a child. The colours were approximate, especially the woodwork, and the white Lloyd loom chairs appeared a little wonky. But she had captured perfectly the slim elegance of the craft, and the tapering curve of the stern towards the water.

Matthew returned to the balcony with the coffees. 'So, Dad, as I was saying, I quite like the idea of part-retirement. It seems like a good halfway house. But I'm not sure being an archivist is the right thing. What does the historian say?'

'Well, the one-time historian says that anything that keeps the bonce ticking over' – he tapped his head lightly – 'has got to be good! What are your reservations?'

'My reservation, I suppose, is that I am not a historian and I feel that an archivist perhaps should be.'

'Well, yes, maybe. But arguably an archivist is essentially a collector. The historian is the writer of narrative, where the archivist is not.' Michael paused a moment. 'But I don't think you should feel inhibited from taking the job. In any case, I am sure, Matty, that your literary training would be useful – your study of a text is exploratory, analytical, interpretative…tentative. Ideal qualities.'

Matthew nodded. 'True. But what are the distinctive disciplines of the historian, Dad?'

'The analysis of sources, I guess. And the shaping of these into some kind of narrative…which is the antithesis of literary narrative. Novelists and dramatists can invent people and places and events, whereas we historians are bound by what the evidence will support.'

'Sure, but the historian can slant his interpretation of his sources, and presumably has to invent – or at least speculate – where there are gaps in his evidence. When joining two dots, where there are some missing dots in between, he can draw completely the wrong shape.'

Michael chuckled, and allowed Matthew to continue.

'But picking up on your distinction between literature and history. Plutarch obviously gives us a fuller account of the life of Mark Antony than Shakespeare does, and no doubt, you would say that Plutarch's is a truer account. But arguably Shakespeare gives us more insight into Antony than Plutarch.'

'I'm not sure I'd agree with that. But you are right that the historian's interpretation of a series of events relies to a certain extent on an act of imagination…I tell you what, Matty, let's go for a walk. I need to stretch my legs. We'll continue this.'

As they walked by the river, Michael spoke animatedly about the grand sweep of historiography, from the works of Herodotus to the more recent musings of E.H. Carr, who had briefly taught him at Cambridge. He explained that Carr had divided facts into two categories: 'facts of the past', which he defined as the historical information that historians decided was unimportant, and 'historical facts', information that historians deemed important. He contended that historians arbitrarily determined into which category facts fell, according to their biases and agendas. He claimed, in his famous example, that millions of people had crossed the Rubicon, but only Julius Caesar's crossing in 49 BC had been judged noteworthy by historians.

Listening to his father as they walked along the towpath, Matthew imagined that this was the way that he spoke to his students. But he did not feel patronised, rather was grateful for the clarity of his father's 'tutorial'. In the months ahead, he would often refer back to this afternoon's discussion, extracting and distilling comments his father had made into protocols of guidance for his role as archivist.

By the time they approached Marlow lock on their return, the sun was low in the sky, shadows seeping from the ground, the river a ribbon of light. The trees on the far bank and the steeple of All Saints Church were silhouettes now, their reflected inversions smudged by the slight rippling of the water. Further west, the tops of the blackened trees were separated from the gun-metal clouds by a peachy streak of dying light.

He left his father by his front door, squeezing him tightly as he embraced and kissed him goodbye. 'Thanks, Dad. You have been brilliant, as ever.' His father squeezed his arm in reassurance.

'Just a word of caution, Matty. History is never complete…and your archive is bound to have gaps. I know you love completeness, Matty, need it perhaps, and always have since you were a child. I think that is perhaps why you went for literature rather than my discipline – because you are allowed to fill in the gaps left by the author. Because you as reader are in control of your interactions.'

Matthew wanted to argue, to dispute this most strongly. But it was late. His father was probably tired. So he kissed him once more, thanked him again and took his leave.

As he drove away, he saw the dim, frail figure of his waving father, diminished by the rear-view mirror and receding rapidly. He wondered how many more such farewells there would be.

For some days Matthew reflected on his discussions with his father. He was particularly struck by Michael's comments on E.H. Carr's *History of Russia*. In the 1950s it had been admired by Marxist historians as a monumental work of historical scholarship. But more recent verdicts, said Michael, had been negative, damning even, suggesting the work to have been little more than an apologia for Stalin – a piece that highlighted the facts that placed Stalin in a favourable light and ignored the more uncomfortable ones.

If the writing of history was indeed such a subjective business, open to the vagaries of interpretation and the provisionalities of judgement, then it was not so unlike literary scholarship, thought Matthew.

And so the following September he took up his role as School Archivist. In the early days he had spent most of his time cataloguing and preparing existing archive items for proper storage: removing ancient paperclips and staples that had stamped their rusty imprint on documents, disposing of the corroded elastic bands that had left their rubbery worm casts behind.

He was surprised how much he enjoyed the job; bringing order to the haphazard collection proved unexpectedly satisfying. He liked the quiet of the Archive Room, the lack of disturbance; and working his way through the mountain of poorly preserved documents, magazines and photographs had given him a slowly expanding knowledge of the school that he had never had as a teacher. There were always new materials to catalogue, enquiries of various kinds to be answered, the odd tour of the older buildings to conduct. As his first year turned into a second and the second into a third, he continued to make discoveries, working out new connections between what had hitherto been unconnected, seeing the history of the school emerge with increasing clarity and sharpness, like a slowly developing photograph. Most of the discoveries he made were mundane.

Until one day he uncovered the beginnings of the trail, an enigmatic fragment of letter, which would lead to the visit of Tommy Cooper that morning.

The discovery had reminded him of his father's account, four years earlier, of Carr's classification of 'facts'. The unimportant facts of the past. Or historical facts, elevated to such status by the whim of professional historians. In following up the stray page of letter that had fallen from a long-buried file, amateur archivist Matthew Agnew was attributing some significance to these cryptic snippets of information. On a whim? A hunch? Idle curiosity? Difficult to tell. In the months to come he would puzzle over the motivations that spurred his quest for a fuller knowledge of the incomplete letter.

*

The Agnews left the Headmaster's drinks party early. Matthew had not yet had the chance to tell Rachel about the visit of Tommy Cooper and wanted to talk it through when they got home, wanted her advice. He relied on her good sense and her equable temperament. She had a natural reticence, the contained nature of a subtle mind that would assess the intricacies of a situation so that it could move to a balanced understanding. She tended to be calmer in her reactions to drama or crisis than Matthew. Sometimes this would infuriate him, when he thought she needed to step up and meet the true scale of the drama. Other times he found her unruffled, measured responses enormously reassuring.

Her slow and steady apprehension of things was often sharper than his. He liked quick assessment, whereas she favoured considered judgement. On the other hand, she could be quickly and deeply intuitive, seeing in an instant a truth that he might be slowly and reluctantly creeping towards. They counterbalanced each other. 'We're two sides of the same coin,' he sometimes said. 'And what is the coin?' she would ask in well-rehearsed routine. 'A farthing or a golden guinea?' They would both admit that whatever the coinage, it was somewhat tarnished and chipped with age these days. And although she had never discussed this with Matthew, she had observed in him in recent months a certain uncharacteristic hesitancy, a loss of the old self-confidence.

As they entered the front door they were greeted by Foxy, their young sheltie. She gave a few joyous bounds around the hall and then an affectionate muzzling against their legs.

He poured two whiskies, his a larger measure and less watered than hers, and sat beside her on the sofa. As he told her about his strange visitor, he apologised for not telling her about the letter he'd sent some days earlier which, in his view, had triggered the visit of Tommy Cooper.

'Oh, for God's sake, Matty, what on earth did you do that for? Why? Why? You were told to leave well alone. By me. By your dad. We said that there was nothing to be gained. That it was not your business. You are a fool, Matthew.'

Matthew was looking in her eyes as she spoke. They were a reliable weather glass of her mood. Her grey and blue and green eyes were the colours of a changing sea; sometimes they suggested the mystery of the sea, sometimes a tempest, but most often a calm clarity. Like a sailor he had learnt to read those colours and chart her moods. Mildly cross, he decided, at the moment.

'I'm sorry, darling. It was silly…But you know me.'

'I do! You never let go. You persist and persist. You're stubborn. Your imagination…your imagination is over-fanciful. Ridiculously over-fanciful!' The eyes are smiling now. The sea is calm tonight.

'Do you think I should be worried?'

'No. No, not at all. In any case, what is the point of worrying? Assuming the whole thing wasn't some silly wind-up and was a real warning, then so long as you heed the warning that is the end of it.'

'You think?'

'Of course, darling.'

Rachel's words could not wholly extinguish Matthew's anxieties. And in any case, his curiosity had been aroused. What had he stumbled upon?

*

As he lay in bed that night turning over the events of the day, the oversized image of his mysterious visitor came at him repeatedly. He thought back to the brief encounter. After Tommy Cooper had told him that Special Branch could 'magic' people away, he had made a plosive popping sound with his lips. Matthew had been tempted to thrust his arms towards the man, palms down in the famous Tommy Cooper gesture, and say in a gruff voice, 'Just like that!' But he felt that the implied levity might be inappropriate. His harbinger of doom did not seem to be the kind of man who would brook much teasing; he had probably been ribbed a thousand times about his similarity to Tommy Cooper and would long ago have got heartily and perhaps brutally sick of it. On the other hand, maybe in using the word 'magic' he was playing up to the similarity, expecting a resulting piss-take. Who could tell?

Matthew would have preferred to think that his visitor had been the cleverly incompetent Cooper rather than, as he suspected, a Special Branch goon conjured up by a Minister of State at the Home Office, one David Chapman, an alumnus of the school.

CHAPTER 2

The spectral figure of Tommy Cooper had flitted through Matthew's dreams throughout the night. So, setting off for work, he had decided for the time being to banish any thoughts of the man. Later in the day he might look at the file he had been compiling on David Chapman. To check whether anything he had said in his letter might explain or justify the rather extreme response of a Home Office thug being sent down to demand that Matthew 'desist'. If it really was a Home Office thug. And if indeed the visitation of Tommy Cooper had anything at all to do with David Chapman. For now, more pressing was the need to send off some research notes he had been compiling earlier in the week.

One of the things that he had quickly learnt was that an archivist, a school archivist at any rate, was more than a mere 'collector', which was how his father had described the role when differentiating it from that of the historian. The archivist, Matthew now realised, was also a researcher; and what he did with his researches needed sensitive judgement. The nature and needs of the enquirer sometimes demanded careful selection and tactful editing to spare unnecessary hurt or to forestall the misplacing of an emphasis about a person or an event. And it was in that very selection, that editing – 'shaping' his father might call it – that the blurring of truth began. The whole truth and nothing but the truth? Rarely.

Compiling the research notes that he had been working on earlier in the week had posed a dilemma. Christopher Evans had left the school in 1955, having made very little impression in any sphere of his scholastic life. A career in investment banking had made him a very rich man. And now a brief biography was being written about him by a charitable trust to which he had left a considerable bequest when he had died.

The salient details of Evans' dull and mediocre schooldays were readily extracted from his school record. However, it was the small sub-folder at the back of the record that was of real interest (perhaps), and which required an editorial judgement to be made. It concerned a dispute about a hockey stick – trivial enough, you might say – which either had or had not been purchased by the boy at the school shop, which had billed the parents for it. After a tortuous correspondence between the Headmaster and the father, who was becoming increasingly indignant and angry, the boy's housemaster was brought in. His written submission to the Headmaster confirmed that the boy had not bought a stick at the school shop, instead bringing one back from home. But, said the housemaster, Mr Evans was a tiresome old fellow with form in writing rude letters to the school. And young Evans was a rather obstinate and conceited boy. And a bit of a loner, always in search of friends.

Matthew was unsure whether to send details of the correspondence. Why send it? It was trivial. Yes, yes, but it did give some insight into both father and son. Important information for a biographer, surely? No? But, just supposing...just suppose that Evans did bring his own hockey stick back, which was the one he had used that term…but that he had also bought the one from the school shop – as adamantly claimed by the shop manager. Just suppose.

…Matthew sees young Evans, short hair slicked back in 1950s style. He enters the house common room, where his peers are assembling before going to supper in the school refectory.

'Hey, chaps!' Few eyes turn towards him; they recognise the whiny voice. 'Listen, chaps, would anyone like a brand new hockey stick?'

'How much?' A drawling, half-interested voice.

'Nothing. For free.'

Young Evans is now a focus of attention. The boy closest to him reaches out an arm. 'I'll have it.'

Evans holds it out, with a delighted smile on his face, inviting, pleading friendship. The stick is snatched from him roughly.

The face crumples. 'You might say "Thank you".' There are groans from the other boys…

When Matthew asked Rachel for advice, she thought he was being over-fanciful and was going beyond his remit as archivist; she thought that the whole matter was deeply trivial, that the correspondence about the hockey stick was irrelevant and that Matthew's elaborations were ridiculous.

'You're not in a position to make your supposition, Matty,' she'd said. 'It's pure speculation. You may be right, you may wrong. It's one thing editing, another thing entirely speculating in the way you are.'

'But surely the correspondence about the hockey stick is something the biographer needs to see, so that he can decide on its importance. It's a decision for the biographer, not the researcher, which in effect is what I am. He needs to see everything that is there. Then he can make his own judgements, his own speculations. An impartial historian needs all the evidence he can get. His task is limited if he is reliant on evidence that has already being pre-edited.'

'Evidence? You have no evidence whatsoever for your imagined scenario!...And for goodness' sake, Matty, you are talking very grandly about a biography which in reality will be little more than a pamphlet offering a mere snapshot of the man. No doubt upbeat and celebratory, without any ambiguities or shades of grey. Hagiography rather than biography!'

As so often, Matthew took her advice: the correspondence would not be included in the material he sent to the trust.

Choices. Decisions. Matthew had made those when writing his letter to David Chapman. Had he made the wrong choices, the wrong decisions? The visit of Tommy Cooper had suggested that possibly he had. Or hadn't.

*

He occasionally went for break to the Senior Common Room to maintain some kind of visibility. In the scheme of things, contributing to the school archive was a very low or non-existent priority for most staff. Even when he went for coffee, he was hardly noticed by the majority of them, who were instead grabbing hasty conversations with fellow teachers about pupils and work that could not rely on email communication.

In former times, when the school was turning out young men to administer the Empire and to spill their blood on the battlefields of Asia and Africa and Europe, the SCR would no doubt have borne some resemblance to a London Gentleman's Club. Buffed and scuffed leather chairs, heavy well-made tables, portraits on the wall, elegant lamps. The modern age required something more functional. Rows of pigeon-holes, a cluster of computers, white-painted walls to lighten the room. And women teachers, whose civilising influence had helped to dispel the traditional public school ethos, with its silly customs, its barbaric prejudices, its inward-looking elitism. Not that the elitism itself had been banished; it was merely more outward-looking these days, pointing the school's young leavers towards top universities and well-paid jobs in the City or the Law or medicine or the media. Or government.

As he was pouring his coffee, there was a tap on his shoulder. It was the Headmaster, asking about the previous day's tour. Matthew wasn't sure if anything lay behind the question and was unsure whether or not to mention the strange interloper. He decided not to.

'It was fine. Same old same old.'

'Oh. I ask because one of the party popped into my study before leaving.'

Oh dear. Was this whole business suddenly going to take on a completely new layer of complication? Had Henry Baines caught sight of yesterday's strange visitor after all? And mentioned something to the Head? Matthew cleared his throat and, attempting nonchalance, said, 'Was it Tommy Cooper who called in on you?'

The Headmaster looked momentarily puzzled, and then his face broke into a smile of recognition. 'Tommy Cooper? Yes!...But without the fez!' They both laughed.

'What did he want?' Matthew asked, trying to sound casual and confident, keen to hide the mild apprehension that he actually felt.

'Oh, he just said what an interesting tour it had been, what an excellent chap you were. And how I should be careful not to lose you.'

'Oh. Right. Nice.' Matthew wondered if the Head would detect the tremor in his voice. 'Well, make sure you do take care of me, then!' he said with an unconvincing laugh.

But the Head was already gone in search of someone else.

*

Time to look again at his file on David Chapman, Member of Parliament, Minister of State at the Home Office. He had left it out on his desk for his return after break. Four months in the making and growing, it contained a print-out of a Wikipedia biography, newspaper clippings, and some records from his schooldays. The important documents in the file were the stray page of letter that had launched him on his enquiry in May, a sheet of paper containing the notes he had subsequently made as he had delved into the provenance and significance of this mysterious fragment and, finally, a copy of the letter he had sent to Chapman a fortnight earlier. Would this fateful letter prove the fulcrum of the investigation, the moment when Matthew had flushed his prey from his cover? A grand notion, for sure! But that is what the visit of Tommy Cooper was perhaps suggesting. That Chapman had something to hide.

As he climbed the seventy-one steps to the Archive Room, Matthew remembered the schoolboy he had taught. A tidy, well-groomed boy with a striking self-possession. A bright, articulate boy with a subtle mind, too subtle for politics, perhaps. A penetrating intelligence, certainly, but one too coldly clinical to study literature with a fully imaginative engagement; to Matthew the intellectual precision of Chapman's essays seemed unsatisfyingly detached. And his contributions to the Socratean, the invitation-only discussion society for the finer minds at the top of the school, were similarly astringent. He had delivered a memorable paper full of surprising and provocative angles on the philosophical nature of terrorism, but the sharpness of his responses to the papers of others tended to inspire a fearful caution: of his quickness in unpicking flawed arguments, of turning ideas in new and unforeseen directions.

After leaving the school and before going up to Oxford, he had done a stint as an intern in the House of Commons, dogsbodying for an MP friend of his father's who had once worked alongside him in the City. His beginnings in politics.

*

When Matthew reached his room, he found Mary, the cleaner, finishing her weekly hoovering. She apologised for running a bit late. Matthew told her not to worry and asked after her husband, who had recently had two coronary stents fitted.

'Same grumpy old sod as ever!' she said. Matthew laughed. She glanced at the desk and pointed at the Chapman file. 'I'm sorry, Matthew, I knocked that onto the floor while I was dusting. You might need to rearrange the papers. I didn't know what order they were in.'

'Not to worry.'

She glanced at the file. 'David Chapman. Isn't he that Tory feller? One of them posh Tory lot, eh? All the same, in't they? Hands in the till, helping theirselves.' She cackled.

'I don't know about that, Mary. I'm sure there are lots of honest ones.' She snorted in response. 'This chap, David Chapman,' he continued, 'is an Old Boy.'

Another snort. 'Really? God help us! Another snotty git! Some of these kids just don't know they bin born. The mess they make in their rooms, just leaving everything to be cleared up after theirselves. And you should hear the way they talk to us sometimes. Like we was something they'd scraped off of their shoes.' Another cackle.

A harsh judgement, thought Matthew. A sequence of images flickers through his mind: Chapman with a gaggle of local ladies canvassing with an easy charm the streets and roads and long drives of the constituency. Smiling, nodding faces of householders giving him the thumbs up; quizzical or uninterested faces closing doors politely after the briefest of exchanges; doors being slammed roughly in areas of hostility to the Tory party. The beaming smile on election night and the warm, appreciative kiss of his wife Sarah.

'You've been here a while, Mary—'

'Thirty-two years!'

'Perhaps you remember him…here, have a look at this.'

Matthew took a cutting from the file. It was a story from a local paper announcing his victory in the 2010 General Election, and carried a charming picture of Chapman and his wife, with their two children. It was posed in the large garden of their house, an old rectory that had belonged to his parents. The shadows of trees are playing on the lawn. Chapman and his wife Sarah are standing behind an elaborate stone bench on which the children are seated. The kids are quite smartly dressed. Care has obviously been taken over the choice of their clothes. By Mum? Or by a nanny? Sarah is wearing a flowing, flowery summer dress and has one hand on the back of the bench. She is looking admiringly at her husband, smiling warmth and openness. He is standing a little behind the bench, leaning forward with both hands resting on it. He is the most casually dressed of the foursome. Navy blue polo shirt and sand-coloured chinos. He gazes directly at the camera. It is an honest look. It speaks confidence. It says,

'I'm comfortable in myself.' It says, 'We are part of each other's lives. You're welcome. Make me welcome.'

Mary has been peering at it. 'No. Don't recognise the face…Or maybe…Some of the boys is all right. Some quite polite, truth be told. Dunno. But she looks lovely. And the kiddies! Suppose he looks all right. But he has to…for the camera! Tory toffs!' She cackled again.

'He worked for MI5 before becoming an MP. Anti-terrorist work.'

'Keeping us safe, eh!' She peered again at the photograph. 'Now.' She put a finger to her mouth. 'I do remember him…I used to clean his study when he was in the Sixth Form. Nice boy. Good manners…Nice, mainly. But I do remember going into his study once. I did knock. And there was him and another boy and a younger boy. And the littlun looked very distressed. He'd been crying. Maybe he'd been roughed up. The older boy looked embarrassed. Like he'd been caught doing something he shouldn't of been doing. But Chapman, he just stared at me and said something like "It's not convenient now. Will you go, please".' Mary seemed deep in thought, reliving a long-forgotten memory. 'So. So he's a Tory big-wig now! Figures! Always like to be in control, eh!'

She chuckled and said she must be off. He heard her descending the stairs, clacking the hoover behind her.

And into his mind now comes the clickety clack of expensive leather-soled shoes as Chapman walks the halls and corridors within the decaying grandeur of Charles Barry's gothic fantasy. The shoes muffled, of course, when he reaches the green carpeting of the House of Commons. The high ornate ceilings of the main rooms of the building are well suited to Chapman's vaulting ambition. An ambition that the careful and carefully ambitious Chapman would surely never allow to o'erleap itself. Except. Except.

…The clickety clack of expensive leather-soled shoes can now be heard echoing across Old Palace Yard as Chapman walks towards the Victoria Tower Gardens. In his breast pocket is a letter from a former teacher of his.

Just beyond the extravagantly decorative Buxton Memorial Fountain, sitting on a bench overlooking the river, is a man who has made the short walk from Thames House, the headquarters of MI5. Chapman hails the man as he approaches. The man looks round, his square face creasing into a smile, his large blue eyes twinkling a welcome. Chapman sits beside him on the bench.

'It's good to see you, Tommy'

'And it's good to see you, sir. Still climbing the greasy pole, eh?…I am assuming you want to see me because you've got a bit of bother. No?' The large blue eyes look curiously innocent.

'A minor irritation.'

Chapman explains the letter he has received from his former English teacher who has been rootling around in the school archive. 'It's nothing particularly serious, but I don't really want this chap Agnew creating a nuisance of himself.'

'Leave it to me, guv. I'll put an end to the…er… botheration.'

Cooper has seen service in Northern Ireland and over the years has developed a spectrum of strategies to put an end to what he calls botheration. The harsher end of the spectrum does not bear thinking about.

'A gentle warning will suffice, Tommy.'

'Right you are, sir.'

*

Matthew's notes on Chapman suggest that his career is progressing very nicely; that he has built up an impressive CV with some care. After Oxford he joined the Conservative Research Department – a finishing school for bright, ambitious young Tories seeking to fast-track themselves towards political preferment – where he became a Special Advisor to the Defence Secretary. After eighteen months he took a break from politics and joined MI5, eventually working for the Northern Ireland Counter-Terrorism Unit at the propitious time when the Northern Ireland Peace Process was being forged. Would he have been involved in direct talks with the IRA as the Government worked its way towards the Good Friday Agreement of 1998? Quite possibly.

He was lured back to party politics by the founding in 2002 of a new Tory think tank, Policy Exchange, fermenting ideas of reform with other notable modernisers of the party. A failed bid for a seat in the West Midlands in the 2005 General Election was followed by the assiduous courting of the local Conservative Association for a safe seat in the Cotwolds. Matthew can imagine the process: the targeting of it shortly after his 2005 defeat, the entertaining, the glad-handing, the cultivating of the local press, the boning up on issues of local concern. And the heady delight of those summer days in 2010 as the Tories led the first coalition government for many decades.

And now? The most recent press cutting Matthew has added to his file is from *The Independent*. A profile of the handful of the 2010 intake of MPs tipped for great things. Chapman's work as a party moderniser is noted, as are his many useful connections. His expertise in counter-terrorism is seen as a key asset; the article is broken up with a large-type block quote with apposite words from a blog he wrote for Policy Exchange in the aftermath of the 7/7 bombings. There is comment on his excellent relationship with his immediate boss, Home Secretary Theresa May.

The article speculates on the outcome of the 2015 election and picks its riders and runners for any subsequent Tory leadership election. George Osborne, with Boris Johnson coming up on the rails, would be favourite in the short term, but David Chapman is included in the larger group of MPs who would be fancied runners in the longer term. A man to watch.

*

As Matthew wanders from his desk to open a window, he catches a glimpse below of someone stepping into the entrance hall of the tower. He appears to be wearing army fatigues. He is carrying what looks like a rifle in a long, thin case.

The narrow, tubular nature of the spiral staircase that leads up to the Archive Room amplifies every tiny sound from the lowest level. Matthew hears a slow, resonant tread ascending the stairs and freezes for a moment. Then rushes for the door. He will leave his room and take refuge in the room above, the top room of the tower.

Damn. He has forgotten his keys. Rushes back to his desk, fumbles, dropping the keys, picks them up again and hurries up the spiral staircase, another thirty steps. The foot treads are getting louder, but it is impossible to tell how many steps below his pursuer might be. The amplified sound is misleading: the man in army fatigues could be fifty steps below or perhaps a mere ten. Matthew unlocks the door to the top room, then decides he might be safer on the roof of the tower. Fumbles again for his keys. Climbs the last short flight of stairs that spiral within a dusty, cobwebbed wall.

He unlocks the door. Steps onto the roof one hundred feet above the ground. Below him is the roof of the Grand Hall. In the distance, looking tiny beyond the arboretum, is his house. There is nowhere to hide here. The parapeted roof contains nothing but a flagpole and a huge water tank.

Matthew has left the door to the roof slightly ajar so that he can hear what is going on below. If the man comes the whole way up, Matthew will slam it shut at the last moment and lock it. Then he will shout down to the ground for help. But he is hoping that the man will find the Archive Room empty and that he will decide on an immediate descent of the stairs, mission aborted. The man. Could it be Tommy Cooper? Doubtful. Cooper would surely send an underling, a henchman.

The Chapman File! Matthew suddenly remembers that he has left it on the desk. Prize enough for the man, surely. And an end to Matthew's amateur sleuthing, no doubt.

But the footsteps continue, a little slower now; and now Matthew can hear heavy breathing. Suddenly a torso appears, grey-haired, army fatigues-clad, a thin long case slung over his shoulder.

'Aaaarrgh!' The pitches are different, but the strangled sounds of startled surprise are emitted simultaneously by both men.

'Fright you gave me!' says the man, clutching his chest. 'Wasn't expecting anyone to be up here!'

Matthew is almost speechless. The terror of the man's sudden appearance and the shock of his unexpected yelp have for a moment sent a paralysing bolt through him. He gulps in a breath of air. Realises this is no assassin. 'Jeez. And you frightened me, too…I was just…I was just looking down on the roof of the Grand Hall,' he mutters unconvincingly, adding, as though to add some conviction, 'I'm…the school archivist.'

The man has recovered from his surprise, but is still breathless from his long ascent to the roof. He speaks in fractured phrases. 'Checking the…water tank…clearing… the roof drain.' He unhitches the long thin bag of plumbing rods from his shoulder and drops it on the floor. 'Mike Platt…Platoon Plumbers,' he says, index finger stabbing a logo on his khaki sweatshirt.

'I'll leave you to it…Sorry to have given you a fright!' Matthew smiles weakly and leaves. His heart rate is no doubt still raised, but the cold terror he felt as the torso of the plumber appeared around the spiral staircase has been replaced by an embarrassed feeling of sheer foolishness.

He returns to the Archive Room. The Chapman File is exactly where he left it.

*

It is the stray page of a letter to a former headmaster, now in the Chapman file, together with Matthew's subsequent notes, that are of interest now, especially in the light of Tommy Cooper's visit.

In May he had received a routine enquiry into Christopher Harper, former headmaster of the school who had unexpectedly taken early retirement at the end of 1991. To answer the enquiry properly, he had needed to look at Harper's file, which, along with all staff records, was kept in the school strong room. When he retrieved the file, he was surprised to see that it was much scanter than most of the files of former staff. It appeared to have been culled; there was none of the routine correspondence that most files contained and – most unusually – no letter of resignation.

But as he flipped through the papers – the CV, the application for the headship, the references – a loose page of cream-coloured writing paper untucked itself from between the tightly stapled pages of a reference and fluttered to the floor.

It was the second and final page of a handwritten letter. Without the first page it was impossible to tell its date, and the only clue to the writer was his first name in the subscription. A puzzling extract, for sure:

> no alternative but to follow the course of action we did. It was expedient and, in my opinion, not wrong. An eminent man's reputation was saved, a promising boy's future protected, and the school spared from scandal (to say nothing of the generous donation David's parents have agreed to make).
>
> I am sure this whole unhappy episode will blow over in time. You must not fret.
>
> In the meantime, Janet and I wish you a very happy retirement.
>
> With all good wishes,
> Tony

The archive had many documents whose full meaning or significance Matthew had failed to discern, but this snippet had intrigued him. He had decided in May that he would investigate further. That he would delve.

And now, four months later, as he headed down the spiral staircase for some lunch, fragments of a famous line of Eliot's floated through his mind: fragments indeed. Fragment, at any rate. But ruin? Ruin? Whose?

CHAPTER 3

There was a knock on the door. It was Toby Dogget. 'Seeing you in break yesterday, Matthew, reminded me that there was something I wanted to see up here. The William Smith map.'

William Smith's 1815 geological map of Britain was one of the treasures of the school archive, perhaps the only real one; it had been donated by the same ironmaster who had endowed the school in the 1850s. It had spent most of its life in the school library but was now kept in the archive, carefully stored so that its vivid colours and precious paper were properly protected from bleaching lights and the dirty hands of school pupils.

'Matthew, if it wouldn't be too much trouble, I'd like to have a quick look at it. The governors want my view on whether we should sell it or not. I gather it could be worth as much as £90,000.'

'Of course, Headmaster. It takes a bit of time to lay out because of its size and the care one needs to take of it.'

In the centre of the Archive Room, four large office desks formed a huge rectangle. This was a useful space to lay out materials for sorting, cataloguing or, as in the case of the William Smith map, to inspect sizeable objects. The eight-by-six-foot map filled the space. Its fifteen panels were mounted on fine linen arranged in three sections that folded for storage into a marbled slipcase.

It was always with considerable anxiety that Matthew laid out the map. Terrified of damaging it in some way, he tentatively explored the arrangement of folds until finally all three sections were before him.

He could sense Dogget's impatience. He was an impressive man, in many ways. He dressed smartly and held himself well. His succinctness of speech, his directness of gaze and his briskness of gesture and movement no doubt filled prospective parents with the confidence that this was the man to whom they could safely entrust their children's futures. But he was not the man to have hovering over you when you were attending with cautious, slow and painstaking attention to the complicated patterns of fold in this precious artefact.

Eventually all three sections were laid out. As Matthew was completing the third section, he said to Dogget, 'Toby, I do hope that the school doesn't sell this. It was a donation. It is a wonderful thing to have. It surely should be regarded as an educational asset, not a monetary one.'

'We're a business, Matthew, as well as a school. We must never forget that.' Dogget leaned over the southern part of the map, eying it quickly. 'Very pretty,' he muttered. 'Well, thank you, Matthew. We'll see what the governors have to say.'

As he heard the diminishing sound of Dogget's descending footsteps, Matthew looked again at the map. He was always staggered by the beauty of what he saw. Produced as a work of science to aid mineralogists, coal field owners and, indeed, ironmasters, this was a piece of art, an object of stunning loveliness. The swirling shapes suggested an abstraction of colour and form rather than the precise delineation of a geological landscape. The watercolours, finished by hand, were surely as brilliant today as they had been two hundred years earlier. The Cotswolds shone a glorious sunset, with the red of Under Oolyte and the egg-yolk yellow of the Great Oolyte. Matthew's eye was naturally drawn to the mint greens of the North Wessex Downs, where he lived and worked, the darker colour denoting the under layer of chalk, the lighter indicating the flint-strewn upper layer. More subdued were the browns of the clays, sand and gravel of south Berkshire, where he had grown up.

As a boy, he had been given an old atlas by his Uncle Douglas. Douglas had been a soldier. He had taken part in the brief and calamitous invasion of the Suez Canal in 1956 and for the next decade had been posted to some of the other notable flashpoints of British imperial decline. As Douglas pointed out to his nephew, the world had once been covered in swathes of pink. From north to south, from east to west. Much later Matthew had acquired a newly published historical atlas; the changing names and boundaries fascinated him. Anatolia, Arabia, Bohemia, Transylvania. And Roman kingdoms, showered by a fawning Antony upon Cleopatra like so many trinkets: Cappadocia, Paphlagonia, Pont, Comagene, Mede, Lycaonia – kingdoms indeed were clay on this dungy earth. Peoples absorbed, digested into larger entities, spat out and vomited sometimes when their rebel refusals contained the taint of poison. A glance at his old atlas would have found no trace of Yugoslavia, and nor indeed would a contemporary one. But Iraq would be there. How real was that? And how long, indeed, before the nomenclature of the United Kingdom itself required the cartographer's alteration to update these changing histories?

The most personally painful evanescence of place concerned Hyghcliff, Matthew's childhood home. A six-bedroom Victorian house with a large garden and a six-acre paddock, it had acquired a kind of sacredness in his memory. It had been a childhood idyll, an open-house where different branches of the family came and went, an enchanted garden, theatre of his developing imagination. He still dreamt of the place, grieved for its loss. When his father had put it up for sale, a developer had snapped it up and built a large housing estate of 'executive' homes. Another job for the map-makers.

Hyghcliff was also the locus of his most powerful memories of his mother. How true were they? Like the boundaries of dissolving empires, the changing shapes and disputed memories of one's past are largely a collection of faded fragments, incomplete and open to all kinds of misinterpretation. Inevitably a remembered mother of childhood is an amalgam of solipsistic understanding and a projected persona of motherhood.

Who was his mother? In the thirty years since her death, as he had increasingly thought about her at various stages of his life, her image had sharpened, acquired more contours, more definition. But how reliable? He retained a vivid memory of her taking him to the cinema – he must have been about five. He saw the pair of them leaving the house and walking to a bus stop. He pictured the clothes they were wearing. And the curious thing was that it was as though he was walking behind them, seeing himself and his mother hand in hand as they disappeared up the road. But there was no movement. It was more like the still from a film than a film itself.

There were avenues of research into her life that Matthew wanted to explore at some stage. In the meantime, the school archive was what dominated his attention. The school archive. And the Chapman File.

*

At the end of his first term in the Lower Sixth, in 1989, David Chapman had asked his parents to invite some of his teachers to their annual Christmas drinks party. These included the Agnews and Ben and Angie Macpherson. Ben was Chapman's academic tutor, an affable and civilised historian with a sharp intellect and an impressive learning, especially in the field of politics. His relationship with Chapman was a rich one, the pupil worshipping the tutor, the tutor nurturing his promising pupil.

The old rectory dated from a time when vicars were the younger sons of the gentry. It was a substantial and attractive building and, if its clear Georgian lines had been compromised somewhat, this was because of the accretions over the years, intended to make it that little bit larger or that little bit grander. As the Agnews approached the stone pillars of the elaborate entrance gate, they were greeted by an almost blinding incandescence. Every tree and shrub along the curving gravelled drive had been decked in Christmas lights and luminescent decoration. Radiant reindeer leapt over bushes, while lucent partridges perched on the boughs of trees.

There were a number of large portraits hanging in the entrance hall. Matthew assumed they were of Mr Chapman's family. His pedigree included a nineteenth-century industrialist who had created the family's wealth and, later, some members of parliament who had no doubt protected that wealth. Mr Chapman's own contribution to the family fortune was by working in the City as a fund manager of some kind.

The Agnews were greeted by a waistcoated waiter who offered them a choice of mulled wine or non-alcoholic punch.

'Is there anything else?' asked Matthew rather ungraciously, drawing an elbow in his ribs from Rachel.

'Yes, sir. If you go through to the left you will find a table with a large selection of drinks.'

A little further into the hall David Chapman and his mother were greeting the arriving guests. David, tieless but otherwise impeccably smart in a well-cut blazer, reached a hand forward to Rachel and then to Matthew. 'Mum, this is Mr and Mrs Agnew. Mr Agnew is my English teacher.'

'Ah, yes,' she said, taking Matthew's hand and looking him directly in the eye with a hint of a smile. 'David has told me lots about you. He says you're fun to argue with. He loved…what is the river book, David?'

'*A Bend in the River.*'

'Oh yes. Not to be confused with *Wind in the Willows*! He loved *Bend in the River*. But not so keen, are you, David, on that miserable old Philip Larkhill.'

'Larkin, Mum!' Chapman spoke gently to his mother, correcting her mistake.

'Yes, yes, Larkin! Not much larking there, though, by all accounts!' She laughed at her own wittiness.

'I think she is just winding you up, sir. She is actually very well read!'

There was a gleam in her eye. She was an attractive woman. Matthew imagined her as a girl. She would have been fun to teach. And there was something about her – was it a disguised knowingness? A mischievous spontaneity? – that reminded him of his own mother.

The room to the left did indeed contain a long table full of drinks, mostly wines to suit a variety of tastes. On the other side, an expanse of table-clothed trestle tables were borne down with the most extraordinary selection of food that Matthew had ever seen. A feast for the eyes, for sure, if nothing else. To help their guests navigate the exotic concoctions, the caterers had helpfully listed them on menu cards. Matthew cast a quick eye. There were mini seared fillet steaks with salsa verdi on toasted croutes; cocktail dill scones topped with flakes of smoked trout, horseradish crème fraiche, and spears of chive; for vegetarians, there were mini herb scones topped with Dolcelatte and black grape. There were glasses filled with food – 'They are called verrines,' he'd heard someone explain to her friend; seared scallops with Julienne thai flavoured salad. And much, much more. Matthew marvelled at what he saw, muttering 'Amazing!' to Rachel, and wondering what the desserts would have in store.

The food would wait. He wanted to meet some of the guests. Putting his arm on Rachel's shoulder, he led her to the larger of the two reception rooms, both of which were filled with people chatting in pairs or small groups. As they entered, Rachel tugged his arm. 'Look!' she said, nodding subtly towards a man talking earnestly to two elegantly dressed women. It was a well-known television presenter who had made his name as a print journalist before being given his own political talk show on television. A little beyond him was another face Matthew recognised, or thought he recognised. He was pretty sure she was, or had been, the editor of an influential Sunday tabloid.

As Matthew moved through the room he saw other faces to which he could put a name, including the local MP. But it was the political talk-show host that he was most interested in. Having helped himself to some choice canapés and had his wine glass refilled, he made his way back towards the man, lurking until a conversation came to an end and an opening presented itself.

'Presumably you're off-air for the Christmas and New Year break,' Matthew said, reaching for a lightness of tone rather than lumbering in with an off-putting question such as 'Why are you always so very aggressive with your interviewees?' or 'Why do you never let them finish answering your questions?'

'Yes, indeed. We never broadcast during the parliamentary recesses.'

'It's a shame. In a way. Especially now, with so much going on. I saw your interview with Douglas Hurd after the fall of the Berlin Wall. Stirring stuff! The wall coming down, not Douglas Hurd!'

'Yes, remarkable times.'

'Do you think the whole Soviet block is under threat?' Matthew was beginning to warm to his theme.

'I think anything is possible in the present climate of unrest.'

'Yes. Yes. It would be ironic, though, wouldn't it, if the Soviet Union were destroyed by a kind of domino effect. When you think that, after the war, what the West feared most was that the non-communist countries of Asia would fall to the domino effect of the communist onslaught… Mind you, I guess the Tory party is suffering its own domino effect. Hurd is the third Foreign Secretary of the year, isn't he? Ministers dropping like nine-pins, to change the image. Who knows, perhaps at the end of the line, the final domino…' Matthew paused while a witticism floated into his mind. 'The final dominatrix…will be Maggie Thatcher.' Matthew had become garrulous. Probably the wine. Taken too quickly.

The television personality smiled indulgently, but Matthew could see his eyes looking beyond him, over his shoulder, no doubt hoping for rescue.

'I'm sorry,' said Matthew, 'this must be like a busman's holiday for you. I must go and find my wife.'

'Fine. Fine. Good talking to you.' Another indulgent smile.

An hour or so later Rachel suggested it was time to go. She was tired and didn't want to leave the forty-five-minute drive home until too late.

She had spent much of the evening speaking to Angie Macpherson. 'And I had a good chat with David's father. A very nice man. Utterly charming, and very interested in the school. Oh, and I had a long chat with Kitty Harper.'

Kitty, the Headmaster's wife. It seemed that both the Headmaster and Henry Baines, the Head of History, had been at the party, though Matthew had not noticed them.

'That's interesting,' he said. 'Neither teaches David. I'll tell you what. I bet their intended role there was to witness the impeccable behaviour of an embryonic Head of School. I bet that's what the parents were thinking.'

'That's very cynical! But I have to say that David is an absolutely sweet boy. A real credit to his parents.'

That was true. Throughout the evening Matthew had noticed him moving amongst the guests, checking their glasses, talking briefly and charmingly to as many as possible. Effortless charm, wonderful poise. Except. Except for a moment when Matthew had heard him making an unkind comment about Henry Baines to his mother, something about it was only a matter of time before the collar of Baines's clean shirt became stained with the blood of his restless mole.

A fox ran out in front of the car, a flashing glint of eye, but it was never in danger of being hit; Rachel hated driving in the dark and drove frustratingly slowly.

But eventually they were home.

As they lay in bed, ready for sleep, Rachel said in a dreamy voice, 'What a lovely house. I'd love to live somewhere like that.'

It must have been that comment, or the house itself, that prompted Matthew to dream that night of Hyghcliff, his childhood paradise. He would periodically dream of the place. The narrative would normally be a happy one, but he would sometimes wake up with a sense of heaviness, of loss.

Hyghcliff was the home that Matthew's parents had moved into when they got married. An elegant Victorian house, with large grounds and a spectacular, towering Wellingtonia tree, it had been a wedding present from Matthew's maternal grandfather, an enterprising carpenter who had left Cork after the First World War. Starting as a small jobbing builder in the northern suburbs of London, he had quickly prospered. In the housebuilding boom of the 1930s, as ribbon developments had radiated out from the capital like the tapes of a spinning maypole, he had seized the opportunities and created a successful building firm that quickly made him a great deal of money. He had sent Matthew's mother to be expensively schooled by nuns and, when she had got married, had insisted that she have the means to keep the horses that had been an important part of her childhood and which would have been unaffordable on Michael Agnew's salary as a junior university lecturer.

It was a love match of opposites. A deeply cerebral man and an adventurous, spirited, passionate young woman, with an untutored but curious mind. Her birthday was in late September and, many a time, had he told her lovingly that she was 'the last gift of summer'. Though his mother's Celtic temperament would prompt the occasional fiery outburst, Matthew had never heard his parents have a serious argument. His childhood had been entirely happy and secure.

His dreams of Hyghcliff almost always centred on the rockery and pond that separated the house from the lawn. Matthew had collected Dinky toys from a very early age and had acquired a sizeable and prized collection. In winter they found themselves tracking around the patterned carpets of the nursery. In the summer their domain was the garden. The master of the domain was Matthew. This was his world. A world he had created, a world he controlled.

An army convoy treks along the rockery roadway that Matthew has constructed, with indulgent leave from his parents. In the bushes beyond lies an enemy army of plastic soldiers moulded into various positions of combat. On the commanding heights of the rockery, a Centurion tank dismounts its transporter, takes cover between two rocks and starts firing matchsticks towards the enemy.

Sometimes imaginary bombers are allowed to drop stones on the roadway. This is a roadway that has been built with great care. A red Dinky Blaw-Knox bulldozer has scraped a path, mostly but not always avoiding Mrs Agnew's plants. If his mother had demurred, Matthew would have explained that the driver of the bulldozer had no head – he had lost it when dropped on a crazy paving pathway – and therefore was blind. A Bedford tipper truck with red cab and beige platform has removed the spoil and has deposited it to create a bank; the banking serves nicely when it is time for a day of Le Mans. The roadway is completed not by the green Aveling-Barford steamroller (whose driver benefits from the protection of a die-cast hood) but by Mrs Agnew's trowel, which flattens and compacts the soil much better than the light Dinky toy.

*

In the dream on the night of the Chapman Christmas party, two Dinky toys are moving quickly across the rockery roadway. A Commer fire engine and a black Humber Hawk police car. With the help of Matthew's nimble hands, they are heading towards a fire. Aflame is a small heap of straw, taken earlier by Matthew from the stables, and set fire to with a match found on a table top in the kitchen. It is rather fiercer than expected; a bold little boy is now beginning to panic as a clump of shrubs begins to blacken and singe.

Suddenly his mother is there. She is shouting angrily, 'Matthew, you little fool, what on earth are you doing?' Appearing in the doorway behind her is his father.

Matthew awakes with a start. He is relieved that there is no fire. Relieved there is no angry mother. No castigating father. As he emerges into complete wakefulness, and before the dream slips away like a late frost on a sunlit lawn, he realises that the woman shouting at him at the pond side was not his mother at all, but Mrs Chapman. The man in the doorway was not his father, but the political talk-show host from the previous night's party.

Matthew puzzled over the dream: he was not a pyromaniac; neither his mother, nor Mrs Chapman were frightening people. He decided, as he remembered with embarrassment button-holing the political talk-show host, that the fire-raising dream was to do with his sense of foolishness at prattling away to the man.

He remembered, with a smile, Mrs Chapman's comment about Larkin's poetry. She had said that David had not enjoyed studying Larkin. Which was not how Matthew remembered it. David had been the only member of the set to notice and comment upon Larkin's sophisticated versification, noting subtle rhyming and rhythmic patterns that other pupils had failed to see. He had argued that because most of the poems adopted a persona, one could not necessarily deduce much at all about Larkin as a person. He might well be a very jolly old chap. Matthew had reminded the class of D.H. Lawrence's famous dictum: 'Never trust the artist, trust the tale'. A strange injunction from the author of the largely autobiographical *Sons and Lovers*. Or a completely understandable injunction.

Earlier in the term, Matthew had been driving to a conference for English teachers in Bristol and had listened with interest to an edition of *Desert Island Discs*, whose guest was Seamus Heaney, recently appointed Oxford Professor of Poetry. Heaney spoke with a careful precision, a scrupulous attention to saying nothing untruthful; to capturing, to pinning down with exactness what he wanted to say. When asked about the Northern Ireland question, he had abjured any direct involvement in the conflict, insisting that he would never be a spokesman for any cause. He desired, he said, to conduct himself honestly.

He spoke warmly of his mother and aunt – his 'two mothers', he called them. Much of what he said was a celebration of his Irishness, making Matthew wish that his own mother – dead now for four years – had been alive to hear the broadcast. One of Heaney's musical choices had been a song by John McCormack, a favourite of hers.

Honesty and directness. Fidelity to truth. These were what Heaney stood for. In class the following week, Matthew tried to promote a discussion about the truthfulness of poetry. He photocopied a couple of early poems of Heaney's on childhood to give the class a sense of a poet reaching deep into his memory and trying to record accurately the detail and texture and feeling of that experience.

'We've looked at a number of Larkin's poems where the speaker is not Larkin himself but an invented persona through whose vision and voice the content is filtered. What I want you to consider is whether the directness of

Heaney's voice, and the immediacy of the detail, make Heaney's poetry more truthful than Larkin's.'

As the class considered the question, some gazed vacantly at the photocopied poems, others started annotating the sheets or doodling; David Chapman, meanwhile skimmed the poems quickly and then sat immobile, eyes pitched upwards a little, waiting for the discussion to begin.

He was the first to speak. 'In a sense it is a pointless question because, while both poets might be attempting to say something true, that truth is being mediated through a particular voice and a particular vision. It is still Larkin speaking through his invented persona, ventriloquising, if you like…and who's to say whether that is any more or less truthful than what Heaney sees and articulates? In any case, the truth is always diluted by the sheer artifice of poetry. Poetry is not really one of the great pathways to truth.' His voice was matter-of-fact. There was no condescension, no undercurrent of cynicism. But the seeming authority and finality of his comment had intimidated the rest of the class. Matthew would have challenged Chapman's proposition, but did not want the discussion to descend into a mere duologue, with the rest of the class left as voiceless spectators. Stilled by the voice of Chapman.

Chapman who, one day, like the newly-weds of Larkin's *Whitsun Weddings*, would arrive in London, with its figurative fields of wheat, in post code SW1A. There he would begin the next important stage of his life. And no doubt those beginnings in Westminster would have all the ambiguity of Larkin's conclusion to the poem, with the arrow-shower sent out of sight, somewhere becoming rain. Transmuting those figurative fields of wheat into something harvestable.

Or so it had been mapped out.

CHAPTER 4

Chapman's alma mater, Matthew's place of work, lay in the North Wessex Downs. Chalk grasslands climbed away to the north-west, and to the south-east grew an ancient forest. The main buildings overlooked a river that marked the northern boundary of the grounds, and running westwards was a well established arboretum. Every day Matthew walked through these trees on his way to the Archive Room, noting the minute seasonal changes.

The oldest tree was a Spanish Chestnut, deemed to be ancient in the 1750s by a notable county antiquarian. Several times a year Matthew would closely inspect this huge, untidy being, never tiring of the new discoveries to be made. The immense base, reaching little more than ten feet, consisted of a wide and contorted trunk, its thick and ancient solidity appearing fluid, like molten wood spilling to the ground. It was largely a conglomerate of burrs, varying in size and shape, conjuring up changing and fantastical figures. Some of the outgrowths had small bosses and holes, suggesting the faces of gargoyles or the heads of grotesque creatures that might have illustrated a medieval bestiary: a winking monkey face, a wide-eyed owl, a placid duck. One live but decaying branch, seeming to lie for rest upon the massive trunk, looked like an aged elephant's outstretched leg, scarred and wrinkled.

Trees like this ancient chestnut were both mysterious and straightforward. Their mystery stirred the imagination, while their straightforwardness lay in their admirable fidelity to their history. Their past was contained in their present, the old coexisting with the new. Their growth rings were their annual diaries, their damaged limbs the scars of storms past, or of droughts or of human intervention. This tree spoke of survival, of a determination to renew itself endlessly.

*

It is May. Still some months before Matthew writes to Chapman. Some months before the visitation of that sinister square-jawed, blue-eyed visitor. Matthew's investigation is in its infancy. The fragment of letter, accidentally left in Christopher Harper's filleted file, needs interpreting. Needs decoding. And there are undoubtedly clues.

> no alternative but to follow the course of action we did. It was expedient and, in my opinion, not wrong. An eminent man's reputation was saved, a promising boy's future protected, and the school spared from scandal (to say nothing of the generous donation David's parents have agreed to make).
>
> I am sure this whole unhappy episode will blow over in time. You must not fret.
>
> In the meantime, Janet and I wish you a very happy retirement.
>
> With all good wishes,
> Tony

Mystery and fidelity to history.

While there was no hint as to what the 'expedient' course of action had actually been, it was clearly to avoid something whose exposure would damage the school's good name. 'An eminent man's reputation'? A visitor to the school? A parent? A governor, perhaps. The governing body had a number of members whose qualification for governing a school was their 'eminence' rather than any real knowledge of education. The writer of the letter was Tony. And Tony was married to Janet. The 'promising boy' might or might not be 'David'. David, whoever he was, had rich parents. That was clear.

Matthew knew how he would proceed with his unpicking of the clues offered by the fragment of letter. He would look again at Christopher Harper's early retirement. He had always assumed it was for health reasons. Perhaps it was. Perhaps not. He would find a list of governors at the time of Harper's retirement and see if any were called Tony or Anthony. And he would see how many boys at that time were called David. It would be a start.

First the school magazine. Harper had retired at the end of the Christmas term of 1991. Mid academic year was an unusual time for a Head to step down, which was why Matthew assumed it was for health reasons. The magazine for the summer term contained an account of Speech Day. And there it was. The Acting Chairman of the Governors announcing that for personal reasons the Headmaster would be stepping down at the end of the following term. A sentence or two summarised the Chairman's fulsome praise of Harper's exceptional contribution to the school's development…'deep sadness at the unexpected resignation…all good wishes…'

There followed a lengthy summary of Harper's speech. He had a habit of framing his speeches to parents with some kind of metaphor, often elaborate. On this occasion it was rather uninspired. Or perhaps that was the summariser's fault. Parents and pupils were invited to think of the river that ran along the northern perimeter of the grounds. They were to imagine the river's spring, a tiny trickle; to imagine it gathering size, overcoming barriers and obstacles on the way. If adult maturity was the river's estuary, with its quiet, powerful expansiveness, the stage that pupil leavers were at today was a weir. A sharp drop might lead to some turbulence and uncertainty, but in no time the waters would be broadening and smooth.

Matthew would have been in the marquee for the speech, but could remember nothing of it, not even groaning at the dull, laborious nature of the metaphor. After the introduction of the metaphor came the bread and butter stuff of Speech Days: another good year…blah blah…lots of success…blah blah…the carefully crafted farewells to leaving staff, with all the exaggerations and omissions customary to these eulogies…blah blah… wonderful Head of School, David Chapman. Ah. Matthew had forgotten he had left the same year as Harper. He had remembered that Chapman had been Head of School, not which year. His memory for faces and names was good, but he often shuffled them into the wrong year groups.

He rose from his desk to put the magazine back on its shelf. Glancing out of the window he saw a heron standing in the shallows of the river. A grey-gowned pedagogue, with white-topped mortar board, hunched over a student to peer intently at his work.

Matthew now looked at the Christmas term edition of the school magazine and read Harper's *Valete* entry. There were two pieces, the first by a senior teacher. Without doubt Harper's career had been successful. Economics teacher in a Grammar School, with occasional time off to play Minor Counties cricket. A move to the independent sector, where he quickly became a housemaster. His first headship in a middle-ranking school. And then what would be his final post. His contribution to the school was noted – the driving up of standards, the building programme – and there was considerable affection in the tone of the piece. But no mention of illness.

The second article was more perfunctory. There was nothing in it that hadn't been said or implied in the first piece. What arrested Matthew's attention was the byline: Tony Marshall. This was a name he remembered. Marshall – Dr Marshall – had been senior partner in a local GP practice. As far as Matthew could recall, he had also been a governor at some stage. Matthew located a school roll for 1990/1991, which contained a list of governors, and there he was: Dr Anthony Marshall, MB BS, MRCGP, MSc.

A quick search in the archive catalogue located a *Valete* to Marshall. He had stepped down in the summer of 1991. The piece wished him and…and his wife Janet(!) all the best. Matthew was thrilled. He enjoyed his searches of the archive and always felt excitedly satisfied when he solved a problem or successfully reached the end of a trail. Not that this was the end of a trail. It was the beginning. That's probably what was exciting him now.

Another catalogue reference referred to an obituary on Marshall. Matthew would not be able to repatriate the stray page of letter to its writer.

He looked again at the list of governors. He remembered some of the names and could put faces to one or two. At the beginning of the academic year, Lieutenant-General Sir Peter Gilbert, KCB, KBE, DSO, MC was chairman of the governors but, for whatever reason, was no longer chairman by the year's end, when an acting chairman had officiated at Speech Day. That was something to check at some stage.

In the meantime, he had established the name of the letter writer. And there was at least a possibility that the David mentioned in the letter was David Chapman, a promising sixth former at the time and the son of wealthy parents.

Reading about Speech Day had jogged Matthew's memory. He had a hunch that David Chapman was to be the guest of honour for the approaching Speech Day, a hunch confirmed when checked in the termly calendar. A happy conjunction. Matthew might be able to ask him, if he could find a delicate way of putting it, what catastrophe was avoided in his final year at the school. Assuming that affairs at the Home Office did not detain him on the school's great day. Nor any distractions over the Scottish independence referendum which, by the time of Speech Day in late June, would be less than three months away and exercising the minds of the Coalition government.

*

The next day Matthew visited a country manor house in Dorset, which had a grand staircase and some panelling commissioned from the same Venetian woodcarver who had crafted the work in the school's Grand Hall. Matthew hoped he might learn more about the Italian master, and he had signed on for a tour that had been organised by the owner of the manor, who now lived in one wing of it.

It was a pleasant drive down through the vibrant Dorset countryside, the agreeableness of the views broken only by the unwelcome frequency of the lurid yellow rapeseed fields. Rightly or wrongly, Matthew felt that rapeseed was alien to the countryside, as alien as the cursed gaudy green, shrieking, screeching parakeets that were colonising west London, where his son lived.

The tour guide – the lord of the manor, so to speak – was an elderly, rather scruffily dressed gentleman. On the portly side, he wore baggy brown corduroy trousers and a loosely fitting tweed jacket of some age, sagging at the front from the distortions of over-filled pockets. A watery trickle ran from his left eye down his florid face.

His knowledge of the staircase and the carved panelling was good and Matthew took notes. His fellow tourists were equally attentive, clearly impressed with what they were seeing and what they were hearing.

At the bottom of the staircase the two large balusters – newels, were they called? – broadened into plinths, and on each of these stood a bronze, each about twenty-four inches high.

Could anyone identify the bronzes? asked the lord of the manor. He was standing halfway up the staircase, his audience clustered at the bottom. Some faces looked left, some right.

'Is that Edward VII?' said someone.

'Indeed it is. He used to come down here as a guest when he was the Prince of Wales, for shooting parties… And whatever else he used to get up to…' he added with a sly grin. 'And the bronze on the other side?'

'Is it…Is it one of Queen Victoria's daughters?' suggested a little old lady who had been engrossed in everything she saw and heard.

'No,' said the lord (who wasn't a lord).

'It…looks…like…Marie Antoinette.'

Matthew couldn't see who had made this suggestion.

'Correct! Marie Antoinette. A replica of a bronze by the famous French sculptor, Houdon.'

'Did she used to come here?'

'No, no. Indeed not. No doubt she would have told the estate workers to eat cake!' Mein host let out a maniacal chuckle. 'Now, for many years I was puzzled by the conjunction of these two figures. And then, about five years ago I visited Warwick Castle. Going through the various rooms, I came to one which had a number of photographs of Daisy Warwick...'

A woman in the audience tugged the sleeve of her partner and nodded. Clearly they too had had made a similar visit.

'Now, what I knew, when I went there, was that Daisy Warwick was a favourite mistress of the Prince of Wales. What I didn't know, until that visit and seeing the photographs, was that she liked to dress up as Marie Antoinette, especially for masked balls.'

His audience was now smiling in recognition, some anticipating what he was going to say next.

'So, I like to think that these statues were put here as an affectionate private joke! Now, I have no idea whether my theory is true or not, but it seems plausible and satisfying. And it makes a good story to tell visitors!'

History as entertainment. The awkward ruffles and bulges smoothed into a linear narrative, the lacunae of missing evidence filled with fanciful invention.

As the man chuckled at his own mirth, a beam of light caught his rheumy left eye, which glistened a splinter of silver.

Matthew refused to humour him with even a smile. History as mere entertainment. So quickly, the whimsy of speculation had hardened into 'truth'. Often what was believed to be true, or told to be true, was merely the plausible, sometimes no more than merely the possible.

*

Rachel, who was a year younger than Matthew, had a May birthday. If Matthew's father had called his wife the last gift of summer, Matthew regarded Rachel as one of the many gifts of spring. It was a season that got into its stride in the garden with the flowering of the lilac tree, the pink little beads of the spaced florets looking like exploding raspberries. Its end was marked, for Matthew, by the strewn leaves of a large holm oak which dominated the bottom of the garden. His immigrant settler, he called it, a settler which maintained its continental custom of shedding its leaves at just the wrong time of year, littering the lawn when it should have been at its most luxuriantly splendid. The frequent task of raking the fallen leaves created a sound like a gentle tide running onto a shingle beach or, if they had lain without rain for a while, they rustled more aggressively with a harsh rasping. Nevertheless it was a tree he loved; the graceful twist of its branches, its dark, gnarled, elephantine trunk. And the chore of leaf-sweeping was rewarded by the evergreen cheer the tree offered in the cold depths of winter.

Matthew had decided to set himself the challenge of preparing Rachel a chateaubriand steak for her birthday meal. But first there was the present to sort. He had bought a silver picture frame in which he would put a photo of the two of them from their earliest years together as students. The large sideboard in the dining room was full of pictures of family and family events, but there were none of the young Agnews in their first flush of love.

He spent some time going through boxes of old prints. Most were monochrome, but there were some colour ones from the first holiday they had taken together. They had hitched down through France and Spain and taken a ferry to Tangier, memories of which had disappeared in something of a Moroccan haze. On the way back they had stopped off at Granada. Two photos showed them dressed up in Arab clothing. Matthew looking ridiculous in a fez, a foolish grin on his face; Rachel looking mysterious in her yashmak.

He progressed through the boxes, flipping quickly through the photos, pausing every now again to gaze in wonder at the beautiful woman who would eventually marry him.

He smiled as he came across her standing on a plinth with the name Picasso on it, distorting her body and presenting her head side-on and gurning with bent mouth. Another photo showed her smartly dressed, standing with Matthew's best man, toasting together the camera. To a happy future!

He finally found a promising series of sharp, black-and-white prints. How young they looked! He was surprised at how thin he was, especially in the face. Almost handsome! But Rachel, Rachel was stunning. Film-starrish. A surge of melting warmth hit him. And gratitude.

He settled for a photograph of them standing together on the towpath of a river or canal – he couldn't remember which or quite where it was. What he liked about the photograph was its air of youthful optimism. Two people on the threshold of shared lives.

*

She opened her present with the same inscrutable expression she reserved when feeling mixed emotions. Her natural reticence made her uncomfortable when looking at photos of herself. 'That's lovely,' she said. 'And you look fantastic!' She raised the frame to her lips and kissed the glass.

'And you look absolutely stunning, sweetie!'

'I don't!' she said unconvincingly. But he could tell that she liked the photo, including the image of herself.

After breakfast, they walked Foxy in the school grounds. Spring had reached its characteristic stage of strident aggressiveness. While there was always something impressive and uplifting about it, Matthew these days felt that the amplified volume, the absolute glut of it, could be too much; the sheer full-on-ness of mid May was a rowdy, gaudy reproach to those, like himself, in declining years.

But not to young Foxy, who was scampering in all directions, vainly trying to catch squirrels or hopping crows. And then she saw a green woodpecker stabbing its beak into the lush greenness of a playing field. She hurtled towards it; startled, it erupted into the air and flew away in its rhythmic wave motion, cackling its disdain of Foxy's feeble effort at capture.

As they walked, Matthew told Rachel about his visit to the Dorset manor house earlier in the week. While describing the owner, their guide, he exaggerated the portrait, turning what had irritated him into a comic narrative, making Rachel laugh.

'Did you learn much about what you went there for – the staircase, was it?'

'Oh yes, he was good on that…And then he invented some implausible story – well, possibly plausible story – about a couple of bronze busts at the bottom of the staircase. Outrageous. And then he starts cackling like a banshee on laughing gas, pleased as punch with his own cleverness!'

Rachel smiled. 'What larks!' And then, with a mischievous grin: 'Of course, I can't imagine anyone I know inventing some implausible historical story!' She laughed as he did a double take.

'Bollocks to that!'

*

Home, and time to make the beurre maître d'hôtel which, according to the recipe Matthew was following, was an important part of the chateaubriand dish. He'd been shopping the day before, buying all the ingredients he needed. The fourteen-ounce fillet steak had looked wonderful; but when the butcher had told him the price, had suddenly looked like something else: a very expensive mistake waiting to happen.

Come evening, he got down to work in earnest, preparing the meat and making the sauce. Shallots, thyme, bay leaf, mushrooms and wine. Reduce. Stock. Reduce. Add the beurre maître d'hôtel and a pinch of cayenne pepper. The meat meanwhile grilling and resting.

There was a precision to everything Matthew did when cooking. The kitchen was a domain, and temporally he became its master, controlling it as completely as he had once controlled his fleet of Dinky toys at Hyghcliff. In this controlled world, he was the master creator.

When it was time to serve the meal, he watched Rachel cut into a slice of the beef, douse it in sauce and taste. Again, the same inscrutable expression. And then, 'Mmm. It's gorgeous!' And he dared taste it too. And, yes, it was gorgeous.

'Tell me how you made it, darling.'

He took her through the menu, the preparations, the cooking. 'You know I sometimes think that there are similarities between cooking and running the archive—'

'Really?'

'Yes. Certainly. When you are cooking, you collect the ingredients, you lay them out like the various documents of an enquiry. You assess how much weight and emphasis to give to each item. And then you blend and shape them into a culinary narrative.'

She smiles. 'Interesting...I must remember that next time I cook. It will help dispel the sheer repetitive dullness of it all! Culinary narrative!' Perhaps noticing some reaction on Matthew's face, she quickly adds, 'You're sweet, darling…And this chateaubriand, by the way, has a very strong narrative! I love it!'

They paused between courses, and Rachel asked how things were going in the archive. 'Apart, of course, from the lord of the manor, who you've already told me about.'

'It's mainly routine stuff. Chasing stuff up, cataloguing, answering enquiries from former pupils. But I did come across something quite interesting the other day.' Matthew explained about the stray page of letter, and his sleuthing so far.

'It doesn't seem that important,' said Rachel.

'I don't know. You may be right. I just wonder, though. I'm rather intrigued by it. It looks like the school might have hidden some potential scandal.'

'Oh, Matty! Off you go again, you conspiracist! It's probably completely random, completely innocent…And in any case it's not really your job to disinter old skeletons. If that's what it is.'

'I disagree. I think it's very much my job…Not so much to dig up old skeletons as to pursue the truth. And I think Dad would agree.'

'Have you mentioned this to him?'

Matthew shakes his head. 'And anyway, who's to say that this is a question of a clean, interred skeleton and not in fact a question of a half-buried corpse stinking to heaven?'

Rachel laughs. 'You do exaggerate, Matty! You have such a…such an inventive mind!'

'And perhaps you have a surprisingly unsuspicious mind for someone who used to be a workaday solicitor!' Matthew has been unable to keep a slight edge from his tone. 'So,' he says, 'what I've established is this. That an eminent man's reputation was saved. That the school was saved from a scandal. That some wealthy parents made a significant donation to the school. That the Headmaster resigned shortly afterwards and that the Chairman of the Governors resigned that same year.'

'When did he resign?' Rachel has decided to play along with her husband. She would rather that they were not talking so earnestly about archive business during her special birthday meal, but she senses a familiar intensity rising in Matthew; she has long felt that it borders on neurosis and she wants to bring the conversation to a quick and calm conclusion.

'I'm not sure. I haven't checked that.'

'Well, that's your next task,' she tells him.

*

At four o'clock the next morning Matthew wakes abruptly with a complete and clear sense of what had happened in the summer of 1991, an éclaircissement unsettlingly but thrillingly unexpected. So convinced is he that he has been delivered the pertinent details that lie behind the letter from Dr Anthony Marshall to Christopher Harper, Headmaster, that he slides quietly out of bed, goes to his study and makes some notes.

- Harper summons David Chapman to his study, early summer term. Tells DC that a complaint has been made by a parent whose son has been beaten up by DC and another boy. Conduct not consistent with being Head of School. DC must stand down.
- DC tells parents, who (presumably) see this as an impediment to future political success. Parents make contact with Chair of Govs, Gen. Gilbert, an old friend of family.
- Gen G. tells Harper not to sack DC. H refuses, says boy can no longer be Head of School.

- G. fires H., who will step down at end of following term.
- Dr Ant. Marshall, friend of Harper, resigns in protest.
- DC parents make donation to school in gratitude.
- Gov. body feels school needs to move on after sorry business. Gen. G agrees to resign too.

Even as he writes the notes, Matthew can feel the certainty, so clear and strong as he had awoken, draining out of him.

*

The next day, Matthew checked in the school magazines of 1991 to see if there were any references to the Chairman of the Governors, General Gilbert. He was surprised to see that what he had missed was not a resignation announcement, but an obituary in the same Christmas term issue which contained Christopher Harper's *Valete* piece. He had died suddenly of a stroke in May that year. Chapman's last term as Head of School.

That was something else to ask David Chapman when he attended Speech Day the following month.

CHAPTER 5

Speech Day, 2014. Tommy Cooper has not entered Matthew's life yet. Matthew has yet to speak to Chapman. But he is about to, he hopes.

The skies are clear blue, the sun shining hotly on the colourful, summery crowd that is filing into the huge marquee. Elegant dresses for the mothers, stylish and more daring dresses for the daughters who will leave the school today. Linen suits and lightweight jackets for the men. Dark suits for the boys who will return in September, smart casual for the leavers. Loud striped blazers for the top rowers and cricketers. An unchanging ritual parading itself for another year.

Inside, as people take their seats they see with relief a ripple run through the thin inner drapes of the great tent: there is a slight breeze. At the front, which is the middle of the longer side of the rectangular structure, is the stage. Speakers at the back, half hidden by banks of carefully arranged flowers and greenery. Three smart chairs, chosen for style and for comfort over the two-hour ceremony. Two microphones. And to the left of the stage a large baize-covered table creaking under the weight of cups and trophies and piles of books.

The Headmaster enters the marquee with his party.

Governors and their wives, honoured guests and, of course, the Guest of Honour, one David Chapman, Minister of State at the Home Office. The governors and wives take their seats in the two reserved rows in front of the stage. The Chairman of Governors leads the way onto the stage and stands behind the central microphone. The Headmaster shepherds Chapman up behind, and gestures him towards his chair, then takes his own seat.

A welcome to parents and guests, a special welcome to the special guest – about whom more later – and then the announcement of the traditional start to proceedings, a polyphonic anthem from the Chapel Choir, who file up onto the stage. The eyes of libidinous fathers will be drawn to two of the girls, whose short dresses allow probably too much thigh to be displayed. The ears will note the relative weakness of the tenors, who are being out-sung by the full-throated trilling of the girls. Perhaps there are too few tenors. Or perhaps they are simply out of sorts this morning.

It is time now for the Chairman of the Governors. He is the CEO of a large local company, but for some reason is a poor public speaker. He stumbles through a forgettable summary of the governors' thinking for the future and then introduces the Headmaster.

This is Mr Dogget's seventh Speech Day and he follows an efficient and well-practised formula. It is not a dull speech but, to use one of the clichés he is fond of using about prospective staff he interviews, it is not going to set the Thames alight.

Throughout the Headmaster's speech Matthew has been watching the Guest of Honour closely. Chapman has been sitting very still, face appearing to be fully attentive. Occasionally a flicker of a smile. A slight cocking of the head at some surprising or interesting detail in the speech.

But not much is being given away. Sitting on the green benches of the Commons, with cameras ever-present, must make for a careful demeanour. Or not. There are certainly enough of Chapman's colleagues who are happy to slouch for hours on their benches, to snooze even, and to bray absurdly when the Pavlovian trigger is pressed.

The Headmaster has concluded his rather dull speech and it is now time for him to introduce the Guest of Honour. He is, says Mr Dogget, a distinguished alumnus of the school, noted while a pupil for his academic brilliance, which was justly rewarded at Oxford with a First. His career, since graduating, has been on a steadily upward curve. Dogget concludes with a quotation from a recent *Daily Telegraph* column. 'If I wanted to place a bet on an outside chance of who would replace David Cameron, should he lose next year's General Election, I would think very seriously of putting money on David Chapman. He has risen swiftly through the ranks since being elected in 2010, has formed alliances with some powerful friends in the party, and is certainly a man to watch.'

Matthew continues to peer at Chapman. No change in the facial expression as these words are spoken, but again that slight, almost imperceptible cocking of the head.

He wonders what it must be like for Chapman to be back at his alma mater, Guest of Honour on a glorious sunny day. Is he thinking back to his school days? To his successful academic career, his final year as Head of School? It had been a turbulent time. In the early nineties, the independent sector was grappling with a significant drugs problem. Most prospective parents were terrified their children might succumb, and veered away from schools with a perceived issue; most headmasters, therefore, were unyieldingly tough on those pupils caught. In his year as Head of School, Chapman had been asked to assist the Headmaster in an enquiry into a senior boy who was known to be bringing cannabis onto the campus. He did as he was asked. He was thorough, structured and clinical in his enquiries, passing names and details to the Headmaster. The deeper the questioning ran, the clearer it became that there were boys in the junior years involved. In accordance with the policy of the time, more than ten pupils, seven of them from Year 10, were expelled. The consequent attentions of the press resulted in fewer prospective parents looking over the school; and it led to a subtle shift in policy that allowed for more leeway in future episodes of the kind. Did Chapman regret the zealousness of his investigation? Who knew?

*

It is time for the prize-giving. The pupils have their names read out in twos or threes and mount the platform to shake the hand of Chapman and perhaps have a few congratulatory or exhortatory words spoken to them. There is poise and charm to the way that he is conducting himself, but also, Matthew feels, something slightly automatic. There is less mobility in the face than he remembered in the pupil.

And then the speech. Chapman starts by saying how refreshing it is to be back at the school and amongst real achievers. His children, he says, made him sit and watch England's dismal World Cup performance against Costa Rica three nights earlier. The team has returned having not won a single game. He is grateful, he says, to have been at a school like this, where one was taught to strive, to take nothing for granted and to persist until successful.

He tells a joke – one that Matthew has heard before – that hinges on whether 'fly' in French is a masculine or feminine noun. Some of the audience laugh quietly, one or two loudly. Some appear not to have got the joke. And some perhaps simply find it unfunny.

The main thrust of his speech is advice for leavers. University is a place of freedom. Freedoms of all kinds, but especially intellectual freedom. These are not years to be wasted down at the pub, but to be cherished and used fruitfully. And he speaks about the importance of face-to-face communication. The passages and corridors in the Houses of Parliament contain miles and miles of cabling of one kind or another, much of it for communications. There are all kinds of modern and sophisticated ways to communicate, but nothing can beat talking to someone face-to-face. Matthew is strangely encouraged by this advice. He is, after all, intending to talk to him man to man about the events of the summer term of 1991. He is still in turmoil, however, about how he is going to broach it. He has spoken nicely to the Headmaster's Secretary to wangle himself an invitation to the Governors' lunch for Chapman and other guests.

*

Speeches were at an end. It was time for the Chairman of the Governors to direct parents and guests to their pre-lunch drinks before picnicking in the grounds. But he had a surprise to spring. The new teaching block, completed a year earlier, was still unnamed. The governors had agreed to call it, in honour of today's speaker, the Chapman Centre. David Chapman, he said, would return in the autumn term to unveil a plaque.

Very strange, thought Matthew. This had never been mentioned before. It seemed that the decision had been made on the fly. When? Why? Interesting.

Drinks were held on the main lawn in front of the school. A large rectangle, with curved corners, it was enclosed within a gravel pathway. In the centre of the lawn a small square of yew hedge contained the stone memorial to the boys of the school who had died in the two world wars.

He noticed for the first time – where had he been located during the speeches? – a man who was clearly of Chapman's party, and equally clearly part of a security detail. He stood in the way these people did, weight distributed equally between his two feet, hands loosely held together in front of him; and his head was in virtually constant slow movement, eyes scanning laterally and looking now and then at the upper windows of the building. Was it Chapman's Home Office work that required security, or his past involvement in Northern Irish politics when working for MI5?

Large banners denoting the different houses of the school had been erected on various parts of the lawn, drinks tables laid out alongside them. This was where parents and pupils were to congregate. Special guests (and Matthew, with his wangled invitation!) were milling around a point by the memorial garden, which is where Matthew was heading, his heart thumping.

He saw Chapman before Chapman saw him. Two or three wives of special guests were talking to him, eyes excitedly animated by their closeness to celebrity. Or celebrity of a kind. They were probably congratulating him on a 'wonderful' speech.

Matthew had a cousin who, like his grandfather, had done very well for himself. In this case, in the city rather than in development and housebuilding. The apogee of his career had come when he had been elected Mayor of Chelsea and Kensington. In his year of office, he had decided to honour the 'old country' (which he had never in fact lived in) by holding a reception for the Irish

Taoiseach, Bertie Ahern, and had invited Matthew and Rachel to the do.

What had struck Matthew most forcibly and memorably was the aura of Ahern. Dressed differently, this stocky, coarse-faced man would have been indistinguishable on a building site from all the other labourers, but here, in the smart Town Hall of Chelsea, there was a sheen to him, an eye-catching presence. Was the magnetism of the man something that came with his position, the patina of power, a kind of seal of office? Or did it derive from some innate quality that had driven him to the top position? Or was it perhaps nothing to do with the man at all, but a merely a projection of the observer?

Chapman had that same aura, that same magnetic quality, that lustre that drew eyes to him. Not that Matthew could imagine him as a labourer on a building site. At that moment, Chapman looked up and caught sight of Matthew.

'Matthew! How nice to see you! It's been such a long time.'

'Indeed,' replied Matthew. They shook hands. 'I don't suppose you find much time for reading improving literature these days. Even if you were so inclined.'

'Oh, I don't know. My wife feeds me the odd book to relax with.'

'It was an excellent speech, by the way,' said Matthew. Oh gosh. Small talk. And so lame. And not even strictly true. It was, if anything, a 'safe' speech. Nothing too controversial, nothing outrageous.

'Thank you. It is genuinely good to be back…Are you lunching with us?'

'Oh yes.'

'Jolly good. I gather, by the way, that you are the school archivist these days. That must be very interesting.'

More small talk. But not lame. Not lame at all. Not from Matthew's point of view. The very opening that Matthew was hoping would present itself.

'Yes, I am and, yes, it's very interesting…Actually, there was something I wanted to pick your brain about. If we have time.'

'Of course. Fire away!'

But at that moment Headmaster Dogget appeared and asked Chapman to come and meet one of his other guests.

'After lunch, perhaps,' Chapman said over his shoulder as he was whisked away.

*

The school caterers had provided an impressive lunch, but Matthew, sandwiched between the pompous wife of a rich landowner who was a governor, and the Headmistress of a school in outer London, was too preoccupied to enjoy it. His distraction no doubt appeared rude to the women either side of him and to the others on the table, too, but he was rehearsing in his mind variations of the question he might ask Chapman after the meal. 'What was the hardest part of being Head of School?' Much too vague. Hopeless. 'Were there any crises in your last term at school?' Again, too vague. 'Did your parents give a large donation to the school when you left?' Just plain rude. 'Was there a scandal in your last term at school, which you helped the school avoid?' Direct, certainly. And certainly along the right lines. But would it do? Matthew didn't want to sound like some cheapskate journo on the trail of a local hero.

'Mr Agnew…Matthew…my Head of English claims that *King Lear* is the greatest text of all world literature.' It was the Headmistress. She had clearly had enough of Matthew's aloofness and wanted to engage him. 'She says that nobody should be allowed to leave school without having read it. Would you agree with that?'

'Oh, gosh. Well. Well, I'm not sure that I agree with a league table notion of…you know, "the greatest of all" kind of thing. Ladies and Gentlemen, I present you with the European Champion and World Champion, *King Lear*! Ta da! But I'd certainly agree it is a most staggering piece of literature. It…shows, I guess, the profundity of Shakespeare's understanding of the human condition… but actually I suppose that my favourite, my most admired Shakespeare has changed at different stages of my life. There was a time, for example, when I thought *Antony and Cleopatra* was his finest play…As a matter of fact I taught *Antony and Cleo* to David Chapman—'

'Oh, how interesting. I didn't realise you had taught him. He seems such an impressive man, doesn't he? And destined for great things, of course. Could you see that in the boy? See the successful politician? What was he like to teach?'

'Well. Very bright of course. And, yes, coming from the family he comes from, clearly someone who would take a tilt at the political life. But if I remember, I don't think he much liked *Antony and Cleopatra*. I seem to recall that he found the relationship between the two lovers unconvincing and didn't see their ending as tragic, but he was certainly interested in the realpolitik played out in the drama. Fully engaged in that.'

'Interesting.'

The brief exchange had taken Matthew out of himself. He looked across the room to the top table. Chapman was deep in conversation with someone. The eyes of many at the table were fixed upon him. But it was Chapman's eyes that Matthew was interested in. Even from a distance he could see that they were in contrast to the rest of the face. When the man smiled, the smile was in the muscles of the face. But the eyes were unsmiling. They were not dead, but they had no vitality. They had become a screen behind which all feelings and attitudes could be disguised or hidden.

*

It is time for coffee. When Chapman comes over to Matthew, it is a relief. He has been dreading having to manoeuvre an opportunity to talk to him again.

'Matthew, you had a question for the archive?'

'Yes. David, I was looking at a file in the archive recently and came across the name of General Gilbert, Chairman of the Governors. He died in your final term, didn't he?' Where has that come from? That isn't the question he'd intended to ask. But. But.

The tiniest flicker of…What was it? Surprise? Alarm? Irritation? Too quick a flash to know. The politician's mask – the product, no doubt, of assiduous training by a media management coach – is quickly in place. The muscles of the face relaxed, the mouth with just the merest hint of a smile. *You must at all times appear friendly.* And the eyes. Yes, the eyes have it. *The eyes are what need to be most carefully trained. They need to have a look of directness, of openness, of cheerful confidence, without giving anything away about how you are feeling.*

So, before he knows it, Chapman is looking into Matthew's eyes, no longer any trace of a man who, for a micro-second, has seemed to be discomfited. The mask is back in place.

'Oh. I don't remember. Sorry…Is that it? Is there anything else you wanted to ask?'

But Matthew doesn't have the nerve to continue.

CHAPTER 6

The image of Chapman, that momentary flicker of the eyes, stayed with Matthew. He could not dislodge it.

The previous month, another politician, Ed Miliband, Leader of Her Majesty's Opposition, had been out campaigning in the local elections. He stops for a quick bite at a small café in New Covent Garden. The shutter of a pointing lens clicks. A frozen moment of the man clumsily eating a bacon sandwich. Online, the image goes viral and in the press it is paraded endlessly. An image which, unfairly, no doubt, will come to define his ineptness.

For Matthew, the freeze-frame image of Chapman has, rightly or wrongly, come to define a sense of something shifty in the man. Or, if not shifty, something not quite right. A secret of some kind. That was what his gut instinct was telling him. Hunch. Instinct. Intuition. Whichever it was.

Dislodge it or not, further enquiries would have to wait. Speech Day marked the end of the school year, and the following day Matthew and Rachel would be visiting Michael Agnew in Marlow for the weekend.

The drive eastwards, in dazzling summer sunlight, was pleasant. As they headed north up the A404, increasing numbers of red kites could be seen circling for the roadkill that no doubt was plentiful on this fast-moving road. They were larger than the buzzards that Matthew was familiar with at home, and yet more agile; they used their forked tails like kestrels, making small adjustments to give themselves a fine manoeuvrability.

The plan was to head downstream on his father's slipper launch *Farewell*, and lunch at The Ferry inn in Cookham. Too frail these days to do it himself, Michael had asked a friend to prepare the boat. The seats had been scrubbed clean, the varnished woodwork buffed to a gleaming amber in the midday sunlight.

Matthew drove the boat with his father beside him, Rachel sitting in the back with Foxy on a tight lead. It was the dog's first boat trip. They passed All Saints' Church on the left and the curving weir on the right before heading into Marlow Lock. Foxy was fascinated by the process: the people on the lock side disappearing slowly; glistening green algae deepening as the boat gently lowered with the emptying of the water. The lock keeper waved a large narrowboat out first, before signalling to Matthew. He manoeuvred the craft out past the development of white ship-lapped waterside homes with roofs angled in the shapes of sails. More elegant than the development where Michael's flat was, but busily noisy throughout the summer months when the lock filled with bumping boats and shouting people.

Matthew did not want to mention his dilemma over Chapman until later in the day. He talked, instead, in generalities about the previous day's Speech Day. 'It was pretty much the same as ever. Headmaster's state of the nation speech. Prizes. Guest's speech. The guest, in fact, was an old boy who I taught in the early '90s. Chap called Chapman...He's done well. A minister in the Home Office.'

'Chapman. Yes, I've heard the name…Did he speak well?'

'In the manner of most ambitious or high-flying politicians. There's something of the automaton about them. One imagines they could give these speeches in their sleep.'

'Yes, politicians are a peculiar breed. You know, I read a book not so long ago – I don't remember what it was called or even who it was by – but it was examining the psychopathy of leadership, arguing that models of leadership in various spheres are drawn these days from the business world, which in turn derives from the modern capitalism of the global economy.'

'What spheres?'

'Parliament, naturally – especially for career-politicians – and, increasingly, academia. The book contains a checklist of the attributes that define a psychopath, and finds interesting overlaps with a checklist that might define a successful modern CEO.'

'That sounds interesting! What are the overlaps?'

'Oh gosh, what were they? Well, in general, the qualities that deny one's humanity. Oh dear, Matty, I'm sorry, my memory is not so good these days. Not for the fine detail.'

'Dad! Even assuming I ever reach your age, if I am half as sharp as you in my mid eighties I will be very happy.'

'Sweet boy, Matty.'

A duck squawked noisily. And then two swans floated by with a line of well-ordered cygnets in tow.

'Have the swan-uppers been through yet, Dad?'

'No, not yet. Another couple of weeks, I think.'

Although *Farewell* made very little wash, Matthew slowed as a Ladies Four approached, the crew red-faced from their exertions in the sun.

'Now, the key indicators of the psychopathy of

leadership,' said Michael, adjusting his ancient and somewhat frayed panama hat to keep the sun out of his eyes. 'The absolute trademark is lack of empathy. Lack of empathy. A lack of kindness. A lack of remorse. Manipulativeness. Glibness. Superficial charm...Not all the overlapping attributes are negative. A proneness to boredom. A need therefore for busyness might be seen as good, leading to a compelling desire to improve the business. But that in turn leads to such people moving on quickly to do the same again with another business.'

'That's really interesting. It's certainly true that, in the time I have been teaching, the typical head of an independent school is a very different person from in the past. The modern head is a manager first and a teacher second. And the management structures probably owe more to business that to the traditional school, where one could perhaps get by with a gentlemanly amateurishness.'

'And what about Chapman, Matty? Is he a psychopath?'

Matthew's shocked reaction drew a laugh from Michael.

'No, I don't think so, Dad, but...Well...he is emotionally a cold fish. I remember when I taught him being surprised at his complete lack of emotional engagement with a text.'

'Interesting. The last Vice-Chancellor before I retired from the university was the new kind of CEO type. Business orientated. Clinical. Heartless in many ways.'

Was now the time to mention his suspicions of Chapman to his father? He decided against it.

But that momentary flicker of unease. What image was it that had ambushed the mind of David Chapman at the mention of General Sir Peter Gilbert? Matthew replays, with slight adjustments, the scenario that had awoken him that night in May, shortly after discovering the incriminating letter.

...'Come in, David,' says Harper. 'Take a seat.' He tells Chapman that there has been a complaint from the parents of a boy who had been expelled for drug-taking earlier in the year. 'They are adamant that you beat a confession out of him.'

Chapman's face clouds. 'Beat? That is not true, sir. It's nonsense. I questioned him. He answered my questions.'

Harper explains that there have been similar, if slightly less serious, complaints from other parents, parents of existing pupils. He tells Chapman that he must stand down as Head of School. For the good of the school.

Chapman's parents know that being sacked as Head of School will be a blot on Chapman's school record, a possible impediment to his future political progress and eventual success. But they are well used to operating the levers of power. They are well connected. And very soon Mr Chapman is on the phone to General Sir Peter Gilbert.

General Sir Peter Gilbert is a sick man with arteriosclerosis. He doesn't know it, but soon he will be dead. But he is a helpful man. He is a mover and a shaker; and he is keen to help out other movers and shakers – that is the way the Establishment works. 'Leave it to me,' he says in a voice made weak by his struggling heart.

When he goes to see Harper the next day, he does not get the co-operation he wants. That he expects.

'Peter, I do not believe what you are asking me to do,' says Harper. 'Asking me to reverse my decision about David Chapman is not the right thing to do. The Head of School has to be tough, of course, but there are lines that cannot be crossed. Chapman has crossed a line.'

Sir Peter, a sick man with only weeks to live, lacks the energy to argue his case. He says, in a wheezy voice, 'You will do as I say, Christopher, or I will sack you.'

Christopher Harper is a man of principle. He will not

yield. He is told by Sir Peter, Chairman of Governors, that he must step down from his headship at the earliest possible moment, which will be the end of the Christmas term. He is told that David Chapman will remain Head of School. There is, however, some collateral damage. While most of the governors acquiesce to Sir Peter's ordinances, Dr Anthony Marshall, friend of Christopher Harper, resigns in protest. But there are benefits, too, from the whole sorry affair. The Chapmans have agreed to make a generous donation to the school...

Matthew's reverie is broken by his father's voice. 'How's Foxy Lady doing?'

Foxy was doing well. Sitting up on the back bench, head facing forward into the breeze of the boat's movement, ears back, eyes half-shut, tongue lolling out for coolness on this hot day. 'Fine,' said Rachel. 'A veritable sea dog!'

They passed The Bounty, an attractive riverside pub on Cock Marsh, with mock Tudor façade. Boats were moored two abreast on the large landing stage; the terrace by the waterside was bustling with cheerful people enjoying the summer sunshine. Some waved as *Farewell* went by.

A large, expensive cruiser passed them, going much too fast and creating a huge wash. 'Bloody fools,' muttered Michael. The bloody fools were sitting on the top deck, wine glasses and beer mugs in hand. As *Farewell* hit the spreading V of the wash, it lurched and rocked a little. The movement always reminded Matthew of being on horseback, something he'd done for much of his childhood at Hyghcliff, hacking out with his mother or, under her watchful eye, jumping in the paddock. They were happy days and he loved his closeness to the horses. His first had been a Welsh Mountain pony called Cari. Small and scruffy, and savagely wilful; it wasn't until Matthew progressed to something larger and better schooled that he began to acquire the finer skills of horsemanship. When older, he was sometimes allowed to ride Merrion, his mother's most prized horse. Powerfully built, perfectly schooled, soft in the mouth, high spirited, he was wonderful fun if ridden properly; if not, he would misbehave outrageously. Not long into his teaching career, Matthew had decided that the relationship between teachers and taught was somewhat similar to that between riders and ridden. A dull plug of a horse was like a stupid, lumpen class that needed goading and pushing if it were to make any progress. A class of bright, curious, slightly mischievous adolescents was like a classy horse of good mettle that needed to be ridden with skill. Whatever the challenges, the bright class, the classy horse was always to be preferred, the challenges to be embraced, the rewards to be enjoyed.

The wash subsided and soon the road bridge linking Cookham to Bourne End came into view. Matthew took *Farewell* just beyond and then swept back in an arc. There were no mooring spots free, but a man on the back of a narrowboat was waving to them, indicating that they should pull up alongside him. When they were close, Rachel threw a rope to the man, and Matthew nosed the launch gently alongside.

Michael had booked a table overlooking the river and Cookham Bridge. 'This is where the ferry used to go from before they built the bridge. Hence the rather obvious name of the pub!' he explained.

'Cliveden Reach is just round the corner downstream, beyond the next lock, isn't it?' said Rachel. 'The children used to love going there. The picnics...'

'And the rain, too. They loved it when Dad put the canopy up, feeling secure and cosy.'

'*African Queen!*'

They sat beneath a large rectangular sunshade. Foxy was lying under the table for additional shade. But not invisible. A small girl spotted her and tugged her father's arm. 'Daddy, that dog looks like a fox!' She scuttled over, squatted on her haunches and peered at Foxy. Who never spurned attention. Tail wagging, she launched herself towards the little girl. 'What's she called?'

'Foxy. Foxy Lady is her full name.'

The little girl turned back towards her father. 'Daddy, it is a fox!'

'I don't think so, poppet,' he said.

'No,' said Matthew. 'A sheltie. But she does like chicken! It's her favourite,' he added.

The food was arriving at the table so, after being allowed to stroke Foxy, the little girl returned to her father.

As they were waiting for their desserts, two women walked by, one of them pausing as she saw Michael. 'It is you, isn't it? Michael Agnew. I thought it was you earlier.'

Michael seemed to recognise her immediately. He stood and bowed to greet her. 'Catherine!' She was an attractive woman, despite her age, which Matthew guessed was early seventies. 'This is my son, Matthew, and daughter-in-law, Rachel. Oh, and Foxy the dog.'

'What a beautiful little creature! Such a pretty face!'

They talked for a few minutes, exchanging news of what each had been up to in recent years and then the two women departed. Matthew had sensed a real charge between his father and this Catherine.

As they clambered aboard the narrowboat to return to *Farewell*, Matthew began to worry that his father would struggle to get onto the launch, which was lower in the water than the narrowboat. He had found it difficult to make the big step up when they had arrived. And Matthew had noticed how slowly he had eaten his lunch, seeming to labour over his food. He seemed frailer than when they had last visited.

But with Rachel in the launch to steady him and Matthew taking his weight as he lowered him down, they managed to get him safely aboard. When underway again, Michael was soon in typical good humour. He explained who Catherine was, that he and she had once had a close relationship, sharing much of their lives together, if not their homes.

'You never told us about her, Dad.'

'No.' He grinned. 'I didn't think it was a matter to concern you with.'

*

Michael had prepared a beef casserole the day before and now he and Rachel were in the kitchen making the final preparations for the supper. His shopping had been done by his cleaner, Betty Knowles, who came in twice a week. She would usually bring a treat of some kind for Michael and always the local gossip, chuntering on while Michael nodded his head and chuckled occasionally, only half listening. But she made a very good job of keeping the flat tidy and clean and he was very fond of her.

There was only one item of furniture that was off-limits to her, a nineteenth-century Dutch marquetry chest-of-drawers that stood across a corner of the sitting room. It was a striking piece, with a bombé serpentine front, and boxwood and fruitwood marquetry of flowers and foliage set in a walnut top. Standing on the chest were nine figures of the Meissen Monkey Band, bewigged, clothed in pastel shades of Regency dress, playing their variety of instruments. Only one of the figures was undamaged, a lone trumpeter, playing his instrument with one hand, the other placed rather effetely on his hip.

It was not that Michael did not trust Mrs Knowles. She would have dusted the monkeys to within an inch of their lives and buffed the chest to a shine that would have sent back the sharpest of reflections. It was out of bounds to her because this was a job that Michael liked to do himself. The chest and the band had been objects particularly loved by his wife, Bridget. Both had come down to her by some obscure family route. She thought that they were beautiful and special. And that she should now be the careful custodian of them.

Michael had never been as fond of the chest as his wife, finding its busyness of shape and decoration a little excessive, and believing that the monkey band veered towards kitsch. Nevertheless he now in turn felt himself to be the custodian, a responsibility he took seriously. And when polishing the chest, he always sensed a strong connection to his wife.

*

After supper they sat out on the balcony. As the twilight deepened and lights came on, gleaming flickers danced on the water, their rhythms broken now and then by passing boats or water fowl. Later the disco boats would pass by with their flashing lights and their cargoes of raucous revellers.

Matthew thought back to the meeting with Catherine at The Ferry, and the charge between her and his father. 'Dad, did you never ever think of remarrying after Mum died?'

'No, never seriously. Your mother was so complete for me; she was all I ever wanted. I knew I would never find a woman again that could give me that completeness. So I had relationships, of course, for companionship and for the odd fling. But I never really contemplated remarriage.'

Matthew sensed it would be indelicate to ask which category Catherine fell into. In any case, he thought he knew the answer.

'My memories of you and Mum are of a perfectly contented couple. You never rowed, did you?'

'Not often, certainly.'

'I never heard you.'

'You did. The once. You were in the next room, the playroom, driving your toys around the carpet. And we were having this blazing row, shouting loudly at each other. I'd just discovered that your mother had had a brief dalliance with the young vet who used to come round to treat the horses. I was hurt and angry. And then she got angry. Voices were raised. Suddenly we heard you crying in the next room.'

There is a stunned silence. Matthew is shocked, reeling at what his father has just said.

Rachel, sensing the chasm that has opened before the two men, wants to fill the void with words. She reaches over and takes Matthew's hand in hers. 'Matty, it doesn't matter. It was such a long time ago. So long ago... There's no point thinking about it. No point...'

Matthew notices that his father is looking distressed. 'Matty, I'd always assumed that you knew. That you had heard the words your mother and I exchanged. That the episode – brief and unimportant in the fullness of our marriage – was carried as an unspoken memory by us all. I'm so sorry to have upset you.'

Is that what Matthew's face is showing? Upset, rather than the deep surprise at what he has learnt? He supposes it is. And of course he is upset. The prism through which he has viewed his childhood and his parents needs tilting a little, needs an adjustment so that he can accommodate this new strand of his history.

'When she heard you, she went rushing in to the playroom. She comforted you, and then she took you out to the cinema.'

The cinema? The image of them leaving the house and walking to the bus stop. He can see the clothes he and she are wearing. He sees the pair of them disappearing up the road.

He tells his father about this vividly recalled image. 'But I don't recall anything before this, or after. The film she took me to or anything. It is an isolated image.'

Now Michael takes his hand. 'I'm sorry to bring this upset, Matty. As I say, I thought you remembered the incident. I see now that you have blocked it out for all those years.' He pauses. Is he wondering whether to continue? 'It's interesting, isn't it? When we tell the story of ourselves, we are the most unreliable historians of all. The evidence of our lives is edited…is shaped and reshaped to give us an image of ourselves…a story of ourselves that we can accommodate, that we can live with. Some of the evidence we dismiss. Some, as in your case of not remembering the row because it was so disturbing, we destroy.'

Rachel is very quiet. There is a look of sadness in Michael's eyes. Matthew squeezes his hand and nods.

'The episode had no importance to our future. I forgave your mother instantly. She was a passionate woman. It was a passion I loved. A passion. A curiosity. A zest. She was always very ashamed of what she'd done with the vet. Of how upset she'd made me. And according to her religion, of course, she'd been very sinful. And no doubt she set herself all kinds of penances, to say nothing of the priest. But we soon forgot her transgression. It was nothing.'

Matthew nods again.

When he goes into his father's bedroom to say goodnight to him, he looks at the portrait of his mother that hangs on one of the walls, an oil painting that was done when she was in her early forties. It is simple in some ways. No background setting, instead just colour – a goldy yellow suggesting light and warmth, giving an aura to the figure of his mother. Her hair is arranged in a way that gives no clue to when the painting might have been done, and there is a similar neutrality of fashion to the simple green cardigan that she is wearing.

What is striking in the portrait, striking at least to Matthew, is the expression that the painter has captured. He will have seen the passion, the 'zest' his father had called it, the energy of his subject, but has chosen instead to delineate, both in the mouth but especially in the eyes, a deep thoughtfulness. The gaze is upward and outward, towards the future perhaps, and suggests confidence and understanding.

'Dad, I've looked at that portrait so many times, and I always find it interesting…Do you think it captures Mum?'

'I do. I think we were both expecting something a little different, and I think she was disappointed with it. She wanted something that captured what she called 'the colleen' in her, the Irish vitality, I suppose she meant. But this…' He looks towards the portrait. 'This captures her wisdom, I think…You know, she always felt intellectually inferior to me. Always regretted not going to university. But actually, the untutored mind – if it is a good one, and she had a good mind – is often so much more interesting than the mind that has been taught to jump through the hoops of the examination hall.'

*

Matthew had kissed his father goodnight and joined Rachel in their bedroom. When they turned their lights out, she had moved to his side of the bed and embraced him so tightly and for so long that he knew and gratefully accepted the unspoken comfort she was wanting to give him after his difficult evening.

They left mid-morning the next day.

At breakfast Matthew had discussed Chapman with his father. He explained about the fragment of letter, the morally dodgy 'course of action', whatever it was, the resignations of the Headmaster and the writer of the letter, who had been a governor. And the clear unease of David Chapman when Matthew had mentioned the Chairman of the Governors, Sir Peter Gilbert.

'What are you suggesting, Matty?'

'That something fishy went on.'

'So? Is that important? Is it a concern of yours and, if so, why?'

'I'm interested rather than concerned. Curious.'

'You don't have much to go on, do you?'

'I have the beginnings…What I would like to know is how you would proceed, Dad. How you would take your research forward.'

'I wouldn't. I'm not a detective, nor an investigative reporter. And nor are you. I would leave well alone. In any case, it's not really within your remit as archivist and, even if it were, I would advise against it.' He paused while he took another bite of toast. 'You need to remember that politicians are by nature ambitious people, and ambitious people can be ruthless, especially if they have something to protect. I suspect that Chapman is not a man to cross. You should remember, too, that if he works at the Home Office, he will have access to various branches of the police. And if, as you say, he worked for MI5, he will have come across some fairly unsavoury characters working for the service.'

'Gracious, Dad, I'm not suggesting that a major

scandal lies behind this and that all kinds of nasty forces will be released if I dig a little deeper. You make it sound very cloak-and-dagger!

'No, you make it sound very cloak-and-dagger!' Michael smiles. 'This is so you, Matty! It's that imagination of yours again. You always were a great inventor. When you were a little boy at Hyghcliff, you would invent these wonderful narratives for your Dinky toys and would play alone contentedly for hours and hours. And when you were older, it seemed to me that you opted to read English Literature because you could stay within a world of the imagination.' Matthew opens his mouth to interrupt, but Michael continues. 'There is something wonderful about the imaginative, inventive mind, but when you let it get out of control, Matty, you do tend to see things that aren't there, you see conspiracies that aren't conspiracies...You see some bones of a kitten and in your mind flesh them out to the body of a lion.'

'Dad, that's really not fair. And not true...But I like the metaphor! With regard to the letter, I'm just curious. I found the details in the letter intriguing. It's a puzzle crying out to be solved...And we know, don't we – and it couldn't have been made clearer than by the abuse uncovered in the MPs' Expenses Scandal – we know how corrupt politicians can be.'

Michael paused to choose his words. 'The Expenses Scandal certainly showed that politicians can be venal. As if we didn't know that! But it was small scale. It was petty cash. And in any case, it appears to have been a system with a pseudo legitimacy. If you remember, claiming questionable expenses was a tolerated and even encouraged way for MPs to compensate for poor salaries.' He paused again. 'Now, if you really want a history lesson, I could tell you about eighteenth-century British politics when corruption, real corruption, had become institutionalised. It even has a name: The Old Corruption. But I'll spare you both the history lesson for the time being. All I will say, Matty, is leave it. It's not something that matters really, is it?'

Rachel, who had been pouring more tea for them all, now chipped in. 'I agree with Michael, Matty. I think it's pointless and could get you into deep water. Supposing Chapman complained to Dogget about your sniffing around.' She explained to her father-in-law that Dogget was the Headmaster.

Michael laughed. 'There you are, Matty, you are outvoted!' He glanced up at Rachel, who was bringing him his cup of tea. 'But you know, Rachel, and I know, that when young Matty here has a bee in his bonnet, he will listen to no one. He is persistent, as his mother was, and no doubt has the same standards of absolute morality that his mother derived from her faith. Although Matty has long since been heathen!' He chuckled again.

'So you are not going to give me any advice, Dad.'

'I'll say one thing only. In history, as in law, everything must be underpinned by evidence.'

CHAPTER 7

The movement of water, the movement in water, with its slow, patient progress; the sound of water, the surrounds of water: all had long held an appeal for Matthew. The river trip – but perhaps it was more Michael's discussion about the psychopathy of power, with his mischievous question about Chapman – had given Matthew the desire, when he returned from the visit to Marlow, to read *Heart of Darkness* once again. He had taught the text a number of times over the years, including to the A level class which contained David Chapman. It was a novel – novella – he valued highly for various reasons: the choices – compulsions, perhaps – it seemed to offer for a *modus vivendi*; its glimpse into the crazed greed of nineteenth-century European imperialists; the setting of the two rivers running through it like a bright ribbon.

He wondered if Conrad had thought of the smart Buckinghamshire riverside town when naming his narrator Charlie Marlow. Provisioned by the butcher, protected by the policeman, it was a comfortable, safe place to live. And the Thames, the venerable stream Conrad called it, had a tranquil dignity that offered gentle recreation these days. A far cry from the horrors – the horror – of the heart of African darkness.

The book provoked fierce arguments. He had given it to his class to read over the Easter holidays so that he could begin teaching it at the beginning of the summer term. When he asked for initial responses in the first lesson, a furious girl – was she called Jo? – had erupted. 'I think it's a vile book. How can we be expected to read something, let alone study it, which uses the word 'nigger' and which portrays Africans in such a disgusting way?'

Later, once they had started a close study of the text, Jo had said that not only was the novel deeply and offensively racist, but also sexist, citing the lie that Marlow told to Kurtz's fiancée. She quoted his excuse: "'They – the women, I mean – are out of it – should be out of it. We must help them to stay in that beautiful world of their own." Conrad wants women to be wrapped in cotton wool, to be protected. The fairer sex. To shimmer for men and not trouble their pretty little heads…Urgh! Why are we studying this nonsense?'

'Are you suggesting,' Matthew asked, 'that anything that reflects the attitudes of a particular time that differ radically from the attitudes of our own time should not be studied? Should be destroyed even? Literary revisionism? It sounds very Stalinist!'

'But it is racist in a way that is unacceptable now,' someone had said. 'The way that Conrad sets the culture and refinement of Europe against the brutalism and bestiality of Africa.'

'It's not as simple as that.' Things never did seem as simple to David Chapman as they did to others. 'Conrad is actually less interested in the *differences* of culture and more interested in the *similarities*, and kinship, even, between white man and black man. What seems to terrify Marlow is the possibility of his kinship with these beings.' He reads from the text: 'But what thrilled you was just the thought of their humanity – like yours – the thought of your remote kinship with this wild and passionate uproar.'

Somebody else chipped in. 'I think you are being unfair to Conrad calling him racist. He presents a very negative view of the Belgian imperialists as well. Or Marlow does. Let's not forget that it is Marlow's story we are getting.'

Chapman shook his head. 'The very negative view of the Belgian imperialists does not in any way ameliorate the portrait of African man. And the fact that the portrait of Africa is separated from Conrad by the insulation of two narrators does not excuse Conrad. He has not offered any criticism of his narrators – Marlow sits Buddha-like, with all the wisdom that seems to imply – and, significantly, he does not give any alternative frame of reference by which to judge them.' As so often is the case, Chapman's pronouncements have the sound and appearance of dispassionate and monolithic statements of truth, unchallengeable.

He disliked the book, especially the account of the core of the book, Kurtz's discovery of the heart of darkness. 'It's confused, woolly-headed. Look at the way that Marlow – Conrad – uses words such "mysterious" and "inscrutable". They repeatedly do duty for more specific description—'

Some brave or foolhardy spirit jumps in. 'This surely is because Conrad is indicating the ineffable nature of Kurtz's existential discovery, the—'

On the word 'ineffable' there is a grunt of derisive incomprehension from someone, then a snort from Chapman. 'Yes, yes, I know. The limits of my language are the limits of my world, that words are an approximation and all that, but I think Conrad needed to do better than that.'

*

Who were the someones of that class, Chapman's classmates? Matthew never threw away his old mark books (should he give them to the school archive?), and made a trip to the attic to recover the relevant one.

He found the battered, bottle-green ledger – 'Matthew Agnew 1988–1992' – and looked with interest at who was in that David Chapman class. Jo Perry. It was Jo who took issue with Conrad's racism and sexism. And Shakepeare's. And other writers', too. She read with a watchful readiness for prejudice. She had gone on to read English at UCL, if he remembered correctly. And there a name he had long since forgotten, Paul Smedding. The face came back to him. A bored expression normally. A level English was a means to an end for him, a simple end, one that he felt was pretty much the sole purpose of an expensive education. To make lots of money. Quickly.

Matthew looked up a passage in *Heart of Darkness* that he remembered reading to his class. It was about the Belgian colonists:

> these men strolling aimlessly about in the sunshine of the yard... like a lot of faithless pilgrims bewitched inside a rotten fence. The word 'ivory' rang in the air, was whispered, was sighed. You would think they were praying to it. A taint of imbecile rapacity blew through it all, like a whiff from some corpse.

Someone – another someone, Matthew couldn't remember who – had drawn a comparison with the 1980s culture of greed, the 'loadsmoney' culture that characterised a certain aspect of Margaret Thatcher's deregulated Britain. 'Loadsamoney, Paul!' someone had whispered, leaving

Smedding to simmer with an inarticulate rage, his face a picture of dull stupidity.

*

Did Chapman say that Conrad's articulation of Kurtz's horrific epiphany was woolly, was linguistically wanting? Or was Matthew giving licence to his memory as he tried to recapture some teaching days long past? It was difficult to say. What he could say, what he knew, was that he found Marlow's psychic journey into the heart of darkness, man's darknesss, the de-moralising darkness of Kurtz's own heart, compelling and convincing.

He looked again at his old mark book to see what essays he had set the group. One caught his eye in particular. '"Kurtz is destroyed in his final confrontation of what Marlow views as the ultimate truth: that the essentials of experience remain amoral and, even, alinguistic." Discuss.' A critical quote. From whom? No matter. He noticed that Chapman had received a very high mark.

And then his eye was caught by another name. George West. He hadn't lasted the course, expelled in the Upper Sixth, one of the many pupils sent packing after David Chapman's investigation into drug-taking. Matthew had been fond of George. He was quite bright and fitfully hard-working. What Matthew liked in him was his adventurousness. He read with a wide-ranging curiosity, and he argued so that ideas – his own and those of others – might be tested; and he believed that youth, especially that part that belonged to late adolescence, was a time for experimentation of all kinds. Which is presumably why he had dabbled in drugs.

George had loved the Harlequin man in *Heart of Darkness*, loved his enthusiasm and his open-mindedness. He had seen him as some kind of prototype hippy: 'But when one is young one must see things, gather experience, ideas; enlarge the mind.' Where was George now? What did he do? Matthew might check that, out of nothing more than idle curiosity, when term resumed.

*

On the day in early July on which Rolf Harris was sentenced to five years and nine months in prison for various convictions of indecent assault, the Agnews set off for a short break amongst the billowing hills of West Dorset. They had hired a cottage that looked out onto Colmer's Hill. This almost perfectly conical elevation was topped by a small clump of Caledonian pine trees, which sat rooted precariously in the shallow soil that covered its sandstone mass. The unusual symmetry of the hill, with its crowning tuft of trees, was one of Dorset's iconic landmarks. Much painted and photographed, a winter image of it, with a light covering of frost and arising out of a thick and flat mist, had appeared in the *Times*. It looked enchanting, and had set Rachel searching online for a suitable cottage.

Rarely these days did the Agnews seek the exoticism of abroad, preferring the quieter pleasures of domestic holidays. Their requirements were simple. Good food and good walks in stimulating countryside. Nearby Chideock was surrounded to the west, north and east by two horseshoes of hills separated by the Marshwood Vale, and it was in these hills and valleys and woodlands that they spent the next few days. They climbed to the grassland of Pilsdon Pen, where they saw and heard larks, and where they got their first sighting of a burnet moth, brilliant red on black. And they walked along the arching holloways that were a feature of the area, imagining the sheep that might have been driven down these flinty tracks in former times. Golden Cap offered them a fine view of the Jurassic coast and of Lyme Regis in the distance. And for Foxy, it was her first experience of the sea. She loved the texture of the sand beneath her feet, and she enjoyed running towards an incoming wave, challenging it to catch her before springing away with smart agility.

The school seemed a world away. The archive an irrelevance. And Chapman wasn't spared a moment's thought.

*

Once home again, Matthew's mind was dragged back to Chapman. The battered mark book lay open on his desk where Matthew had put it before they had left for West Dorset. He looked to see what essay titles he had set on *Antony and Cleopatra*. No very startling or original titles there. A shame. It was a challenging text to teach to adolescents, who found it difficult to understand the middle-aged lust of the protagonists; many were repelled by the notion of mature people, their parents perhaps, having any kind of sexuality.

The temperamental opposites of David Chapman and George West argued over this text as they had over *Heart of Darkness*. When George had talked about the protagonists' self-sacrificing passion and ennobling love, Chapman could barely contain his contempt.

'This is not at all what Shakespeare is showing us! He is presenting two delusional lovers, each, in the moment of their defeat, claiming a spurious dignity to the sorry ends – the sordid ends – they have led themselves to. He is not glorifying them at all. Their relationship is selfish and distasteful and, if Shakespeare really is trying to glorify their deaths, then he is wholly unconvincing...I read somewhere that the key to the play might be seen in

Enobarbus' comment that "Men's judgements are a parcel of their fortunes".

'Yes,' Matthew had agreed, 'this is a valid interpretation. Antony's judgements, misjudgements, go hand in hand with his fortunes...misfortunes, as he spins uncontrollably to the bottom of the whirlpool. The vagabond flag upon the stream, like a piece of detritus on the sea's surface, going back and forth on the changing tides to rot itself with motion. Like a feather to every wind that blows.'

'I think that's harsh, sir.' George West, the romantic, was having none of it.

'The dissolution of Antony, dislimning like a cloud that is dragonish, is pitiful, certainly, George. But is there enough worth and enough pity?'

Perhaps that was Kurtz, too, his judgements a parcel of his fortunes. But how had Marlow escaped the seductions that claimed Kurtz? When Matthew had asked that question, it had been George West who had articulated Marlow's limited perspective.

'He's obsessed with his tin-pot steamboat. It's his over-riding preoccupation, the saving reality that he sinks himself into.' He immediately corrects himself. '"Sinks" is the wrong word, because actually he makes a point of inhabiting a surface reality. He says he had to keep guessing at the channel, to keep a lookout for signs of dead wood they could use for fuelling the steamboat. And then he says, "When you have to attend to things of that sort, to the mere incidents of the surface, the reality – the reality, I tell you – fades. The inner truth is hidden – luckily, luckily".' Matthew is nodding in approval as George then thumbs his book looking for another passage he has marked. 'He explains why he didn't go ashore for a howl and a dance, like Kurtz. And of course it was because he had to look after the boat. "I had to watch the steering, and circumvent those snags, and get the tin-pot along by hook or by crook. There was surface-truth enough in these things to save a wiser man".

Chapman was gazing out of the window, but most of the class were interested in what George was saying. 'I see it,' he continued, 'that, unlike Kurtz, he is not a psychic adventurer. He has taken a quick and timid glimpse over the edge of the precipice and pulled back. His perspective, therefore, is limited, biased even. He doesn't want to enlarge his mind like the Harlequin man; he wants to limit it.' Were these George's words? Verbatim? Probably not. And did or did not Matthew hear someone muttering quietly 'Likes a spliff!' when the words 'psychic adventurer' were uttered by George? He thought he did remember that.

He pictured the classroom he had taught in for many years before retiring, housed in a 1970s block, ugly and distant relation to the grander buildings of the school campus. Unlike Victorian schoolrooms with their windows set high to avoid distractions, this black-brick building had one wall entirely glazed, the full length windows, ceiling to floor, forming a permeable membrane between the young minds within and the world beyond. The world immediately beyond was an attractive vista towards the Music School which, with its similar 1970s modernity, threw back an echo of the English Centre. Neat borders, with carefully planned and planted flowers and shrubs and ornamental trees, lay each side of the neat gravel path connecting the two buildings. An English-country-garden scene. Quite unlike the millions of trees, massive, immense, running up high and curtaining the heart of Africa's darkness.

Some of the most animated discussions were about the end of the book, and the morality of Marlow's lie to Kurtz's Intended when he returned to Belgium.

'Kurtz is, of course, a very interesting character, but actually I have always found the end the most engaging part of the novel, because of the way it challenges us to think how we should live our lives. With the truth, complete and unvarnished, with all the pain that might involve? Or on the surface, perhaps, to avoid what's disturbing or hurtful? What Marlow calls "surface-truth".

'You're offering a binary choice, sir. It's not as simple as that,' said Chapman.

'But that's what Conrad is choosing to present to us, David. Marlow visiting Kurtz's fiancée as dusk is falling, deepening to darkness. He meets a beautiful woman incredibly needy in her grief. A woman whose faith in her fiancé is intense, her expectation of what she will be told unshakeable. I think that Conrad writes this last section brilliantly. We see the Intended leading Marlow, manipulating Marlow, as she questions him, squeezing the answers she wants from him. And as the hesitant answers fall shakily from him, a dull anger grows in him. Until the final lie is plucked from him: "The last word he pronounced was – your name". Marlow expects the heavens to fall in upon his head for his lie, which of course they don't. And then he wonders if they would have fallen in if he had told the truth. If he had given Kurtz the justice that was his due. But he can't. Why?'

'Because the truth would have been "too dark"! Much too horrible for a mere woman to bear!' The speaker is Jo, whose distaste for Conrad's various isms has jaded her study of the text.

Matthew laughed. 'Not entirely fair, Jo! Okay, the book is sexist, but let's give Conrad his due. It is an important question. How much truth can we bear? How much illusion should we allow people to cling on to? Do you tell a three-year-old child that Father Christmas doesn't exist?'

'That's just silly,' Jo tutted.

'Not entirely. And you are not being entirely fair. Let me read this to you.' Matthew pauses to find the passage. 'Marlow talks about bowing his head before…"before the faith that was in her, before that great and saving illusion that shone with an unearthly glow in the darkness, in the triumphant darkness from which I could not have defended her – from which I could not even defend myself." He is not protecting her because she is a woman but because she is a human, and he sees innocence and illusion as preferable to the corrosive darkness that has eaten into Kurtz's heart. Marlow sees where Kurtz's adventurism has led him. He prefers the surface of things.'

A surface reality. Pottering about. Navigating the shallow coastal waters, avoiding the mysterious deep beyond. Short paces on the stepping-stones of illusion rather than bold exploratory strides into the unfamiliar. A way to live. Who would not prefer the sugar-coated lie to the sharp and bitter bite of toxic truth?

Ah, who indeed? Not the delver, surely, trowel in hand, dusting away the dirt of lies.

CHAPTER 8

The start of the autumn term finds Matthew preparing an archive display to commemorate the centenary of the First World War. Edwardian tranquillity transformed to the horror, the horror of senseless war. He is looking at the journal of one of the many hundreds of former pupils of the school who took part in the war, five hundred and seventy-three of whom sacrificed their lives. Oliver Webb joined the Royal Flying Corps in 1915; his journal records his service for the next three years. A hundred and twenty-three of the yellowing pages of the lined ledger contain written entries. Between many of the pages are insertions of various kinds: photographs, letters, telegrams, military orders, concert programmes and newspaper clippings. The photographs are varied. Many different kinds of aircraft, mostly biplanes, are shown, from the B.E.2c in which he flew from Farnborough to Flanders in the summer of 1915 to the Avro 788 that he spent much of his time flying; there are photographs of comrades, sometimes relaxing, sometimes busying themselves about their base. Most interesting are the aerial photos, interesting because they are the first of their kind. Matthew can imagine the sense of awe they must have inspired, this new form of virtually instant cartography offering the very latest intelligence on enemy positions and enemy movement.

The journal entries themselves have a wonderful immediacy. They convey the sense of excited discovery in the earliest days of his service. Much later in the war, there is a deepening gloom in the tone, an exhaustion, an intense desire for it all to be over.

A memorable entry from the autumn of 1915 describes his first visit to the front line. He has visited the Ypres Salient during the day:

> Ruination on every side, broken houses, pockmarked fields, general desolation. One heavy battery opened fire while we were there, the noise is deafening. Hellish conditions to live in & very little leave, but they manage to make the best of it & have pretty snug dug-outs with the latest pictorials and newspapers about and 'lively' pictures on the walls. We did not go into Ypres but it is a hateful sight, all grey ruin and deserted. It's curious to see the civil population clinging to the villages around & carrying on their farming and other work as usual, children playing around the doors.

Matthew makes notes of the entries he might use for his exhibition, and he scans the photos that will accompany the journal. The most striking is of Oliver Webb standing in front of his Avro. His is wearing his leather pilot's helmet, the straps dangling onto his shoulders, looking directly at the camera. It is difficult to read his expression. There is a hint of boredom in the face. Before the photograph can be printed, Matthew needs to tidy up the scan in Photoshop. A rusty paperclip has left its imprint and the image is further disfigured by tiny cracks of age in the surface of the photo.

Some quick work with the programme's cloning tool and the photograph looks as good as new. A falsification? No, a recovery of the original reality. The reality of the photo, at least, whatever relationship that has with the truth of the instant in which it was taken.

Next he looks at some letters from another Old Boy, Ian Wilson, who was also a member of the Royal Flying Corps and who, like Webb, survived the war. The letters are from 1918. Once again, there is the immediacy that only contemporary documentary evidence can give. The letters are from a young man to his mother. In one he tells her excitedly about his hedge-hopping escape from enemy territory. The engine is playing up, he is being fired at from the ground and suddenly two Fokkers are bearing down on him from above. The tone conveys the exuberance of youth, the sense of complete invulnerability. It can only be the combination of these two qualities that might explain such openness in the letters, a candour that must have terrified the man's poor mother and made her fear for the worst.

Neither Webb nor Wilson was in service at the beginning of the war in 1914. If Matthew's display was to offer a chronological account of the war he would need to find some items of display from its earliest moments. He went to one of his cabinets and pulled out a wadge of school magazines from the 1910s.

As he began to look through them, he heard a slow tread ascending the spiral staircase. A knock. And there in the doorway was Henry Baines, still puffing from the exertions of the climb. Either the mole on his neck had bled earlier in the day, or Henry had not changed his shirt; dried brown blood stained the collar.

'Matthew.' The pointy finger. When Henry wanted something, he had a disconcerting habit of wagging

103

a pointing finger towards his listener. An implied admonition? Or the body language of assertion?

'Henry! How can I help you?'

'I want any stuff at all that you've got on Chris Walters. He's leaving at the end of term and I've been asked to give his leaving speech.'

'Okay, I'll see what I can do and will get back to you.'

'I want it now.' On the word 'now' a pointy finger moves from ten o'clock to eight o'clock.

'Now?'

'Yes. I don't want the fag of coming back here again.'

'Ah. Okay...okay. What you want is Now...What you are going to get is In Due Course. I'm doing something else at the moment.'

Henry looks irritated. 'But I thought your time was flexible. That you could shuffle things around.'

'It's that very flexibility that enables me to shunt your request to a time that suits me. You don't need the stuff for weeks and weeks. I'll email what I find on Walters or put hard copy in your pigeon hole.'

Henry shuffles over to Matthew's desk and leans over it. The shirt is definitely unchanged; there is a musty smell of sweat seasoned sharply with what was presumably last night's supper. 'First World War. A display no doubt. But what actually do you know about the First World War? You're not a historian.'

'Oh for God's sake, Henry, what on earth do you mean, what do I know about the First World War? I know lots about the First World War and what I don't know I can learn about...Look, I've got all this stuff here. I can read. I can learn.'

'But you're not a historian.'

'Blah, blah, off you go again. No, Henry, I am not a historian in the sense that you are. I have not spent three years learning methodologies that could be learnt in a few weeks…But it's not rocket science…No, no, I'm not a physicist, either, before you ask.' Matthew lets out a giggle. 'But then if I'm not a physicist I won't know what rocket science is…So perhaps it *is* rocket science. In which case you are a rocket scientist, Henry. Wow!' His giggle becomes a laugh.

'You are a very irritating man. Very.'

'Okay, Henry, in a few short sentences, tell me what qualities, what competencies, I need to be a historian. Or Archivist…That's what this is actually about, isn't it? What are the qualities?'

Henry splutters. 'Well, you need to know where to look…What you're looking for. You need to know what's good and what is not—'

'What's good and what is not! Whaat?'

'What's valid and what is not.'

'Well, validity: that's a whole big question, for sure. And then?'

'And then organise these things.'

'Organise?'

'In order.'

'In order! Well, thank you, that's most helpful. So. Just so you know. As school archivist, I shall be looking in the school archive for documents and objects relating to the First World War. I know where the archive is. Because I am the archivist, see. So I will know where to find them. And then I will organise them into a display. In order. Whatever that means. Chronological, topical, etc. blah, blah. Or whatever I decide…as school archivist!'

'You're a little shit, Matthew, do you know that?'

'Are you drawing on your historical expertise there, Henry? Yes, you must be! Because you are not a social scientist. Or biologist. Or a medical scientist. Or psychologist even. Various of the disciplines that would contain within their skill sets the ability to identify a shit!'

Henry exhales noisily and aggressively and turns to go. But suddenly his eye catches the Chapman File, half hidden beneath some First World War photographs. 'David Chapman? Why have you got a file on him?'

Matthew had forgotten the file was on the desk. He quickly picks up the file so that Henry can't get hold of it. There would be complications if he did. 'The Ch…er, a file on David Chapman?…Why do you think, Henry? He was our guest on Speech Day. I wanted to do a little research on him to go with a copy of his speech, which I'll archive.'

'Hmm. Right…Let me have the stuff on Chris Walters in due course.' A sigh. And then Henry Baines turns and heads out of the door to begin a slow descent down the stairs.

Back to work. The magazines offered a startlingly bleak window on the war. Pared down, to save paper presumably, they were dominated by lengthy lists in the Rolls of Honour, the honoured falling into one of five categories: Killed in Action. Died of Wounds. Missing Believed Killed. Wounded. Missing.

When, in his teaching days, Matthew had taught First World War poets or memoirs, such as Goodbye to All That, he had always explained to his pupils his complete inability to understand the insanity of the war. The collective psychosis that had allowed the major nations of Europe to squander, year after year, the hundreds of thousands of young lives. Whatever text, or whatever poet he was teaching, he would always give them Ezra Pound's searing summation of the war from Hugh Selwyn Mauberley. Nothing sweet, nothing fitting. Lies. Lies from old mouths, lies from public figures. Countless lies. And countless deaths. For what? For a spent, washed-up culture. A brave young generation was wasted away for a broken civilisation.

The school rightly took great pains to honour its dead in the solemn Remembrance Day Service each year. And it was easy, Matthew thought, to lose oneself in the ritual of the occasion, the powerful stillness of the minute's silence broken by the pathos of the bugler's Last Post, with its haunting final note left hanging in the air. But easy, too, to lose sight of the ghastliness that this ceremony was commemorating. To forget the blood-sodden battlefields and the blood-drenched minds of the soldiers.

*

Beside the war journal, the bundle of letters from Ian Wilson and the pile of school magazines lay another letter. One that fortunately had not caught the eye of Henry Baines. Matthew had written it earlier in the day. It was addressed to David Chapman, MP, c/o The House of Commons.

It had been agreed, when David Chapman had visited the school as its Speech Day guest, that he would return on the second Saturday of the autumn term to open officially the classroom block that had been named in his honour. Predictably, perhaps, this visit was cancelled. A YouGov poll in early September was suggesting that the Scots would vote Yes in the Independence Referendum. If not panic, the jitters were now sweeping through the leading figures of the coalition government, and David Cameron had ordered all hands to the pump. This included David Chapman, though it was unclear to Matthew quite what role this public school-educated southerner might play, and with what success. The cancellation meant that Matthew would not be able to ask some questions that he had formulating, hoping for more success than he had achieved on Speech Day.

On the resumption of term, he had brought his old mark books to the archive and, as he had catalogued them, a subliminal image had come to him, an after-image of the page with the names of the pupils he had taught alongside Chapman. The pictorial memory was of two blank spaces in the column of Chapman's marks for the final series of A level revision essays in the summer of 1991. Strange for such a completely reliable and dependable boy.

When he checked he saw that he was correct about the blanks. He wondered if the archive held registration records from 1991 – few boarding schools took registers at that time – and was delighted to find that they did exist and in fact had been archived. When he looked at Chapman's attendance for the summer term, he found that he had been marked absent for more than two weeks. Had he been ill? And so the search continued.

In front of him now was a sheet of paper with his notes:

> 13 May
>> Govs' Meeting
>> -Gilbert in chair; Marshall present
>> -fee incr. / HM report (expulsions – West!)
>
> 13 May–3 June
>> Chapman absent from school
>
> 3 June
>> -A levels start (C. present on exam days)
>
> 20 Sept
>> Govs' Meeting
>> -replacement of G as Ch of Govs
>> -resignation of Marshall (no reason)
>
> C's pupil record???

It was time to look in Chapman's school file. Matthew wondered why he hadn't done this before. The records of pupils who had left in the previous twenty-five years were kept in the school strong room. Its Cerberus was the Headmaster's secretary. She was actually less like a guard dog and more like a puppy. Or that was the appearance she presented to the world. There would have to be something steelier beneath that benign and sometimes playful manner; she would have been sent on her way pretty smartly by the Headmaster if there weren't.

She never asked whose file Matthew wanted to look at so, after telling her that he would bring it back later in the day, he took it up to his room. With some excitement he began to read through the various papers. The registration form, glowing prep school reference, early reports indicating exceptional promise; GCSE results, all top grades; UCAS reference, again glowing to the point of incandescence; sixth form house reports, Ben Macpherson's tutor reports…'outstanding contribution to the intellectual life of school'; various letters between school and parents at various stages of the boy's academic career. But then, a strange thing: no reports from his final term; no correspondence, such as a parental letter of thanks to the school. And no mention of any illness in his final term.

At which stage Matthew decided he would write to Chapman, imminent referendum or not. He put the file aside. He would return it to the Headmaster's office on his way home. So he began his letter. The tone should be light, he thought, jokey even, without any sort of pushiness and without any hint of the intense excitement he felt about his researches. Quite why, he didn't know. He couldn't really understand why he had become mildly obsessed by this enquiry. It was like an itch that needed scratching and still wouldn't go away.

After two false starts he struck the tone he wanted, and was away.

Dear David,

It was good to see you when you were down for Speech Day. It was a shame we didn't get a chance to chat a bit more.

I was sorry to hear that you could not make it down for the official opening of the Chapman Centre, which is a wonderful addition to the school's teaching facilities. The unveiling of the plaque duly took place but – in your absence – it was a little like *Hamlet* without the Prince! The school caterers put on a nice spread. There were baked meats, of course, but not of the funeral variety. And they were not coldly served! (Excuse the literary allusions. Once an English teacher, etc…Joke: What happens to old English teachers? Nothing! They burble on, their memories of quotations becoming perhaps a little less exact and accurate as they age!)

On the subject of literature, I re-read *Heart of Darkness* in the summer, and it brought back many happy memories of teaching the book to you all those years ago. I know that English was never a major priority of yours, but I have always valued the contribution you made to that set, with your sharp, intelligent, articulate comments and responses. I hope that you have some happy memories, too, of the texts we studied together.

When we met briefly in the summer, I

mentioned General Sir Peter Gilbert, Chairman of the Governors who, sadly, died in your last term. What I meant to go on to ask you was about some scandal in that summer term which would have brought negative publicity to the school and which somehow was averted. I wondered if you were in any way involved in helping to contain the scandal. Or perhaps it was when you were absent from school. I seem to remember that you were ill in the run-up to the exams.

You may wonder why I am asking this and I suppose the answer is simply so that I can get as clear a sense as possible of the school's history, which is, I guess, one of my chief roles as archivist. It seems that 1991 saw a lot of change – a new Chair of Governors, a governor's resignation and, of course, the unexpected resignation of Christopher Harper. So any help you might be able to give me on that time would be much appreciated.

No rush, of course. I appreciate that you are busy at the Home Office and are one of the key players in persuading the Scots to remain part of the union rather than smashing it up. I don't know if you know *Henry V*, but this quote from the Bishop of Ely might make you laugh:

'If that you will France win,
Then with Scotland first begin.
For once the eagle England being in prey,
To her unguarded nest the weasel Scot
Comes sneaking and so sucks her princely eggs,
Playing the mouse in absence of the cat,
To tame and havoc more than she can eat.'

With best wishes,
    Matthew Agnew

Jokey. And naïve. That's how he wanted it to sound. To convince Chapman that this was not a sinister investigation, but an innocent enquiry. He signed the letter, folded it and put it in the envelope he had addressed earlier. He wouldn't post it straight away.

*

Matthew, with a glass of red wine in his hand, was sitting out in the garden. Curving around its eastern edge lay the school arboretum. Fifteen species of tree are visible, many of them rare and beautiful specimens, their leafy fullness offering a subtle palette of greens and an interesting geometry of shapes. The September weather, if not altogether Indian summery, was warm and still. He looked up at the western sky, seeing the evening spread out like… like a patient etherised. Etherised? These days? What would the poet say today? Like a patient propofolised upon a table. Propofol. Milk of Amnesia, to those in the know. Lighter and quicker than ether. The evening was spread out against the sky like…like a fine September evening, streak of pastel pink seeping from the western horizon.

Matthew told Rachel that he would take Foxy for a quick walk in the dying evening sun. In his pocket, unknown to his wife, was the letter to David Chapman. Did he dare disturb the universe? Eat a peach? Start a scene or two? Once he dropped the letter into the postbox, there would be an end to indecision. And revision.

There was a plonk as the envelope hit the bottom of the box.

PART II
CONCLUSIONS

CHAPTER 9

It was the letter, presumably, that had brought Tommy Cooper's visitation: the conspicuous tagging on to the tour of local historians that Matthew was conducting; the ominously simple message to 'Desist. Stop Delving'; and the implied threat of the comment about Special Branch 'magicking' people away. Chapman, perhaps unsettled by the possibility of some skeletons being unearthed, had called in a favour from a former contact of his MI5 days.

...Chapman is sitting in his small little office in Westminster. In his hand is a letter from his old English teacher. In many ways it is a warm letter. Jokey in parts. But it has touched a raw nerve. It makes reference to a scandal that took place in the summer term of 1991, Chapman's final term at school. A scandal that would have brought the school negative publicity if it hadn't been hushed up. The English teacher, Mr Matthew Agnew, is now the school archivist. Clearly he has stumbled upon something. He also appears to have remembered or discovered that Chapman was away from school in the final fortnight before his A levels.

Chapman's mind is filling with unwanted memories. A summons to the Headmaster's study. An accusation of bullying. The consequence that he is no longer Head of School. A tearful phone call to his parents. His reassuring parents, who promise everything will be all right. 'Don't worry, darling, your father is going to talk to Sir Peter Gilbert, Chairman of the Governors,' his mother tells him.

And he doesn't have to worry. He remains Head of School until the day he leaves, his school record unblemished. A day or two later, his parents come to pick him up. They have arranged that he spend the final fortnight before his A levels at home, where he can revise undisturbed. 'Besides,' his mother tells him, 'it is all a bit frantic at school at the moment. Christopher Harper has been sacked by the governing body. A governor has resigned in protest. But you mustn't worry, darling, everything will be fine. Just concentrate on your A levels and secure your place at Oxford.'

It turns out that the favour that Sir Peter has done the Chapmans is his last. Within a week he is dead. A fatal stroke.

But now, twenty-three years later, Matthew Agnew is poking around. He is an amateur archivist without the power to create significant ripples in the political waters of Westminster. But should a journalist start nosing around. Well, that would be different. A splash in the tabloids. RISING POLITICAL STAR BEATS DRUGS CONFESSION OUT OF PUPIL WHEN HEAD BOY OF WELL-KNOWN PUBLIC SCHOOL. And no doubt the donation his parents had made the school would be misconstrued. Time to act.

A phone call to Thames House, the Headquarters of MI5. A meeting in the Victoria Palace Gardens with an old contact. Chapman hails the man as he approaches. The man looks round, his square face creasing into a smile, his large blue eyes twinkling a welcome. Chapman sits beside him on the bench. 'It's good to see you, Tommy.'

Chapman explains the letter he has received from his former English teacher who has been rootling around in the school archive. 'It's nothing particularly serious, but I don't really want this chap Agnew creating a nuisance of himself.'

'Leave it to me, guv. I'll put an end to the...er... botheration.'

'A gentle warning will suffice, Tommy.'

'Right you are, sir.'

*

Rachel had tried to reassure Matthew when they had returned from the Headmaster's drinks party on the evening of the visit. There had been a 'Why on earth?' moment when he had told her about the letter. But she had said that so long as he now left well alone, there would be nothing to worry about.

As it happened, he had lots to do. There was an enquiry into a philanthropic alumnus that was almost complete; and his planning of the display for the First World War centenary was well underway. In any case, the beginning of the school year was a busy time for routine archive work. Chasing up the new school roll, the calendar; amending the database of staff, entering leavers, adding joiners, changing altered internal posts; cataloguing the previous year's house and team photos which had arrived on disc in the holidays. Dull but necessary stuff.

The Chapman file would remain determinedly closed. But Matthew thought a great deal over the next few days about quite why he had sent the letter to Chapman. He delved – now there was word – into the opaque psychology of his own thinking. He decided that there were two kinds of motivation: there was logical motivation and there was illogical motivation. The former could be analysed in retrospect to show that the right course of action had been taken in the known circumstances, even if the outcome was undesirable. The latter category, obviously, was unknowable, embracing spur-of-the-moment decisions and just-for-the-hell-of-it actions.

Was there logic to his writing of the letter? Was it the act of integrity of a concerned citizen? Not really. That was not what was driving Matthew forward. In any case, what was the 'concern'? If there had been any wrong-doing, it was probably of local rather than public concern. Was it perhaps – and this might explain the silly, jokey tone of the letter – mere mischief-making? Strange to classify mischief-making as a logical act; but an act of provocation, poking a stick into the hornets' nest to see what might happen, could perhaps be borne out of a conscious attempt to heighten the excitement of one's life.

Matthew was certainly aware that there was an impish side to his nature. But that expressed itself in the occasional prank, a hoax phone call perhaps, and more commonly in his fondness for wordplay. He was quick to spot any opportunity for punning; the urge to run with a pun would often triumph when a greater seriousness of response was called for. Mostly, though, his pranks were harmless, intended to amuse – himself and others.

However, the letter to Chapman bore no semblance to a practical joke. Despite its lightness of tone, its jokiness even, it was clearly aimed at finding out what scandal had taken place at the school. Matthew had rather pompously suggested in the letter that, as school archivist, he was also the school historian. There was a serious element here. There had come a moment in his investigation when he had realised that he was on the point of elevating mere 'facts of the past' to 'historical facts', to use E.H. Carr's distinction of categories of fact, as introduced to Matthew by his father four years earlier. The implications made him feel queasy.

*

A week after the visit of Tommy Cooper, Matthew was laying out in his display cabinets the First Word War exhibits he had selected. He had decided that some of the display should evoke the calm and contentment of the first six months of 1914. There are house photos, containing the smiling faces of many young men who will never experience the joy of fatherhood. The image of the 1st XI cricket team projects confidence, the promise of youth. Two grainy photos show the school cadets on their Field Day, enjoying their break from the classroom by playing soldiers. There are sepia images of that year's Speech Day, the mothers in long swirly dresses and elaborate hats, fathers sporting smart Edwardian suits, waistcoated even on what appears to be a hot day. The Guest of Honour, the Bishop of London, strikes a slightly uncertain note about the future, but there is nothing that hints at the cataclysm to come.

And items from the first months of the war. Groups of old boys gathering to join up together. Early letters from the front written to masters at the school. The common theme is excitement at this glorious opportunity for adventure that has fallen to them. They hope to do their country proud, to do their school proud. And then the early casualties which, as year follows year, mount into the great toll of young life.

There is an interesting letter from an elderly master at the school to the mother of one of the fallen. The tone is ambivalent. It is a war that has to be fought. It is a sacrifice that has to be made. And struggling to come to the surface of the letter, never quite making it, is a sense of the old man's disenchantment, his disbelief at such wastage of the future, the future that he, as a teacher, had tried in his small way to shape. 'It breaks my heart,' he writes in a show of emotion uncharacteristic for the period, 'to learn, week by week, of the deaths and the wounding of young men who, in the recent past, sat before me in class, studious, alert, embracing the future with such optimism.'

The archive display cabinets were housed in the anteroom to The Gallery, the large reception room for school guests and for parents waiting to see the Headmaster.

'Ah, Matthew, do let me look. I somehow expected you to mount a First World War display.' It was Toby Dogget.

'Of course, Headmaster. Ever the topical one, moi!'

Dogget looked at each cabinet in turn. 'Gosh, you have some fantastic photos there. And I like the way you start with the pre-war summer where everything seems the same as it ever was.'

'Yes, it is very poignant. I wanted to get this up as quickly as possible, but at some stage I want to annotate all the house photos with the fate of each boy. As you know, we lost over five hundred old boys in that conflict, so a significant number of those in the photographs will have lost their lives.'

Dogget grunted an acknowledgement of some sort. 'Anyway, Matthew, well done. A splendid job...I must be on my way.' And he was gone. As ever, during any interaction, he was already mentally onto his next. A busy man with a school to manage. And meetings to attend. And management policies to formulate.

Matthew returned to the Archive Room to continue with some routine cataloguing. In the middle of the afternoon, the quiet was disturbed by a sudden cacophony of church bells. A bell-ringers' practice in the school chapel. The notes piled quickly and tunelessly upon each other. But slowly a rhythm emerged as each bell found its moment to chime, and soon the practice peals rang out joyously. Clarity from chaos.

*

Matthew had always been a vivid dreamer. Whereas Rachel rarely could remember dreaming, Matthew woke up most mornings with a dream fresh in his mind, and he would almost always try to work through it, either simply to recall it or, if he felt it merited it, to analyse it. He valued his dream world. As a source of filmic adventure; and occasionally as an oracle. By their nature dreams were filled with illogicalities and improbabilities and impossibilities. Their non-linear narratives could be absurd. And yet for Matthew there were truths to be discovered; if one looked properly, or listened. Listened to the whisperings of the undervoice, that quiet voice, so quiet as to be often unheard; that subterranean intelligence, so much wiser than his conscious mind, that emerged in his head from what it seemed was nowhere; a voice of objectivity, of wisdom. It seemed to rise up from somewhere deep within, like a spring bubbling to the surface in a secret place. Waking up from a dream in the morning was like waking to an overnight fall of snow. Sometimes gone without trace before first light. Sometimes a slight covering that survives into the day, to give shape and shadow and offer a fresh perspective.

Although it is over three years since Matthew last taught, his dreams these days frequently inhabit the classroom. And although it is two weeks since the visit of Tommy Cooper, more often than not it is his phantom which is flitting across the dreamscape. Not as Tommy Cooper, former (current?) employee of Special Branch, but in various guises and forms. Tommy Cooper is protean. A scowling pupil sitting at the back of class, pale blue eyes peering out of large square face, gruff voice dripping disdain, menace even. The Headmaster, differing from the scowling pupil only in size and age, knocking on the door of Matthew's classroom to say he has had complaints of a disturbance. 'Keep it quiet, Mr Agnew.' A square-faced, blue-eyed parent complaining gruffly of Matthew's treatment of his child. 'You're pickin' on 'im, Mr Agnew, and I don't like it. It must stop. Desist.'

Sometimes there is a particular pupil, normally sitting in the front of the class, wearing a pinstripe suit and expensive leather shoes. He is saying nothing, but he has a smug grin on his face, a face that is half familiar. A face which both is and is not the face of David Chapman.

*

When Matthew arrived home, Rachel was standing over the kitchen sink holding her left hand under the running cold tap. A vortex of bloodied water was swirling around the plug hole. On the worktop to the side was an abandoned knife and a blood-spattered carrot. A trail of blood led across the floor to the work top the other side of the sink where several scrunched up pieces of blood-sodden kitchen towel lay discarded.

'Jeez, what's happened, darling? Are you all right?' Unnecessary questions. It was obvious what had happened and equally clear that she wasn't entirely all right.

'Thank goodness you're back! This just won't stop bleeding.'

'Let me have a look, sweetie. Poor you!'

She kept the hand under the running tap and leant to one side so that he could have a good look at the cut.

'It's very deep.'

She nodded.

'Do you think I should take you to A & E?'

'It'll probably be all right. And in any case we'll probably have a long wait.'

'I'll tell you what, I'll ring the school san. There'll be a nurse on duty and if she's not busy with pupils she might agree to see you. I know the san is not really for staff, but she might at least be able to advise us whether you need to go to A & E.'

*

When they had left for the san, they had forgotten to put Foxy away. So, on their return to the house, they saw that she had helpfully tidied away the mess of blood that had been on the kitchen floor. The san sister had been solicitous to a fault, disinfecting the wound, closing it with butterfly stitches and bandaging it up securely and neatly.

After Matthew's impromptu performance in the kitchen – eschewing the bloodied carrot and instead cooking a simple omelette – he and Rachel sat on the sofa together. He held her injured hand in his, in the other a tumbler of whisky. Rachel held a tumbler of whisky in her right hand, the two glasses forming a pair of shimmering gold bookends. 'You must take care, sweetie,' he said.

*

That night he dreamt he was cycling down a long school corridor. Strangely it was from his own school days. The corridor becomes a hospital corridor and he is no longer on a bicycle but is hobbling towards a ward...He is in bed at home. But now he is digging in a flower bed in the garden. Suddenly there is a thump as he brings the spade clumsily down on his foot, slicing through his wellington boot. He is in a hospital bed. George West (?) is smiling cheerfully from the bed opposite.

'Hi, sir! What are you in for?'

And then a doctor is bending over him, eyes peering piercingly at him. Pale blue eyes. And the large, square jaw starts moving. 'You should take more care, Mr Agnew!'

CHAPTER 10

There was a slight chill in the autumn air that was quickly being warmed by a bright sun shining in a cloudless sky. The atmospherics were favouring a spectacular mesh of contrails, in various stages of formation and dissolution. Some were sharp lines, others thicker trails with the appearance of ribbed piping; there were zipper tracks, smudged streaks, and wide gossamers, unable to hold their visible shape, dislimning into invisibility. The sky was full of these brief histories at different stages of the telling.

The Agnews regularly walked in The Forest, which was a short drive away. And it was The Forest that beckoned on this glorious November Saturday. They parked the car at the bottom of Kingsland Lane and headed towards Blacktail Wood. To their left were fields and, straggling to the right of the lane for about three hundred yards, houses. On the Ordnance Survey map, this place was called, incongruously, New Town. It was no town, not even a village; more a small, ramshackle settlement cut into a gently sloping hillside. No two dwellings were the same and almost all had outbuildings of some kind, wooden or tin and in various states of disrepair. There were rough stony areas for parking a variety of vehicles, mostly old and functional.

The largest house was an attractive, well-maintained building with flinted brick walls. It would have been of a piece in the nearby village, but in this setting looked a little out of place, the rich uncle forced to live with his lowly relatives. The lowliest of these, the scruffiest dwelling, was set a little further back from the lane. The front elevation of the first floor was built in pink brick, whitened in places by patches of efflorescence; unpainted render had been slapped on the upper storey. The flaky woodwork looked long neglected. Vehicles lay all over the front garden: an old Land Rover, a trailer, two ancient tractors, a rusting pick-up, a car under a grey tarpaulin. And two quad bikes, somewhat newer looking. There was no logic to where the vehicles stood. They looked to have been abandoned rather than parked, though probably most were still in use. Some were on grass, some on an improvised driveway and some on a surface that had been lent a greater solidity through the random placing of broken blocks of paving stone.

Towards the end of this short ribbon of development, the buildings were higher, set back and shrouded by trees and shrubs. Beyond the last house, the tarmac ceased and the lane narrowed into a loose-stoned track that led to the woods.

It was mainly oak and beech, with some ash, that grew in Blacktail Wood, so the autumn palette on this soft November afternoon was muted. The leaves of the ash trees had dropped, leaving the russet keys starkly visible. The oaks appeared in two minds, combining some summer season greens with the dark ochres that would cling on until December. But the beeches, backlit by the sun, were glowing a rich brown. Foxy was exploring the natural history in her own way, tracing a fox here, a deer there, racing occasionally into the undergrowth after a squirrel. The track followed a course that had been gouged through the chalk by ancient geological action to create a gentle slope from the grass downland to the valley below. Either side of the path, the wooded, shrubby ground rose more sharply.

Suddenly they could hear a roar coming up the track behind them. A vehicle of some kind was approaching. Foxy was on one of her sorties, unseen somewhere amongst the trees. Matthew called her; her traffic sense was untutored. Eventually she came darting out just as a quad bike came into view around the corner below them. It was a young boy driving, podgy faced and with a pudding-bowl haircut. He did not slow down, seeming unconcerned that there was loose dog by the side of the track.

As he sped past, Matthew shouted angrily at him. 'Slow down, you stupid idiot! Can't you see there is a dog here?'

The boy braked sharply, skidded into a U-turn and came back alongside Matthew. 'What did you say?' He spoke in a half-broken voice, uneven in pitch.

'I said you were driving too fucking fast, you arsehole. It's dangerous to drive like that when there are people and dogs walking here.'

'Fuck you. I'm going to get my brother…He's got a gun.' And he was off, a backspray of stones spurting up behind as he accelerated quickly down the hill.

'Darling,' Rachel said, 'you shouldn't use language like that. He was only a boy.'

'Boy, my arse! What's he driving that thing for if he's a boy? Bloody maniac.' He put Foxy on the lead and they walked on, the roar of the quad bike diminishing to a drone.

As they approached a fork in the track, the left path heading deeper into the woods, the right towards the farmland, they heard the drone again. But the sound was thicker and, as it came closer, it was clear there were two vehicles. And the sound was becoming a roar.

'Bloody hell! He *is* bringing his brother back. What do we do now?' He picks up Foxy. He and Rachel dash behind a tree for some kind of cover. But it will not render them invisible.

He sees what comes next. Foxy barks. She scrabbles free of his grasp. Springs away and bounds down the slope towards the two brothers, the older with a rifle strapped to his shoulder.

There is a shout in a half-broken voice. 'Shoot the little fucker.' And a shot. And a brief silence. And then, 'We better get outta here.'

'That'll teach 'em silly buggers.'

There is a roar and a screech and the sound of loose stones scattering as the two quad bikes skid around and head back down the track.

Matthew's heart is pounding. Rachel is sobbing quietly. As the noise of the bikes fades away Matthew comes out from his cover and walks down to the track. Foxy is lying still. Blood is oozing from a small round hole in her neck and pooling beneath her. An open eye already has a dull glaze. As he picks her up, her head flopping slackly forward, he notices that the other eye is half closed and encrusted with dirt.

Or not.

As the quad bikes had approached, and before they came into view, he had scooped Foxy up and run into an overgrown path with her in his arms, Rachel close behind. They then squatted behind some scrubby bushes, through which they could see the approaching brothers. Matthew knew that Foxy hated being constrained tightly and would struggle and eventually make some noise of protest. So he loosened his grip, placed her carefully on the ground and hooked a finger lightly around her collar, hoping this greater freedom would satisfy her. She was not a yappy dog. And now was not the time, he prayed, for her to become one.

They could hear the brothers talking below them. They had stopped at the fork and were debating which track to follow. The older boy, who looked to be in his late teens, did indeed have a rifle strapped across his shoulders. They looked up towards Rachel and Matthew and Foxy, but did not see them. Either they did not know about or had forgotten this overgrown path that cut back along the ridge. They decided that their prey had headed up the track towards the farmland.

'We'd best follow this path,' said Matthew. He kept Foxy on the lead and they picked their way up to the top of the ridge, where the woodland became field. The path here, a little less overgrown, kept just within the wood, offering some kind of cover. Matthew was still in shock. His heart was racing and he felt a little breathless. He realised he had been in a state of deep panic. He'd been given a sharp taste of fear, fear of an intensity that he had not experienced since he was a child. Had almost forgot the taste of fears.

They kept walking at a brisk pace, hardly talking. Rachel pointed out great clumps of Butcher's Broom that had spread itself out in regular patches to the left of the path, as though it might have once been a hedge or some kind of boundary marker. Its spiny leaves were inhospitable; when Foxy, seemingly oblivious to the preceding drama, brushed against some, she sprang away sharply with a small yelp of protest.

After a while they heard the quad bikes below. They stopped and waited, readying themselves for a dash into the thicker undergrowth if necessary. But the noise passed and diminished. Their hunters were returning to base.

Matthew began to relax and was soon deep in thought. He was thinking about a man – two men – he hadn't thought about since they had dropped out of the news several decades before: Norman Scott and Jeremy Thorpe.

The facts were a little misty in Matthew's mind. But then they had always been misty, not to say murky, both in the press and in the famous Old Bailey trial of Thorpe, in which he had been acquitted. The facts were as misty as a Cornish fog. Was it Bodmin Moor where a hitman, hired allegedly at two removes by Thorpe, shot the dog of Norman Scott? What was the name of the dog? Minka? Not sure. Facts…Facts. Norman Scott, with whom Thorpe had allegedly had an affair at a time when homosexuality was outlawed, was now being troublesome and making unreasonable demands on Thorpe. Jeremy Thorpe, by now leader of the Liberal Party; and who was entertaining thoughts of entering a political coalition with Edward Heath; and of being rewarded with the post of Home Secretary or even of Foreign Secretary. Jeremy Thorpe, who could not afford the risk of any whiff of scandal.

Who were the alleged go-betweens? What was the name of the hitman? And, what had the prosecution argued? That the hitman had been hired to kill Scott? Or to intimidate him by shooting his dog? Matthew couldn't remember.

'Rach, do you remember the Norman Scott affair?'

'Not really, darling. Well, vaguely only. Something about a dog.'

'Yes, Minka, I think it was called.'

'I really don't remember.'

'I must look it up when we get home. If I recall, the trial was seen by many to be a massive cover-up by the Establishment. Of the Establishment by the Establishment.'

'What made you think of it now?'

'I don't know. I mean…I guess seeing that chap with his rifle made me wonder if he would have shot Foxy…which brought Norman Scott to mind.'

'You're not suggesting—' A definite note of irritation in the voice.

'No, of course not!…But it does remind one that the Establishment—'

'Just leave it, Matt.' There was a rising note of exasperation in Rachel's voice. So he left it.

*

He awoke in the middle of the night. He assumed he had had a bad dream, but couldn't remember any details. For a while he lay in a mildly disturbed state of half-wakefulness. And then realised he had been awoken by a noise.

Someone was in the house. He could hear them creeping about. Which room were they in? The spare bedroom? Rachel's upstairs study? He froze, hardly daring to breathe. Hoping to make himself invisible.

And now the creaking was on the landing. Turning his head carefully so as to make no noise, he looked to the bedroom door. Someone was there. Standing in the frame of the doorway.

By now he was fully awake, and his eyes had become accustomed to the darkness. There, hanging on the back of the door was his dressing gown. And creaking away in the cold of the night were the contracting central heating pipes and old floorboards.

He had indeed forgot the taste of fears. Had forgotten how terrified he became in his younger years at Hyghcliff when chilly nights played havoc with the pipes and the floorboards and his childhood fears.

*

The next day Matthew had arranged to see two visitors who wanted to examine the carved panelling in the Grand Hall. Sir Anthony Curran was the recently retired director of one of the great metropolitan art galleries of the north. He brought with him Tamsin French, a young and strikingly beautiful companion who was a junior lecturer at the Courtauld Institute.

Both were very charming. But the first thing that Matthew noticed about Sir Anthony was his quick, hungry eye, which had a quite extraordinary capacity to notice and to absorb. The man seemed to take in every detail of his surroundings, filtering out in an instant what was not relevant, focusing instead on what was of interest. On the short walk from where he had parked his car to the Grand Hall, his eyes were constantly busy. He walked past a Coade stone vase and without seeming to even glance at it rattled off the figures of its decoration to his companion. Not only was he remarkably observant but also voluble and articulate. No doubt, once he recognised the facing figure on the vase he knew immediately what would decorate the rest of it. But it was the speed of retrieval of that information that impressed. They passed a Katsuru tree that had not yet lost the last of its leaves, pink now in their final days and without any longer the characteristic autumnal smell of burnt sugar. Sir Anthony immediately asked what it was. This was a man who seemed unwilling to allow any item of interest, however small, to go unidentified. In the entrance hall, he stopped to inspect the stone fireplace, elaborate and delicately carved, commenting on the exquisite detail, approving unequivocally every aspect of the piece.

But it was the Grand Hall that Sir Anthony had come to see and it was here that his great mind appeared to go into overdrive. There was a contained excitement as he pored over each panel, speaking most of the time, or listening to Tamsin. The purpose of his visit was to extend his research on the Venetian wood carver who had fashioned the intricate panelling. He'd done some homework before coming down to the school and now simply wanted to see the detail and craftsmanship in the lustrous walnut.

He offered a continuous commentary on the imagery and symbolism of the carving. There was nothing that Matthew could say that would add anything to the shared knowledge of these two people. He could simply watch and listen. Listen to the tall man with a full head of grey hair and a sharply defined face with eager eyes. Listen to the petite woman, blonde, a somewhat décolleté white blouse contrasting with a black suit. She was like an attentive pupil to Sir Anthony, listening keenly, chipping in brightly as though to prove her worthiness of his patronage. Matthew was left the excited eavesdropper.

He imagined that most women would find Sir Anthony deeply attractive. He was elegant, dynamic and charming. And Tamsin? The combination of stunning good looks and a fine mind was surely a winning one to any man of good taste. They were a striking pair.

*

When he got home that evening, Matthew told Rachel about his visitors. He tried to explain the excitement of standing there with them, listening to their erudite conversation. The exhilaration of being in the presence of a wonderful mind which still, in retirement, was minutely curious, instantly assimilative, fluently lucid. A mind that was a treasure house of a lifetime's scholarly learning.

In truth, as he lay in bed that night, reviewing his day,

he had to admit to himself that, while thrilled to listen to Sir Anthony, he had also been curiously disheartened.

Sir Anthony's quick eye made Matthew all the more aware of his own lack of observancy. He had been asked, when they had been in the Grand Hall, about an elaborate mosaic that was mounted in a blind transom beneath the large perpendicular window. When was it installed? Matthew had told him that it was part of the original 1850s building. As he was taking his guests back to their car, they stopped to look at the archive display cabinets in The Gallery. After looking at a photograph of the hall, dated 1888, Sir Anthony had gently asked if the dating was correct.

'Yes,' Matthew replied. 'It's part of a well-known series of the school taken in May that year.'

'In that case,' said Sir Anthony, again gently, 'the mosaic cannot have been installed by the original architect in the 1850s. Look: the mosaic is not there in the photo, so it must be post-1888.' Matthew had been shamefaced. Any tiny bit of credibility he might have started out with now lay in ignominious tatters. He had told every tour group he had ever hosted that the mosaic was part of the original building.

He wondered what else he had missed or misinterpreted. He could have introduced any number of errors into his records. Things he had written would be taken as gospel by his successor, he presumed. And would a future historian of the school identify mistakes, inconsistencies? Stratum upon stratum of error. Members of staff would be unlikely to spot them. Teachers took little interest in the archive. For them, education was about the future, not the past. One could dwell, of course, on a successful rugby season or an exceptional set of exam results. But not for long. The eye was quickly drawn to the coming year when, like Sisyphus, one began to roll the great boulder of learning once more up the hill.

The mood of dejection chimed with a more general malaise he had been feeling in recent months. It was a sense of an increasing distance from his teaching career, a remoteness that gave him a deepening sense of the ineffectiveness and futility of most of what he had done. The full-onness of the classroom, of preparing for the classroom, of giving leadership to colleagues in the department, left little time for introspection. One did what one did what one did. Till the last syllable of recorded time.

He could see now, with a clarity that he had never had time for, the artificiality of so much teaching. Preparing a text for an examination encouraged a way of reading and a way of thinking that was unnatural. Artificial. Language tasks set to younger pupils had a similar artificiality to them. And relationships? How good were they? The assumption was that pupils liked you, assumed because it was easier to accept their liking than their dislike. The assumption was that you were teaching them wonderfully, because to falter in that belief – that way madness lay.

Matthew could grab these heavy, gloomy thoughts, clutch them to himself, and they would drag him into spiral of descent. But his moods of dejection rarely survived a night's sleep. Mostly, he took a sanguine view of his insignificant, ineffective past. Ultimate insignificance was the lot of all men. Ozymandias. Willy Loman. Matthew Agnew.

CHAPTER 11

With Christmas a little over two weeks away, the autumn term was drawing to a close. Matthew was finalising a collection of materials he had put together on a former pupil, a well-known actor, whose biographer he was meeting the next day.

A knock at the door. It was Leo Beamish. A fine English teacher. His name had an almost Dickensian appropriateness to it. A great mop of light brown hair, untouched by decades of changing fashion, was swept back in a leonine mass; in the set of his face there seemed to be a permanent smile, accentuated by his genial disposition. He was ten years younger than Matthew, but from the first they had, at least in their professional lives, been soulmates. They often thought the same thoughts, and their teaching styles were similar.

Leo's great passion, outside the classroom and occasionally within it, was Bob Dylan. His knowledge of the Dylan canon was encyclopaedic and he could, if allowed, talk at enormous length about the thousands of hours of bootleg recordings he had collected over many years. A Dylan fan himself in the past, Matthew had stopped buying his albums when the man got God. He and Rachel had been to one concert. Earls Court, 1978. It had been an occasion, the first visit to the UK by his Bobness in nearly a decade. Dylan was backed, unusually, by a huge band, and the set list had been virtually a Greatest Hits compilation of his sixties songs. What had struck Matthew had been the almost religious fervour of the audience, a sense heightened when, *en masse*, they held aloft thousands of flaming cigarette lighters to show their idolatrous devotion to their man. In retrospect, having got to know Leo, the religious fervour and the idolatrous devotion were no surprise.

Leo maintained that Dylan was the most important creative artist of the second half of the twentieth century; that his lifetime's oeuvre offered as powerful a chronicle of the journey through life as any of the great poets, Yeats included; that the scope of his writing was Shakespearean in its breadth and in its deep understanding of growing up and growing old. Leo brought, as most Bobcats did at some stage (Bobcats? Was that the right term?), the testimony of Professor Christopher Ricks to his support.

On the occasions that their arguments about Dylan had gone beyond the stage of banter to contain something of an edge, Leo would be upset and not speak to Matthew for at least a day. 'You talk about Christopher Ricks,' Matthew had once said. 'But do you know, Geoffrey Hill, no less, Professor of Poetry at the great University of Ox-en-ford, has said that he could not understand Ricks' advocacy of Dylan. He said that Dylan was a skimmer. "Skimmer". Perfect word for someone who implies learning and wisdom through a wide range of reference, but who really knows very little because nothing, absolutely nothing, has been explored in any depth…*Desolation Row*: Eliot and Pound's kerfuffle on the bridge—"

'Tower.'

'Whatever. How much of Pound and Eliot has he actually read?'

'That's unfair. Dylan is very well read. It's well known.' The argument wasn't resolved. They never were. One or other of the two would say that he was supposed to be somewhere else, was late, had to dash, and would leave. With one hand waving free.

But skimming was the way these days, eyes down, scrolling quickly through the Internet, flitting at breakneck speed through social media, seeing a great deal, absorbing very little. It was difficult to imagine Sir Anthony Curran wedded to an iPhone or to a tablet.

Leo and Matthew's friendship was unshakeable. And the two wives got on well, though very different in temperament. Sandra Beamish, Sandy, was a singer. She had some classical training, but had not seen it through, leaving to join a band, hoping eventually to make the breakthrough to solo success. It never quite happened, and she quickly became a backing singer, mostly for studio sessions, but occasionally for touring bands or soloists. It was when she was backing a well-known Canadian singer on a tour of the UK in the mid 1980s that Leo had first cast eyes on her, and fallen instantly in love. He said it was the way she completely lost herself in song, playing second fiddle to the main attraction, swaying from side to side, or bobbing, eyes closed and hands hanging down by her sides like an unstrung puppet. Her voice, a countrified, angelic soprano to the gravelly growl of the man known to some as the Prince of Dirge, was truly heavenly to Leo. And after the show, he had joined a crowd of people at the stage door, mostly young women wanting to offer themselves to the Prince of Dirge. When Sandy came out, he introduced himself, said how much he had enjoyed the show and how brilliant she and the other backing singers

138

had been. He asked her to join him for a drink. And they never looked back.

It was unusual for Leo visit the Archive Room. Matthew asked him how things were going in the department.

'Much the same. Good things, bad things.'

'Are the new syllabuses any less restrictive? Any less of a grind?'

'Not really. Still Assessment Objectives, lots of boxes to tick. You know the drill.'

'Tick-box teaching!'

'Arsehole assessment!'

'Check-box coaching!'

'Instant instruction!'

'Simplistic syllabuses!'

'Lifeless literature!'

'Easy education!'

'Procedural pedagogy…!'

'Er. I think we've drained that swamp. Um…'

'Mormon!'

'Ah!…Varmint!'

'Foetal mouse!'

'Crab louse!'

'Plonker!

'P-p-p-pundit!'

'Aaagh'

'Well. That passed the time.'

'It would have passed anyway.'

'How time flies when one has fun!' Which seemed to bring things to a conclusion. 'So,' said Matthew. 'What brings you up here, Leo? Have you brought me some priceless treasures for the archive?'

Leo looked sheepish. Leo Beamish's beam uncharacteristically absent. 'Erm, the thing is, Matty,

I have been a bit foolish. And I want your advice. And perhaps your help.'

'Okay.'

'Well. I…I had a brief thing with…with Sass.' Saskia Quinlan was a young member of the English Department. She had joined the department as a rookie teacher two years before Matthew's retirement, and had always been grateful for the help he had given her in settling in to the job and honing her teaching skills.

'A brief…thing.'

'A one-night stand. When we were both a bit pissed. It was at half-term and Sandy was away with the kids seeing her mum. There was a booze-up in the SCR bar and—'

'Just a one-night stand?'

'Well…two…twice.'

'Jeez, Leo! What induced you? Once is a mistake. Twice surely suggests intent.'

'Oh God, I don't know. She'd been coming on to me for a while. And she is sexy.'

An uninvited image of her sitting in a departmental meeting, legs crossed, skirt creeping up a little, came into Matthew's mind. Well-shaped, well-toned thighs. Yes, sexy. She was.

'So you shagged her and that was the end of it?'

'Well, yes, I thought so. I felt deeply ashamed, and I told her after half-term that it had been a mistake, and I thought that was that.' ['Been a mistake.' She must have loved hearing that, thought Matthew.] 'But she has been giving me evil looks for weeks and asked me yesterday if I'd told Sandy about our fling. And when I said no, she gave me this look…a sense of 'Aha, I have you there.' She and Sandy will probably meet at the staff Christmas do on Friday and I'm terrified she'll say something.'

'Well, you just have to fess up to Sandy. Pre-empt Sass.'

Leo's face crumpled into a mobile display of panic and dismay. And when he brought his hands to his face, the misery was so complete that for a moment he looked like the famous gargoyle on the bell tower of New College, Oxford.

'Matty, I can't do that. I really can't. It would hurt her so much.'

'But, Leo, you've got to live the truth. You've done what you've done. You've got to face up to it. If you didn't want to get in this mess you shouldn't have played away.' As he spoke the words, Matthew knew they were simplistic, the dregs of the absolutist Catholic faith he'd long since abandoned. 'I don't know, Leo. You said you wanted my help. I don't see what I can do. Would you like me to talk to Sandy?'

A wail. 'Nooooo.'

'Well, what?'

'Can't you talk to Sass, talk sense into her? I know she respects you. Likes you, admires you. She'd listen.'

'I'm not sure. I'll give it some thought. In the meantime you've just got to keep on keepin' on…Empty your buckets of rain. Life is doleful, life is broken'

'Yeah. Everything is broken.'

"No. It's all good.'

'Don't ya tell Henry!'

'I'll keep it with mine!'

'I'll remember you.'

'Most likely you go your way and I'll go mine.'

'Bye…and bye!'

During this exchange, the gargoyle has been banished and a delighted beam has been spreading over Leo's face. 'You serious? You'll talk to her?'

'I'll give it a go. But I must think about it first.'

*

141

The following day, Matthew spent an hour with the actor's biographer who then took him out to lunch in a pub in Avebury. Over the meal, they talked about acting and actors and argued gently over the relative quality of American and British television drama. As they were leaving, a man in a green fleece with long dreadlocks was walking in. He did a double take when he saw Matthew. 'Matthew Agnew!' he exclaimed with a broad grin.

The man was thinner than Matthew remembered him and his blond, now braided hair had darkened a little, but unmistakably it was George West. 'George West! My word! What a coincidence!' The biographer hastily shook Matthew's hand, thanked him for his help and left.

Matthew turned back to George. 'Are you meeting someone here?'

'No, I've just finished for the day. I'm stopping off for a quick bite.'

George was happy for Matthew to join him for drink and a chat while he had his lunch.

'So what are you up to these days, George?'

'I'm a part-time gardener at Avebury Manor, working mainly in the walled kitchen garden. Been there for three years and before that I worked for the Parks and Open Spaces Department of Swindon Council.'

'Is that the direction you went in when you left school?'

'Was asked to leave the school, do you mean?' George said with a smile.

'Okay. I was being tactful!'

'No need. I was well out of that shit-hole. No offence! I completed my A levels at a crammers and then read Modern Languages at Warwick. And then I taught for a while. Got bored. Went to Oz for a few years, generally moving around, not doing a great deal, to be honest, though that is where I started experimenting with – you'll laugh at this – Rap. And it is where I got my liking for the outdoors. And then my mother died and I came home and…stayed…But I knew I wouldn't make much from the music and I knew I wanted to work outside, so I got a job as a general dogsbody groundsman at some local playing fields. And then joined Swindon Council and got some qualifications. If I've got to make money to support my writing, then working in a park or on gardens is ideal. I need to be outdoors.'

'Like Biff Loman.'

'Sorry?'

'Biff Loman. *Death of a Salesman*. Willy Loman's elder son.'

'I don't know *Death of a Salesman*. I've heard of it, of course, but never seen it.'

'Good play. Biff turns his back on his father's expectations for him – which are considerable – and goes to work on a ranch instead. He says he doesn't want to have to get on the subway each morning, to work in an office all day, to work his butt off for fifty weeks a year for the sake of a short holiday. All he wants is the outdoors, with his shirt off.'

'I can understand that. I must look at the play.'

'Yes, it's interesting. Biff is not the main character, mind. His father Willy is. Willy Loman, a dime a dozen salesman. He kills himself at the end of the play. I remember heated discussions when I was at university and we were looking at the nature of Tragedy. Was Willy Loman a tragic hero? Could he possibly be one? Was he not too ridiculously lowly to be considered tragic? Was the writing of tragedy possible in the twentieth century? The age of the Common Man. All very arid stuff!'

'Listening to you, to the way you are talking, reminds me of you in class. I enjoyed your lessons!'

'*Heart of Darkness*. Harlequin man!'

'Now you're talking, Matt!'

Matt? 'Matthew' was an informality beyond which many former pupils could never go. For some, even abandoning the habitual 'sir' was difficult enough. But Matthew was glad that George called him Matt. A relaxed equality.

'It's really interesting hearing about what you've been up to, George. But wasn't your dad upset when you decided you weren't going to use your expensive private schooling and your university education? He was an army officer, wasn't he?'

George nodded. 'I didn't not use it. You will be amazed to hear how I use my Italian these days. I am translating Dante's *Inferno* into Rap. Check it out on YouTube. Just put in a search for GeorgeWestRap. You'll find other stuff there you might be interested in. Or appalled by!' His large, pale blue eyes twinkled. '*Wittigenstein's WordWhirlpool Rap*, for example.'

Matthew laughed. 'I will!'

'I do gigs locally most weeks. You should come along. Educate yourself!'

'Well...We'll see!'

'But, no, Dad wasn't upset. And I don't think Mum would have been either. You've probably had a thousand parents say to you that all they wanted was for their child to be happy.' Matthew nodded. 'But haven't really meant it, when it came to the crunch.' He nodded again. 'But mine did mean it. They've always been really supportive. And Dad was fantastic when I said I wanted to be groundsman or a gardener.'

'That's great. So you're working at Avebury Manor. I have been there, but that was a long time ago. A roomed style of garden, if I remember, and some impressive topiary.'

George exhaled a puff and threw his hands out in front of him expressively. 'Well, it used to be, yes. Trouble is, we're seeing the first signs of Box Blight, so that is likely to be the end of that. Still, I'm sure they'll find alternatives. Such us Japanese holly…There are probably a lot of other changes since you visited. It's a great place and I love working there…I love this whole area, that's why I moved here. Avebury. Silbury Hill—'

'Yes. It is lovely. I love the downs. And The Forest… You don't consider yourself a little too close to your hated alma mater?'

The same noisy exhalation of breath. 'You know, it was an absolute shit-hole. I don't have anything to do with it. Haven't been back. Never will. There were some terrible people there. Nasty pampered people from privileged backgrounds. They'd never seen the real world, were never going to see it at uni, where they would stick within their public schooly tribe. And would go into well-paid jobs where once again they wouldn't have to lower themselves to mingle with the plebs. And there were some shitty staff, too.'

There was a pause. George's pale blue eyes had no hint of anger. He was looking directly at Matthew, wondering, perhaps, if he should continue. There was a wet beer mat on the table. George dug his thumb nail into it, etching an oozing line, and continued. 'I always liked you, Matt, liked you and your lessons. I liked your teaching style. Lobbing in outrageous comments or opinions to stir us into argument. But you never really got it—'

'Got what?'

'Got what we were about. What we were up to. What we thought. I don't think any of the teachers did. And I don't think you got quite what a shit system you were working for. Propping up the Establishment. Churning out the next generation to take over the reins of power.'

'That's not what I was doing, George. My mission, if I can put it grandly, not so say pompously, was to make my pupils think. To question. To somehow keep alive their curiosity. If I had a guiding motto, it was Socrates' famous comment that "The unexamined life is not worth living".'

'Yes, I can see that. And you were good like that. But nevertheless you were working for a system that protects and promotes the status quo.'

'Yes and no. You'd be surprised how many people there are like you. Who've kicked against the goad...rejected the system. And in any case the rich and privileged need educating too.'

'Of course. But they should go to school with everybody else.'

'But you didn't, George. When you were expelled you went to a crammers to get your A levels.'

'My dad's decision. And he was pretty pissed off with the way the school chucked me out.' There was some vehemence in his voice now. 'That toe-rag Chapman, smarming up to the head man. I was always pretty discreet with the dope, or whatever else I took. I never once offered anything to anyone in a year below me. But David fucking Chapman tricked some of the fourth formers into making confessions and saying I had supplied them.'

Matthew was beginning to feel uncomfortable. There was a depth of anger in George that he clearly needed to vent, and it probably had to be articulated to someone from the school. So he sat tight and let George continue.

'He bullied those poor kids. Frightened them so that they were easier to deal with. And more suggestible. Fucking David Chapman hated me, hated everything I stood for. Because I didn't believe in systems and because I questioned hierarchies. He knew that he could pin dope-smoking on me and wanted to make it all the worse for me

146

by telling Harper that I was supplying. So he told the fourth formers if they confessed, and if they told the Head that I had got the stuff for them, they would not be expelled. So they went along with it. And, surprise, surprise, were chucked out with me.' He dropped his knife noisily on his plate. 'I'm sorry, Matt, you don't want to hear this and I don't really want to talk about it. It's old hat. I have a good life, now…And I don't normally get worked up!'

'It's fine. I'm happy to listen. I have never been one to believe that the sun shone out of the school's collective arsehole.'

George smiled, the pale blue eyes sparkling for a moment. And then they clouded once more. 'But it did upset my dad. He went to see the Chairman of the Governors to appeal – I can't remember his name – but he just supported the Head, who supported fuckwit Chapman, so it came to nothing. I don't think we ever expected it would.'

'No. I think it's quite difficult to overturn these things once they've been decided.'

Another pause, and then. 'He was a strange chap, the Chairman—'

'Sir Peter Gilbert.'

'Gilbert. There were always rumours that he had an eye for young men. I don't know if that's true or not.'

Matthew blinked. He didn't quite know how to process all he was hearing. How to respond. 'Well, I must say, I never heard anything like that.'

They talked some politics after that, speculating on the General Election, now only five months away. The main parties were neck and neck in the polls. George believed in Ed Miliband and was indignant at the treatment he received. 'I can't believe how unfair the press is. Well, I can believe it, but it's not right. The criticism he gets is vile and often for the pettiest of things. It's not serious political critiquing. Okay, I know that Cameron gets it too, but it's much gentler – that he's a bit podgy, that he's a bit too fond of chillaxing, that he left his daughter in the pub.'

Matthew didn't really want to enter the fray on this. His mind was still reeling from the vehemence of George's denunciation of David Chapman. And the incidental detail George had unwittingly lobbed in to the conversation about Sir Peter Gilbert. So shortly afterwards they exchanged warm farewells and agreed they'd meet up again sometime soon. Perhaps.

Driving home, Matthew reflected on what he had heard about David Chapman. Testimony for the prosecution, one might say. But distorted by time? Tainted with the poison of personal animus? Who knew?

*

He looked up George's Rap website, which introduced him with two paragraphs of text and an extensive gallery of performance photos; a lean, braided figure clutching the microphone, a look of real intensity on his face. And there was a collection of audio files and videos of his work. It was clever and entertaining. George: gardener, poet, thinker. Not a bad life!

Matthew's other internet search was into Sir Peter Gilbert. There were numerous finds, mostly to do with the successful climax to his military career. On the third Google search page he found a link to a local paper in Devon, the Exeter *Express and Echo*. In a tiny, single-paragraph story headed 'Officer Acquitted', there was a story from 1951 of a Major Peter Gilbert being acquitted of soliciting in a gentleman's public lavatory in the city.

Interesting. Maybe. But Tommy Cooper's magical reach still held Matthew. No more digging. Had that not been the message of the dream he'd had? In any case, the following day he had arranged to see Saskia Quinlan. Not a task to be anticipated with any eagerness.

CHAPTER 12

There are two armchairs in the Archive Room. Matthew motions Saskia towards one and seats himself in the other.

She looks at him expectantly. It is an expressive face. Its line in profile appears to tilt upwards a little: slightly upturned nose, lips fullish and fine, with a very light and natural lipstick, jaw delicately drawn and sharply defined. The thin arches of her eyebrows are perfectly shaped. Golden brown hair falls either side of her face and onto her chest, framing a silver pendant – is it an owl? – which offers a sparkling contrast to the black jumper she is wearing. 'This is very mysterious, Matt!' she says. 'To be invited up into the Archive Room. Do you have something to show me?'

'Well, I could show you a first edition of Tennyson's *Morte d'Arthur*, which is rather splendid…It's good to see you…Er…how's the teaching going?'

'Fine, fine. Of course everyone is absolutely knackered by this stage. It's such a long term.'

'I guess…I can just about remember!…So…what texts have you been teaching this term?'

'*Hamlet*…Hardy's poetry, *Waiting for Godot…Gatsby*.'

'Ah, *Gatsby*. Great text. And don't you think it has one

of the very best endings to a novel? "Gatsby believed in the green light, the orgastic future that year by year recedes before us. It eluded us then, but that's no matter – tomorrow we will run faster, stretch out our arms farther. . . . And one fine morning. So we beat on, boats against the current, borne back ceaselessly into the past".

'I'm impressed you still remember it. Is that word perfect?'

'I think so. You tell me! You've just taught it!'

'I've got a hopeless head for quotes!'

This small talk is not bringing Matthew to the purpose of Saskia's visit. He wonders whether he can use *Gatsby* to steer towards the topic of her fling with Leo Beamish. Probably not.

'Leo was up here the other day.' She looks at him in a questioning way. 'It was good to see him. We had a good old natter about old times!'

'Right,' she says in sing-songy way. Is this implying impatience? A hint of irritation? Or simply an encouragement to carry on?

Saskia is wearing a short, tight skirt, black with a pattern of silver ferns. Black tights; well-shaped, well-toned thighs. She is desirable. Matthew can understand why Leo lost his head.

He knows he needs to take the plunge. 'Actually, Sass, there is something I want to talk to you about.' The icy water awaits him. He dives in. 'Leo is worried that you are going to tell Sandy what you two…did.' Thank God! He nearly said 'got up to'. 'Did' is more neutral. Much better.

Not that it matters. Her body has tensed and her eyes flash angrily. 'I beg your pardon, Matt. What did you say? What the fuck has this got to do with you?'

'Nothing really, Sass, but I am fond of Leo…I'm fond you both. And I don't want to see him or Sandy hurt.'

'How dare you! How fucking dare you!' And she is up and gone with a noisy slamming of the door.

Matthew wonders why he ever agreed to help Leo out. Help him out in this particular mission. Of course Saskia will feel that he is being intrusive, that it is nothing to do with him. It is nothing to do with him. What was he thinking? He wanted to help Leo. But how ineptly he had gone about it. On the other hand, was there a better way? Saskia would surely have been upset by his intrusion, however he put it. He should never have tried. A misjudgement to have agreed to Leo that he would.

Would she tell Sandy about her fling with Leo when she saw her at the Christmas party later in the day? Matthew would not find out straight away. He and Rachel had decided not to go this year.

That night Matthew dreamt about Saskia. It was not a dream that presented itself in riddles, nor were the participants in the narrative disguised as other people. Saskia was Saskia and Matthew was Matthew; he awoke with a very hard erection and a memory of his hand between Saskia's black-tighted thighs.

*

And soon it was Christmas. On the 23rd, Matthew drove to Marlow to pick up his father and was shocked by the further deterioration he saw in him. More weight lost and now looking pitifully thin. The stoop greater and the walk a little less steady. The eyes, while alert, with less of their sparkly directness. On the journey home Matthew suggested, as Rachel frequently said he should, that Michael come to live with them. They had the room, and Rachel was keen that the pair of them look after him; it made sense. But Michael would have none of it. He valued his independence.

'But how do you use your independence these days, Dad?'

'I like to get up when I want and go to bed when I want and eat what I want…And, anyway, I've arranged for Mrs Knowles to come in for an hour each weekday. So, she keeps a good eye on me. She shops for me, cleans, and sometimes cooks…So you really mustn't worry about me, Matty.' But he did.

On Christmas Eve, son Daniel arrived, bringing with him his girlfriend, Louise. To meet the parents, that was how the visit was being billed. Matthew and Rachel had seen photos of her, but beyond the fact that she looked cheerful and uninhibited, they could tell little of her personality. She arrived with a Poinsettia for Rachel and carrier bag of gifts to be placed under the tree.

There was a relaxed atmosphere at the supper table that evening. Louise was, as she had appeared in photos, uninhibited. And fun. She made them laugh with her banter and her teasing, especially of Daniel. She seemed able to take him out of himself in a way that previous girlfriends had not been able to. Michael's fragile state of health was apparent, and she was sensitive to it, but keen also to engage him. Marlow sounded lovely, she said, and she had heard so much about the launch, *Farewell*, and wanted to know more. And perhaps even would get a ride in it some day!

Her first degree was in History of Art, after which she had done an MA in Curating and Collections, and she now worked in an art gallery in West London. Matthew had been looking forward to telling her about his visit from Sir Anthony Curran, but was surprised and disappointed that she had never heard of him. 'Oh, you young people, what are you taught these days that you know so little!' he teased her.

'Ah, you old people, so knowledgeable, so wise!' she countered. 'At least we're heading in the right direction, Danny, aren't we!' She spoke the last phrase in the creaking voice of age, giving him a clumsy wink at the same time.

Michael went to bed early, Rachel repeating as she kissed him goodnight, Matthew's invitation for him to come and live with them. He told her that her cooking alone would tempt him, but that he was not ready for a move yet.

Early the next morning Daisy rang to wish her parents and grandfather a happy Christmas, and later Matthew's brother and sister both called with their Christmas greetings, wanting to talk to their father. Both were younger than Matthew and both had lived abroad for many years. Diana had married an American academic, brought up three children, and now lived in Boston where her husband taught. Douglas, named after his uncle, had trained as an engineer and since the mid 1970s had worked in Germany, where he had married, settled and brought up a family. Both tried to get over to see their father as often as they could, especially these days, when his health was declining.

Did Michael find the Christmas lunch difficult? Matthew kept a close eye on him. He was eating little and would wince when someone spoke noisily or laughed too loudly. He sweetly acknowledged Rachel's cooking skills once more, and said how wonderful it was to be amongst such a warm and loving family. Between the turkey and the Christmas pudding he asked if he could sit in an armchair in the sitting room and Daniel lifted him gently out of his seat and helped him through.

Sated, they all sat for the Queen's Speech. Reconciliation the theme. Images of the bronze statue entitled Reconciliation, with replicas in Belfast, Berlin and Hiroshima. What a powerful image. Man and woman reunited, on their knees embracing. Nation and nation reunited. And then another powerful image: Blood Swept Lands and Seas of Red, the hundreds of thousands of ceramic poppies that flooded the moat of the Tower of London to commemorate the dead of the First World War. Mention of the Christmas Truce in the trenches in 1914. A tribute to the medics who travelled to West Africa to tackle the Ebola epidemic. The voice linking these images, powerful reminders of humanity and inhumanity, was a voice both completely familiar and yet completely distant, with its tones, its intonations from a bygone age. Finally, the Band of the Royal Marine playing *Silent Night* in the grounds of Buckingham Palace.

As the music plays, Matthew notices a glistening tear roll slowly down his father's cheek. 'Are you all right, Dad? He goes to the chair and squats down, putting his hand on his father's arm.

'Oh, silly me! Silly me!' He brushes the tear away. 'I never weep at these things.' He laughs, an attempt to recover his composure. 'I just found that image of those hundreds of thousands of poppies spilling out of the Tower terribly moving. And then that lovely tune, so beautiful, it just finished me off! Forgive me!'

Matthew squeezed his father's arm. 'I love you, Dad.'

Two days later it was time to take Michael back to Marlow. It was with heavy hearts that Matthew and Rachel left him there. There was a note from Mrs Knowles to say she would be coming in the early evening to prepare a meal for him, and she had put the heating on so that the flat was warm for Michael's return.

When Matthew grabbed his father to give him a farewell hug, he squeezed him a little too tightly and he felt his father flinch and heard a quiet gasp of pain. How thin he felt.

There was little to say to each other on the homeward journey.

*

Once again, BBC's *Newsnight* features items about the terrorist attacks in France that had begun with the murder of eleven *Charlie Hebdo* staff on 7 January, the previous week. Invited to represent the Home Office, and because he is an expert on security, is David Chapman. Smart, as ever, in mind and dress, and glowing with that familiar aura of the powerful.

He is asked what the government is doing to ensure such attacks can never happen in the UK. 'We can't absolutely guarantee, of course, it will never happen again. Certainly the security services have upped their game since the Mumbai attacks in 2008, improving police firearms capability and the speed of military response. The police and other agencies carry out exercises to test the response to terrorist attacks and these exercises include scenarios similar to the events in Paris. It is worth noting, by the way, that the *Charlie Hebdo* gunmen clearly were military professionals with former combat experience, employing infantry tactics and using military gestures. This is clear in the video footage that has surfaced on the Internet.'

The pixie-like presenter, who bears a striking resemblance to Gollum, presses Chapman. Reassuring, yes, BUT, surely the real threat lies in the fundamental shift in the tactics used by terror groups. The big Islamic terrorist organisations such as Al-Qaeda and ISIS are far more likely these days to inspire and promote home-grown terrorists to carry out attacks.

Chapman replies with a measured response. 'You are absolutely right. And this process of decentralisation has in many ways increased the challenges associated with identifying and preventing terrorist attacks. The would-be terrorists are encouraged to take their own initiative in developing home-grown cells – a situation facilitated by the rise of the Internet as the preferred means of radicalisation and recruitment and operation. Police forces and intelligence agencies have had to devote increasing resources to countering an unprecedentedly diverse threat.'

Gollum: 'So how should the government react to this new and increasingly uncertain threat? Is enough being done?'

'Well, unsurprisingly, much of this battle is now fought online as national authorities seek to extend their reach into the chat rooms and social media forums that have become hotbeds for radicalisation, co-ordination and planning. The Government's Counter-Terrorism and Security Bill, currently making its way through Parliament, includes various measures to intervene in online terrorist communication.'

Gollum has spotted a problem here. 'As the security services continue to enhance their ability to monitor online communications, the debate on surveillance and civil liberties comes more into play.' He brings in a spokesperson from Liberty who now appears on a big screen set high before him. 'Surely, given the current nature of terrorism, we need to allow a greater degree of surveillance than we would perhaps like. If our national security depends upon these increased powers, then surely Liberty should not be opposing them.'

The spokesperson of course completely supports the security services in their efforts to keep country safe. She then rattles off a raft of technical details about Internet data, and explains, in ways that Matthew doesn't fully follow, why the lack of clarity in the current drafting is very dangerous. Prompted by Gollum she agrees that the provision is very like an earlier attempt at legislation. 'That was popularly known as The Snoopers' Charter,' she says, 'And, if you remember, that was previously ruled unlawful by the European Court of Justice.' She reads from some notes. '"The indiscriminate powers to require the retention of the communications data of the entire population amounts to a violation of privacy rights." What is currently being proposed still amounts to a major step-change in relationship between the individual and the State.'

So many *Newsnight* discussions are noisy, with voice overlaid by voice as impatient guests disagree with each other. Sometimes Gollum will wade in over the other voices in an attempt to bring order, simply adding to the white-noise of debate. Tonight, everything is orderly. Chapman has merely been shaking his head at much of what he has been listening to, but has not interrupted. Now he is invited back into the discussion.

'These alarmist tactics by Liberty are not helpful,' he says. 'It is nonsense to suggest, as I have heard it said, that we want to allow the government to "snoop on your emails". It is allowing the police and the security services, under a tightly regulated and controlled regime, to find out the "who, where, when and how" of a communication, but not its content; this is so they can prove and disprove alibis, identify associations between suspects, and tie suspects and victims to specific locations. Quite simply, if we want the police and the security services to protect the public and save lives, they need this capability. The Home Secretary, Theresa May, has put it very clearly: innocent lives will be put at risk unless the authorities are better able to track communications of suspected terrorists.'

He wants to continue, begins a point about the uncooperative and misguided Lib Dem wing of the

Coalition which is opposing this part of the bill. But Gollum brings the discussion to a close in the time-honoured way. 'I am afraid that's all we have time for. Thank you both.'

Chapman has been impressive in the way he tends to be impressive. Controlled, articulate, well prepared. There is much to admire in Chapman. Matthew can see why his star is in the ascendant. But the discussion, important though the issue is, has not engaged Matthew. The next item is more to his taste. Apparently #JeSuisCharlie is the most tweeted hashtag ever. To discuss *Charlie Hebdo* and related matters, a well-known English novelist and a Cambridge philosopher have been brought into the studio.

The novelist, either through conviction or because this is the polemical line he has been encouraged to take, says that the current climate of Muslim sensitivity reminds him of the days of the Salman Rushdie fatwa. He talks of a sinister yearning in parts of the Muslim world for a caliphate. In France and in Denmark writers and cartoonists are in the front line, fighting the good fight. 'But,' he says, somewhat preciously, 'it is an unequal battle of the pen versus the gun.'

'Surely,' – the philosopher chips in with a mischievous grin– 'the pen is mightier than the sword. And the gun, even. An unequal battle indeed!'

Gollum addresses the philosopher, who has had an article published in this morning's *Times* suggesting the spurious and unhelpful nature of the #JeSuisCharlie campaign. 'You are unhappy, I gather, with the groundswell of support for *Charlie Hebdo*.'

'No,' he says, 'I completely understand the public abhorrence of the murders. But I think the #JeSuisCharlie phenomenon is glib and facile. I mean, goodness, I heard on the news this morning that George Clooney apparently took to the stage at the Golden Globe Awards last night wearing a "Je Suis Charlie" badge, and pronouncing in a choked voice that he was Charlie. What nonsense! In reality Clooney is not Charlie in anything other than an imagined film role. He is a shiny star insulated within his glitzy Hollywood bubble from the sort of realities that descended on Paris earlier in the week.'

'I think that is a cheap thing to say,' says the unhappy novelist. 'He was showing solidarity with the French. He was telling the world that we should not walk in fear. To me it is an honest thing to say. I think at last we are waking up to the idea that we can criticise parts of the Muslim world without the spectre of Islamophobia rising up. We need to have an honest conversation about free speech. We need a conversation about blasphemy. About mockery, satire…scholarly analysis. Talking and writing is all we've got. Slaughtering each other will bring us to the very gates of hell.'

Gollum turns to the philosopher. 'That's a fair point, isn't it?'

'Well, perhaps…Of course we shouldn't be slaughtering each other, it goes without saying. But there is writing and writing. The problem is that *Charlie Hebdo*'s stance contains inconsistencies. This is a publication that wants absolute freedom of expression of publication, while at the same time relentlessly campaigning to curb the freedom of all sorts of Muslims' rules, for example the way they eat, the way they dress…This is not *Hebdo* treading carefully or sensitively. This is not about freedom of expression any more. It is about licence. Licence to suspend intelligence and fair judgement, licence to suspend any faculties that might restrict anger, confusion or prejudice from being unleashed against a particular target.'

Gollum chips in, '*Charlie Hebdo* is about licence rather than freedom of speech?'

'Well, I agree,' says the novelist, 'that what appears to have been an act of fearlessness by the editors of *Charlie Hebdo* can be interpreted as an act of folly. I think the accusation that they have abused the very freedom of speech they espouse has some validity and is certainly worthy of debate. However, I think is wrong to suggest they are encouraging the suspension of fair judgement or are encouraging prejudice. To me, they are having a discussion about things they find distasteful or just simply unacceptable.'

'Why is the way Muslim women dress distasteful? I can say that it is not to my taste. I can go further and say that if a woman in a full burka, showing only her eyes, walks past me in the street I feel offended. But it doesn't matter. Nobody should abide by what I *feel*.'

'But you, yourself have given offence on many occasions.' Gollum is jumping the rails here, isn't he? Where does he want to take this? Does he know? 'For example, when you said that the Islam had entered the Dark Ages of learning.'

'People took offence. But that does not mean that I gave offence. Or was offensive. What I said was a matter of fact. During Europe's Dark and Medieval ages Islam was the beacon of scientific learning and discovery. It led the world into all kinds of exciting ways of thinking. Where is that spirit of enquiry now? It doesn't exist. It has stagnated for centuries. So what I said was a matter of fact. Whether it upsets other people is less important to me than the nature of the fact. My role is to persuade people to think for themselves and to look at the evidence.'

An interesting discussion. But – predictably, perhaps – it's time for Gollum again. 'I am afraid that's all we have time for. Thank you both.'

The nature of fact. Evidence. What was it his father had said in the summer, when Matthew had asked him how he should proceed in his investigation of Chapman? In history, as in law, everything must be underpinned by evidence.

CHAPTER 13

If the balance of weddings to funerals had been four to one in the famous film of the 1990s, for Matthew these days it tended to be the reverse. Today he was attending the funeral of a retired former colleague, Owen Roberts.

St James's Church lay to the east of the town, serving a Victorian development that had been built after the arrival of the railway in 1864. It was probably attended just as well today as in its earliest years. Built in red brick with stone dressings, the church was unfussy and uncluttered. Large lancet windows gave it an airy and cheerful atmosphere.

But Matthew rarely felt cheerful in churches. The problem was not in the fabric of the building, nor in the mass of people filling the pews. The problem was not even the celebrant himself, though in this instance the man's mannered delivery, with the vowels of words such as 'God' and 'love' stretched exaggeratedly in a nasal sing-song, was really quite creepy. The real problem lay in the language. To Matthew, the religious abstractions were elusive and slippery, like water seeping through the fingers of cupped palms. His mother had given him her Catholic faith and, when this had deserted him, he had felt bereft. These days he merely felt incredulous that such preposterous tenets should survive in a rational and scientific age.

Of course he found funerals particularly difficult. Added to the sadness of loss was the assault of liturgical language which, to mark the interface between this world and the next, became floridly hyperbolic, with its shrill certainties and candied promises.

He never found any comfort in the metaphysical reassurances of the celebrants. More often these days his mind would turn to the literary deaths he had shared with his pupils over the years. It might be dragged back to the dreadful act of self-effacement of Michael Henchard in *The Mayor of Casterbridge*: the nullifying sense of complete worthlessness, of being utterly despised; the lacerating compulsion to crawl away and die, unattended, like a wounded animal.

Matthew was always troubled when the priest asserted, in the words of St John, that 'He who believes in me will live, even though he dies.' Here he might be ambushed by the image of King Lear howling like a dog as he carried on stage the body of his murdered daughter, hoping, in his last delusional moments, that her dead lips were moving with the breath of life. Or he might recall the fevered disillusion of Kurtz as he lay dying in the torrid heat of the Belgian Congo.

Most frequently, though, what came to him these days was the pathos of Willy Loman's demise. The little man unsatisfied by the ordinary achievements of home-building and family life, filled to distraction and madness with enormous dreams of success and significance. The short final scene was unbearable. Wife Linda unable to understand the senseless death and unable to understand why all the people he knew did not come to the funeral.

Willy Loman, dreamer of dreams. Would you blame him? Willy Loman. Everyman.

Sometimes these visitations of the literary departed would be interrupted by a remembered voice, sharp, assertive and with just a hint of a sneer in it. 'Literature is not real. It's escapism. Mere escapism. Make-believe worlds that flatter us into thinking we are becoming wiser, more knowledgeable. At best, it is a pleasurable passing of time. At worst, a complete waste of time.' It is the voice of David Chapman at his most acerbic. The brightest pupil in Matthew's English set is telling his peers that they are wasting their time. George West, psychic adventurer, is having none of it. And Jo Perry, hater of isms of any kind, is having none of it.

'You do talk rubbish sometimes, David. Literature brings you into closer contact with the world, into a fuller understanding of it. A work of literature shines a narrow beam of light into the darkness, illuminating some aspect of what it is to be human...I suppose you're going to tell me next that politics is real. That the baying, braying donkeys in parliament are in touch with the "real"!' She snorts her derision. But David will not rise to the bait. 'Physics: that's real. Economics: that's real. English literature: not real. It's an indulgence!'

Matthew had never felt that. In fact, quite the opposite. We are born with our mother's legs astride the grave, crying that we are come to this great stage of fools. This was what, in Matthew's experience, the great writers had told the world. What was it, he wondered, that had compelled Chapman, with his fine mind, to downplay literature, to deny the glimpses into the shadowy hollows of human existence that literature provided, to forgo its humanising power?

Matthew's reverie is broken by the shuffling of feet and

rustling of orders of service as the congregation rises to sing another hymn.

Today there are two eulogies, one by a son and one by a friend, whom Matthew does not know. The son speaks in measured tones, pausing confidently, looking up bravely to the congregation. He captures the man that Matthew knew as an older colleague: the desire to help younger teachers, a disinterested concern for others, the passion for biology that animated his career, the enthusiastic interest he retained in the school after he retired, visiting frequently and never leaving without an encouraging word to someone. And then he speaks of the father he knew. It is an uplifting and heart-warming tribute. The friend also speaks finely, and he too captures something that is recognisable and true about Owen Roberts.

A final hymn and it is time for the recessional. The coffin is borne away to the strains of Vaughan Williams' *Organ Prelude on Rhosymedre*, an upbeat conclusion to the service, with an appropriate glance at Roberts' Welsh ancestry, of which he had been so proud.

The family leave directly for a private Committal at the local crematorium. They have laid on refreshments in the church hall; it is at functions like these that Matthew is able to keep in touch with many of his former colleagues. As they file out of the church he waves to a smiling Kitty Harper, widow of the man who had been Headmaster of the school in David Chapman's time. He collects a cup of tea from a trestle table and walks over to her.

She takes the cup with one hand and with the other clasps Matthew's arm. 'It seems, sadly, that the only time we get together these days is at funerals, Matthew. And any day now it will be mine!' she adds with a throaty laugh, squeezing his arm.

'Don't say that, Kitty!' After a brief hesitation, he says, 'By the way, I'd really like to visit you…If that would be all right.'

'Of course! I'd love you to come round. It's been such a long time…Archive business?'

'Yes, sort of.'

'Sounds intriguing! Why don't you come round for tea next Wednesday? And Rachel.'

*

Kitty lived about thirty miles away in a small modern house just outside the centre of a small cathedral city. Matthew had decided not to take Rachel. It would complicate matters, diffusing the focus of conversation that he wanted in his visit.

The house was a 1930s semi that Kitty had downsized to after her husband's death. Undistinguished outside, it was rather dowdy within. She had obviously not got round to re-decorating since moving in. Old wallpaper, here and there discoloured, and chipped paintwork. In the sitting room, a comfy-looking but worn sofa and two ancient armchairs in need of re-upholstering. But outside, beyond the French windows, a tidy, well-stocked garden showing the first flush of spring.

Kitty seemed delighted to see Matthew. She brought the tea in from the kitchen on a large tray. A delicate china tea set and silver teapot. Buttered bread beside a pot of home-made plum jam. Some heavy-looking shortbreads she had made the day before.

'It's good to see you, Matthew. I do like to keep in touch with the old place, and I know Chris was always very fond of you. He frequently told me that you were one of his best heads of department.' They talked about the school, about Matthew's family, about her life coping without her husband. And then she said, 'You wanted to talk about an archive matter, Matthew?'

*

An hour or so later he left. The visit had gone…How had it gone? Not well, and not not well. Interestingly, for sure; as he would tell Rachel when he got home.

When invited to bring up his question on the archive matter, Matthew had told Kitty about his discoveries. The fragment of letter to her husband. The 'course of action' that involved Tony Marshall as well as her husband. The implied involvement of David Chapman. David's unease when Matthew had mentioned the name of Sir Peter Gilbert. Sir Peter's death in the summer term.

'It just seems, Kitty, that something happened… something big happened that was covered up. And I just want to know what.'

A look of mild alarm shadows Kitty's face as Matthew is listing his discoveries. The previous warmth drains from her voice. 'But what's it got to do with you?'

'I'm the school archivist, Kitty. The curator of the school's historical documents.'

'Pah. You're being pompous now, Matthew…Why do you want to know?'

Why? Why? That was what Rachel asked. And his father had said as much when they had visited in the summer. Why? Why? That is what he had asked himself after his letter to Chapman had brought Tommy Cooper hotfooting it down to the school. He was aware by now that it was not a question he could answer clearly. He wanted to tell Kitty that he felt driven to clasp and brandish the burnished sword of truth. But he knew it wasn't as simple as that. He knew that his search for the truth about the summer of 1991 derived from some hidden compulsion which he couldn't fully understand.

'Why? I don't really know, Kitty. I just want to know what happened.'

'Well, it's not going to do you any good, and you really ought not to pursue this, Matthew.'

She is in tears now. There is a pause, a deep breath. 'Matthew, there was a terrible accident. Terrible. And then, in the heat of the moment, the panic if you like, foolish decisions were made that we all had to live with. Foolish, foolish decisions. Chris couldn't live with that. He never dropped anyone in it, but he couldn't carry on...Felt he had to resign. And lived with terrible regrets for the rest of his life.'

The tears have turned to sobbing. Matthew moves to the side of her chair, squats down and takes her hand. He doesn't know what to say. He doesn't want to push her any further. 'I'm so sorry, Kitty, I didn't want to upset you. I'm so sorry.'

She dabs her eyes with a handkerchief. 'It's all right. It's all right. Only...Only, please promise me this. That you will leave this matter well alone. For the good of everyone still alive. No good will come of it...Worse, Matthew, you could find yourself in big trouble.' The wraith of Tommy Cooper seems to float into the room. Is that a comic leer on his face?

Matthew pats her arm and stands up.

'Thank you, Kitty, for the advice.'

She offers him another cup of tea, insisting when he appears hesitant.

'I'd like to talk,' she says. When she has brought more tea, she talks about her husband, Christopher.

'You know, we had many conversations in his last year about public schools. About boarding. He was sent away to prep school at such a tender age. He was desolate. But couldn't tell anyone. It was only in retirement, I think, that he ever fully reflected on the experience of boarding and of the damage it can do. You quickly have to learn to survive, he said, and you do this by closing down your emotions, disguising your feelings. Building defences. Appearing tough so that you are not vulnerable to the bullies who always delight in finding weakness.'

Matthew nods. He recognises the portrait she is painting. Some of the colleagues he has taught with over the years – the privately educated ones – have been emotionally shallow men, and often misogynistic as well. 'I know exactly what you mean,' he says.

'These emotionally-buttoned people come out of their boarding schools with a sense of superiority and a sense of entitlement. They expect to form the elite, and they usually do. I mean, look at Cameron's government.'

'Effortless superiority,' says Matthew, nodding. A cliché, for sure.

'Yes. Effortless superiority. But it's fake. They appear more competent and assured than they really are. They are emotionally illiterate. Or emotionally stunted. Grown-up schoolboys. You know, I think that Chris felt very guilty when he looked back on his career. Guilty at having promoted a self-perpetuating elite that lacked the emotional intelligence to lead properly.'

'But he didn't think this when he was a Head, did he?'

'No, I don't think so. But in retirement he thought a lot about it…You know, every time he saw Boris Johnson, he exploded!'

She laughs. Matthew smiles.

'He thought Boris typified what we are talking about. The bumbling appearance a mere strategy. The relationships with women. The smugness...and the little boy haircut!' She shrieks with laughter as she says this.

Suddenly she is looking more serious again. 'So many of Chris's staff were from public schools – women staff, too – and most of the school governors were. And of course Chris's public school code of honour ensured that he would never break ranks.' She stops abruptly, putting a hand over her mouth. 'I'm saying too much.'

'Don't worry, Kitty. I understand exactly the point you are making about boarding schools. I've often thought how emotionally cauterising the experience can be...But it is much better these days.'

Matthew wants to leave on a positive note. He points through the window. 'What is that plant? It's amazing!' He is pointing to a white-flowered shrub with branches arching in all directions, weighted to the ground by their full blossoms.

'It's a Pearl Bush. The Bride, it's called, and you can see why.'

'It's lovely.'

As they stand by the front gate, Kitty takes both of Matthew's hands firmly. 'You've promised to leave this business well alone, haven't you, Matthew?' He nods. He pecks her on the cheek.

*

'A terrible accident', Kitty had said. 'Foolish decisions'. 'Chris couldn't live with that...Felt he had to resign'. Strange words, words that challenged the provisional narrative that Matthew had built up in his mind in recent months. Head of School Chapman summoned. Told he must step down. Parents' phone call to Chairman of Governors. Harper sacked.

'Foolish decisions': the sacking of Chapman? And the

sacking of Harper? But where was the 'terrible accident'? What couldn't Christopher Harper 'live with'? And was it a resignation or a sacking? Certainly it was presented to the school community as a resignation; but then of course it would have to have been.

As Matthew allowed Kitty's words and phrases to sink into his mind, as he played with their meanings and implications, he realised, with some irritation, that his provisional narrative was mere hypothesis; flimsy speculation, the evidential strands of which were few. Matthew was annoyed with himself, embarrassed at the ease with which he has allowed this chimera to flesh itself out into a figure of fact.

*

As ever, when driving, he has the radio on. And as ever, these days, much of the coverage concerns the General Election, which is a little under a month away. For two years the Tory party has been slowly closing the gap on Labour in the opinion polls. Since the New Year the two parties have been neck and neck. Commentators are talking of a hung parliament. The Tory coalition's Lib Dem partners are facing wipe-out – that is agreed. And UKIP, who are showing a consistent 15% in the polls, are deemed to be in with a shout for a handful of seats.

Matthew recalls Leo Beamish's recent comment on UKIP. 'The persistence of UKIP,' he'd said loudly in the SCR, 'is like a large turd that remains in the bowl after flushing, and seems impossible to get rid of.' Not the kind of comment that one might expect to hear on the *PM* programme. But Matthew can imagine Eddie Mair being amused by the remark, and perhaps even saying it himself, off-air.

Today, Mair is chairing a discussion between two junior MPs – Matthew doesn't recognise the names of either – who are working their way through key issues. The Tory is taunting the Labour chap about Ed Miliband's poor performance in the first of the televised debates between party leaders. And then mischievously, he uses the leaked *Daily Telegraph* report of Nicola Sturgeon, denied of course, telling the French Ambassador that the Scottish Nationalists would prefer David Cameron to win the election. No-mates Labour.

The Labour MP doesn't rise to the bait. Instead he lays into the Tory with his own taunts about David Cameron's weak leadership. 'The Tory party is so fundamentally fractured that Cameron has to throw some red meat to his rebellious, Euro-sceptic backbenchers in the form of promising to offer an In or Out EU referendum.' The Tory tries to interrupt, but is shouted over. 'This is weak. It is laughable. No, it is not laughable. It is dangerous. It's monstrous.' There is an attractive musicality to the man's Welsh accent as he stretches and stresses the first syllables of 'laughable', 'dangerous' and 'monstrous'.

'So much for the party of the people! Where are your democratic principles there? Denying the people a say!'

And so they continue, picking over the various policies of their respective parties, prompted and directed skilfully by Eddie Mair.

There is no Lib Dem representation in this discussion and none of the minor parties have been invited. What has happened to dear old BBC balance, Matthew wonders. Actually, he believes that the notion of balance is a spurious one. What it amounts to is an equality of airtime for the major parties, with the minor ones getting their share pro rata. But it is not in any other sense an equality, a balance. The substance, the weightiness, of two three-minute slots on a news bulletin might differ hugely. The selection of material for those slots depends upon what is available. It depends upon the good judgement of the news editor, so say nothing of his conscious or unconscious prejudices. Would the pursuit of truth not be a more suitable criterion than balance? A slippery slope indeed! Whose truth? The truth of some harassed, chain-smoking news editor?

'Facts of the day' and 'newsworthy facts', to paraphrase E.H. Carr. A trickier problem still with television news reporting. Perhaps in the pictorial medium one might draw a distinction between 'events without footage' and 'events with footage'. The latter being the ones deemed worthy of a TV news bulletin. By a news editor. With or without judgement.

CHAPTER 14

A light tread was ascending the staircase to the Archive Room. No knock, the door opens.

'Rachel...Rachel, what is it, darling?' She looks pale.

She moves across the room quickly and clasps Matthew to her, squeezing him tightly. 'Matty, it's your father. He has died.' She starts sobbing.

In the brief moment before the news sinks in properly, he is comforting her, stroking her face, saying, 'It's all right, darling, it's all right.'

And then they are comforting each other. She tells him to sit in one armchair and she takes the other one. 'Mrs Knowles has just rung. She found him this morning.'

The enormity of the news is slowly working through his mind. He speaks haltingly. 'Found him...what...in...bed?'

'No, he was sitting in his armchair. He must have died yesterday, but Mrs K doesn't go in on a Sunday.'

As the shock is about to overwhelm him, his mind seems to make an automatic gear change. He begins to think practically and to speak briskly. 'We must go to Marlow. Now. There'll be funeral arrangements to make. The flat to be sorted. We need to let people know. His former colleagues—'

'Matty, slow down. We must tell the family first.'

*

They head to Marlow later in the morning. Rachel has spoken to the children. Matthew has rung his sister in America and has left a message with his sister-in-law in Germany.

It is difficult being in the flat. It looks so normal. Everything where it was last time Matthew visited, three weeks earlier. Mrs Knowles is there to greet them. She makes them a cup of tea. It seems somehow wrong to be using Michael's kitchen when he is not there, wrong for Matthew to go into the bedroom. The bed is made up, Michael's pyjamas folded on the pillow. On the bedside table, a medicine bottle and a copy *of Sapiens: A Brief History of Humankind* by Yuval Noah Harari; a bookmark pokes out about three-quarters of the way through. His father had mentioned the book on Matthew's last visit; he'd read something about it and it sounded worth looking at. So Matthew had ordered it on Amazon and had it sent directly to him.

On the balcony, in a planter by the French window, is a collection of nerine bulbs which Michael had brought with him when he had moved from Hyghcliff. The spidery pink blooms were a favourite of his wife; they flowered in late September, the time of her birthday, and had remained for Michael an annual memorial to her. The leaves are just beginning to shoot. Matthew touches them. His chest and his stomach are filled with a heaviness that he wants to release. He feels on the verge of tears, but no tears will come.

He thinks back to his last visit, nearly three weeks earlier; remembers it with a sharp clarity. Michael, though frail, had seemed alert and content. He had been listening to music a great deal recently, he said, late Romantic –

Mahler, Shostakovich, Strauss. They had discussed Mahler and had disagreed about which was the best symphony. Matthew had acknowledged the claims of the Second, but argued that the Third was the most complete. He told Michael why he loved the opening of the symphony, Pan's awakening. Brash, brazen trumpets and trombones – an outward display of new growth and progress; and then the slumbering, slow awakening of the strings suggesting a more substantial growth, the old heartwood of an ancient tree, perhaps, once more stirring inwardly. Michael had said that the symphony he came back to time and time again was the Ninth: the quietly disintegrating order of the first movement, the astonishing final movement, where life itself seems to ebb from the music as it comes to its slow and almost imperceptible conclusion.

In the CD player Matthew found not Mahler but Richard Strauss's *Four Last Songs*. He had not heard these pieces for many years and could not remember them well, so he decided to take the disc home with him.

When he returned to the sitting room, Rachel and Mrs Knowles were chatting together. 'Betty was telling me about how she found your father this morning, Matty.'

'I was. You must know, Mr Agnew…Matthew, that he looked so at peace. There was a wonderful expression on his face. It was of…complete happiness…Like nothing could disturb him.'

'How was he when you saw him on Friday?' Matthew asked.

'He seemed all right. He had been quiet these last few weeks and he hadn't eaten much, but he seemed cheerful…in a quiet sort of a way.' Matthew's dry-eyed grief was bubbling within, but still could find no release. Mrs Knowles continued. 'He was a wonderful man, your father, wonderful. He was—' she is searching for the words

– 'very decent.' What a perfect description, Matthew thinks. 'Decent'. Yes, that word will cover many of his father's qualities.

They tell Mrs Knowles that they will see her again when they return to Marlow in a day or two to make arrangements. Then they bid her goodbye. Rachel hugs her, Matthew, rather more formally, shakes her hand.

*

In the days after his father's death, Matthew played endlessly the CD he had brought home with him. He wondered if it had been playing as Michael had slipped away and, if so, which song was playing in those final moments. Most appropriately it would have been *Im Abendrot*, with its final lines: 'How weary we are of wandering / Is this perhaps death?' The closing words are followed by the extraordinary postlude. Slow, solemn, peaceful strings with a luxuriant richness, rising at the end and overlaid by trills of birdsong from the woodwinds. At Sunset. Yes, at Sunset.

But the song he listened to over and over again was *Beim Schlafengehen*. A quiet, low sound from the strings, slowly climbing to bring in the soaring soprano, her voice filled with yearning; the desire to sink into slumber, to slip away. Before the final verse, a ravishingly beautiful interlude, a wistful violin solo weaving its way forward above a lush orchestral accompaniment. And then the soprano's return to evoke an unshackled soul floating free, drawn by a haunting horn.

Two days after Michael's death, Rachel went into Matthew's study and found him sitting in his armchair listening to *Beim Schlafengehen*. She saw tears running down his face; came to him; leant over him and embraced him. An embrace that released a strangled, heaving cry.

Then splintering tears erupt as Matthew lets himself go. By the time he is fully gone, beyond any comfort that Rachel can offer, he is howling uncontrollably.

If music be the food of grief, play on. Matthew remembers when his grandfather died in the autumn of 1966. In the months immediately afterwards, Matthew's mother had seemed to feed her grief with the pop songs that were receiving repeated airtime on the radio. *Green Green Grass of Home* was played constantly and would bring a wistful tear to her eye. 'He did miss the auld country,' she would say, unaware perhaps that the song was not about Ireland or Wales even, but was a lament by an American prisoner on Death Row. And she loved Bobby Darin's *If I were a Carpenter*. 'My Da was a joiner when he started out in Cork,' she'd say. Another incessantly played hit of the time was *Reach Out I'll Be There* by the Four Tops. This song of consolation comforted her grieving mind with the thought of her dead father keeping an eye on her from the next world. Simple music. Sentimental lyrics. But speaking to a heart in need.

If music be the food of grief, play on. Where were the consolations of literature now? It was barely a fortnight since Matthew had been reflecting on the literary deaths he had shared with pupils in his teaching days. No consolation there. Confirmation only of the short and brutish nature of life. True? Not entirely. There was the selfless fellowship of Edgar. The simple loyalty of Abe Whittle. The sensitivity of Charlie Marlow to the psychological needs of The Intended. Humanity. Feeling what wretches feel. Empathy; compassion; touch. Feeling beyond words.

*

Rachel accompanied Matthew when he went to Marlow to finalise the funeral arrangements. A service in All

Saints' Church, followed by burial in Marlow Cemetery. A reception at the Compleat Angler, directly across the river from the church. Matthew had accepted the invitation of the funeral directors to see the body of his father. He had been urged to see his mother after she died and had always been glad that he had; he wanted to say goodbye to his father in the same way.

There was a special room for this. It had the air of a chapel, though there was no religious imagery. Laid out on a covered slab, his father looked recognisably himself. Of course experts at the funeral directors would have known exactly how to achieve the best effect. Nevertheless, there was something consoling in the seeming normality, the stillness, the peacefulness of the body. Matthew stroked the white hair gently and was amazed at how soft it felt. Then he kissed the cold forehead and took his leave.

*

Eulogies presented their own particular challenge. How to soften the rough edges of a life, to overlook the less attractive sides of a subject, while still presenting an account that was true, or at least recognisable to the listeners. As Matthew sat at his desk, working on his father's eulogy, he felt that there were no rough edges to be smoothed, no omissions to be made in the raw aftermath of death. The challenge was to capture the complexity of the man, his subtlety.

In the days that followed, many former colleagues and pupils wrote letters, some to Matthew, some to Michael's publisher and some directly to the flat, assuming that they would somehow reach the family. Matthew knew that his father had been a good historian, a popular lecturer, but what these letters gave him was clearer sense of the nature of the man as academic and teacher. His goal had always been to get at the truth, to garner the facts and to understand the wellsprings of motivation and action. He was insistent on the accuracy of his sources, 'always a stickler' wrote one colleague, 'for assessing the value and the provenance of a source'. Another noted the powerful combination of rigorous scholastic methods, academic integrity and intellectual generosity. It seemed that he had an exceptional command of his subject, underpinning his lectures and his writings with an impressive breadth of scope and a minute grasp of detail. His books, which had never sold well, were commended for a crisp, lucid and authoritative style of writing.

There were some affectionate memories from former pupils. He was generous with the time he gave them, much appreciated for his commitment to the development of young minds. There was a clarity to his lectures, and a gently provocative style to his seminars. 'He loved being answered back, being challenged,' wrote one who had, she said, gone on to be a secondary school teacher and had tried to model her A level teaching on his style.

The letters were helpful to Matthew as he wrote and rewrote his eulogy. But what he really wanted to capture was the man. The father, husband, grandfather. His siblings emailed him with memories and attempts to capture his distinctive personality; so too the grandchildren, with childhood memories of this imposing but fun man. Matthew's own childhood memories would form a major part of the piece. He'd learnt only last summer of one of the rare moments of discord between his father and mother; but that had never been an episode in his memory; he remembered growing up in a household of peace and gentleness and complete security.

When his father worked in his study at Hyghcliff, preparing a book or a lecture, it was an unbreakable rule that nobody whatsoever knocked on his door to disturb him. But he did not expect absolute quiet in the rest of the house; and when he had finished his work, he would come out, sometimes humming, sometimes even singing, and join in wholeheartedly with whatever was happening in the family at that time.

He was a lifelong touchstone of wise advice for Matthew and, they both confirmed, for Diana and Douglas, his siblings. A careful listener, a cautious and tentative judge, an eloquent and judicious giver of counsel. It was the loss of this man that left Matthew feeling so bereft.

When he was happy that the eulogy was finished, Matthew went over it time and time again, noting the places where he might stumble with emotion, the little ambushing details that might surprise him on the day. He wanted to immunise himself against a breakdown in delivery that might mar the important tribute he wanted to pay his father.

*

He does not falter. He speaks strongly and clearly. He has memorised most of the address, and glances down at his text just occasionally to make sure he is not skipping a paragraph or two. The faces of the congregation are upturned, concentrating intently on his words. Rachel is in tears and so is Diana. The funeral is confined to family and close friends. A memorial service may follow later. And suddenly Matthew catches sight of, sitting towards the back of the church, and crying too, of?…Catherine. That's who it was. The woman, the old flame, they had met at The Ferry the previous summer.

Michael had left rudimentary arrangements for his death. One of the drawers of the desk in his study had contained a list of practical arrangements to be made. Details of his bank accounts to be closed, standing orders and direct debits to be stopped, the solicitors holding his will; and some wishes for his funeral. To be held at All Saints' Church; inclusion of Cesar Franck's *Panis Angelicus*, to be sung by the church choir, and the 1920s hymn, *Lord of all Hopefulness*, to be sung by the congregation; burial at Marlow Cemetery, not cremation.

Michael had been an occasional worshipper at All Saints', so the rector had at least a passing acquaintance with him and said some apposite words before giving a homily that combined the notion of Michael's pursuit of historical truth with the notion of God's truth. The Way, the Light, the Truth.

It was a simple ceremony. For Matthew, the highlight was the singing of *Lord of all Hopefulness*. It was an appropriate choice, with its tune, the old Irish folk melody *Slane*, reminding the mourners of the great love of Michael's life, Bridget, his Irish bride. As they sang the last verse, a slow tear ran down Matthew's cheek.

> Lord of all gentleness, Lord of all calm,
> Whose voice is contentment, whose presence is balm,
> Be there at our sleeping, and give us, we pray,
> Your peace in our hearts, Lord,
> At the end of the day.

*

The funeral cortege crept slowly through the town to make its short journey to the cemetery. Some more words were intoned by the rector before the coffin was lowered into the grave. And then Matthew led the mourners in the ritual throwing of earth on top of the coffin. Earth to Earth. There was a brutal thud from the earth and a crack as something more solid hit the wood. Why had the soil not been sifted free of small stones and pebbles? The harsh noise seemed so disrespectful. Earth to Earth.

The reception at the Compleat Angler was a cheerful affair. There were people there whom Matthew had never met, of course, and everyone came to introduce themselves, congratulate Matthew on his eulogy and say how much they had loved his father.

When Catherine approached him she looked hesitant. 'You probably don't remember me—'

'Indeed I do. It's Catherine, and we met at The Ferry last summer.'

'Well remembered! I thought your eulogy was lovely. Lovely. And so well delivered. The teacher in you, no doubt!'

Matthew thanked her and said that Michael had clearly been very fond of her. They had been very close, she said. But they had both moved on. She said it was one of the most satisfying relationships of her later life. 'He was a wonderful man. Wonderful in every way. It's such a loss.'

'Well, yes, but it was a long life and a good life,' said Matthew. 'And he was very active until pretty much the last year.' She nodded and smiled.

Matthew tried to spend time with all the guests. One of Diana's daughters had flown over from America with her mother and she had some interesting memories of her grandfather. 'I remember he took us on his boat to Clifton—'

'Cliveden. Great place.'

'I must have been about ten…and it was just such a wonderful trip. Through the lock – is that what they're called? – and then these amazing woods on this steep hill. And there, sitting on top of the hill is this incredible castle!'

'Well, it's a country house rather than a castle!' Matthew corrects her. 'But yes, it is a very impressive building. And it has the fantastic view of the Thames down Cliveden Reach.'

'Yes! And it's quite a steep climb up from the river, and all the way up your pa and I were chatting, and it was just amazing how much he knew about America. We talked about Boston, where I'm from, and he just knew everything there is to know. I learnt so much about the place from him!'

'Well…that was the man.'

'I do wish I'd known him better. Mom used to talk about him a lot. She's always told me that integrity is the most important quality to have, a lesson she said she'd learnt from Grandpa. She told me more than once about a chat he had with her when she was going through a teenage phase. He told her he didn't mind the scrapes she got into, that was normal for someone her age, but what mattered to him was that if she set herself goals she should never flinch from them and never give up on them, but that, most importantly, she should always pursue them with integrity.'

'He was a wise man. Excellent advice for us all.'

In the evening, Matthew pondered this conversation once more. It had filled with an even greater determination to measure up to his father's expectations. No, not quite that. His father had never burdened him with expectations. Matthew's determination was to measure up to his father's standards.

*

Amongst the papers that Matthew had found on his father's desk when he had been looking for funeral instructions, was a handwritten note. The handwriting suggested a frail hand, but was neat:

<u>David Chapman</u>
Home Office MP
MI5

Evidence? Not much!!
  fragment of letter
  resignations
  unease of C when C of G mentioned

<u>M looked at Death Cert. for C of G???</u>

Notes he'd written after the visit in July, when Matthew had asked his father for advice on how to pursue his enquiry into the goings-on of the summer term of 1991. His father had very bluntly told him not to pursue it any further. And yet…he had made notes. Had he been troubled? Or was this just the note-taking of a tidy mind? He certainly had never mentioned it again.

He imagines his father sitting down stiffly at his desk. When? Immediately after their visit to him the previous summer? Or some time later, an afterthought, a nagging afterthought, burrowing into his mind?

…Michael reaches for a sheet of notepaper and unscrews the marbled Parker Duofold Centennial that Matthew and Rachel had given him for his seventieth birthday. In his neat and precise hand, the letters sloping optimistically forward with just the slightest hint of shakiness, he writes his notes. The heading, 'David Chapman', is emphatically underlined. He writes two salient details about the man and then 'Evidence?' With a wry smile he writes 'None!' And, with a noisy exhalation through his nose, adds another exclamation mark. More salient details. He raises his eyes. A pause. And then he writes 'M looked at Death Cert. for C of G?' Another pause, two more question marks, heavily scored asterisks either side of the note and a final emphatic underlining...

M looked at Death Cert. for C of G??? No, Matthew had not looked at the Death Certificate for the Chairman of the Governors, Sir Peter Gilbert. And, even if he was tempted now, he had promised Kitty Harper that he would not continue looking into the matter.

But that was then. And now, now he has a father, a dearly loved father, a deeply mourned father, calling him to action. And into action he feels compelled to go.

CHAPTER 15

The focus of preparing for the funeral had kept Matthew preoccupied. Since then, each day had seemed to bring a new mood. Sometimes he would feel mildly anaesthetised; his life would have the heaviness and feel of being lived underwater, people appearing distant and refracted. At other times there was a sharpness and immediacy about him that made him feel as though people were on top of him; this made him nervous and impatient, and he would speak brusquely and sometimes angrily.

Rachel absorbed his moods, his anger, speaking gently, soothing him, listening when he wanted to talk. He talked a great deal about Michael, memories mostly.

'He was a wonderful father, always there for me. Always, always. I remember when Mum would bring home a new Dinky toy, I would want to show it to him before beginning to play with it. And however preoccupied he was with his research or lecture preparation, he would give me his whole attention. He would inspect the model closely and would marvel at the accuracy of detail, and that would always make it all the more precious to me... And when I went to university...I think he was a little sceptical, if I'm honest, about my reading English, but he supported me completely and took an interest – he was pretty well read himself.' The memories spin randomly into Matthew's head. 'When I was small and had that little ragamuffin pony, Cari, he would always listen to my adventures, laughing, smiling. And although he had no interest at all in horses, he would sometimes come and watch me in the paddock, saying how much pleasure it gave him to see me ride.' The heaviness in chest and stomach has been increasing as though some thick, strong membrane deep within him is being inflated. Suddenly he wails. 'And now he's gone.' And then sobs.

Rachel comforts him, cradling his head in her arms until the tears subside.

*

The Agnews were driving the cross-country route to Oxford to lunch with their daughter Daisy, a date they had arranged at Michael's funeral. It was a warm sunny day, with a slight haze in the air. The radio was tuned to a local station. The election, of course, now a little under two weeks away. Three party representatives were booting around the football that the NHS traditionally becomes in the run-up to a General Election. Charge; counter-charge. Promise; counter-promise. Pass the ball. Kick the ball. Pass the buck. The presenter keeps trying to bring the discussion back to his central question. How are the increasing burden of an ageing population and the rising cost of modern healthcare going to be funded? All the parties are promising an increase in funding, the Lib Dems offering an extra lip-smackingly huge sum of £8 billion each year. The lack of any prospect whatsoever of a Liberal Democrat government assuming power means that this pledge is as easy to make as promising to bring back Elvis Presley from the moon.

In the sky beyond, above a small copse, a buzzard is being mobbed by three rooks. Sometimes Matthew has seen these raptors weaving or tumbling elegantly to avoid their irksome pursuers, but there is something majestically confident about this buzzard, which holds it course like a large, invulnerable bomber, immune to the attacking fighter planes.

The three party spokesmen drone on. Most of the time they are hacking at each other's ankles, occasionally making contact with the football that is the NHS.

There is a sudden bang and hard jolting as an overtaking van glances the front wing of the car, knocking Matthew off the road. He just misses a reflector post and, before he can correct the steering, is sliding down a bank and tearing through a low and narrow hedgerow. Rachel lets out a stifled squawk. A second later a series of large bomb-like bangs comes from the road, with fainter sounds echoing behind.

The bank is shallow and dips into a field of brashly flowering rapeseed. Matthew brakes and brings the car to a halt about twenty yards from the field's margin. He realises with relief that they are safe and squeezes Rachel's arm.

'Jesus Christ! Are you all right, darling?'

A nod.

'Thank God we're okay. What happened? I don't think it was my fault…I think the van just came too close.'

Rachel is hyperventilating noisily. 'I…I don't know.' She exhales with a violent puff of breath. 'What do we do now?'

Matthew sits still for a while, saying nothing. He then gets out of the car and walks around it, bending to inspect and touch the dented front wing. Leaning into the car, he asks Rachel if she has any water. She nods, reaches in her bag and passes him a half-full bottle. After a couple of swigs, he gets back in the car.

'I think it's fine...' He points. 'There's a gate over there. We can drive along the edge of the field and take it from there.'

Matthew backs the car along the swathe of flattened rapeseed, straightens, and then heads along the overgrown margin of the field, the tall rough weeds screeching underneath and scuffing the side of the car. When they get to the gate, they find it is unlocked, and turn into a trackway heading away from the main road.

His mind is racing. There was the terror of the split seconds as he came off the road when he wondered if he was going to get dreadfully injured. But now another panic is rising in him. Is the bumping off the roadway a random accident, or was there intention behind it? Is this another warning, a ramping up of the threat from Chapman's henchmen?

'Darling, you don't think we were bumped off the road on purpose, do you?' he asks.

Rachel groans. 'I don't know. I don't know...Let's just get home, can't we?'

'Okay.' But he is aware now of a racing pulse and an acute fluttering in his chest. He stops the car and feels his pulse. A hundred and ten per minute, strong and weak and irregular. He's had a similar episode once before and recognises what is happening.

'Darling, I think you are going to have to drive. I think I've got AF.'

'Oh, gosh, shall I take you to hospital?'

'No, let's get home and see if it settles. You better ring Daisy to say we're not going to be able to make it.'

*

As they tried to rejoin the Oxford road he could see a stationary 4 x 4 across his lane of the road. In front of it stood a large man in jeans and sweatshirt, waving something in his hand. Matthew realised, with the panic once more rising in him, that they were being flagged down. He looked behind. Nothing. Could Rachel make a quick U-turn and speed away? No, she was too close to the blocking vehicle now. While she reversed, the man would have time to jump in his car and give chase.

For some moments the air had been filled with the distant sound of sirens. It was clear that these were increasing in number and intensity and that emergency vehicles of some sort were heading in their direction. Matthew felt safer now, believing that the man would not do anything stupid with police cars so close by. Rachel slowed to a stop as the man waved the air as if patting a dog.

Three-day black stubble on his face; in his eyes, beneath thick black eyebrows, a look of concern. 'There's been a terrible accident just up the road. You must turn back.'

'What? An accident?' Matthew paused. And then suddenly understood the confusion. Somebody must have seen him come off the road and assumed the worst. 'No, that was us…We're fine. Just a slightly dented and scratched car. Have a look for yourself.'

A puzzled look. 'No. No, it can't be you, there's a car crushed under a lorry half a mile up the road.'

The fear that this man might be a Chapman henchman subsided, but any relief Matthew might have felt at this realisation was drowned by the increasing discomfort of his racing, irregular pulse.

*

Rachel had rung Daisy to cancel the lunch, saying nothing about the car being driven off the road. She explained that Matthew's heart disturbance required a hospital visit but that there was absolutely nothing to worry about; she would ring again in the evening. She had then dropped Matthew at the hospital, agreeing reluctantly to his insistence that she leave him there and go home rather than waste the rest of the day.

He had been examined quickly in triage and sent up to an assessment ward, where he was to await a consultation with a cardiologist.

On one side of a large reception foyer was a ward and on the other an open-plan waiting room. Matthew had no book with him and was resorting to a favourite activity, people-watching. In hospitals, this could be somewhat dispiriting. The patients were often very old, sometimes with a decrepitude or a vacancy of gaze that suggested an ambivalence towards their continued existence. Hope was a timid and infrequent visitor to places like this. He was glad his father had died in his chair at home, music he loved playing him to his rest.

He decided instead to concentrate on what was happening in the foyer rather than the waiting room. Every now and then a trolley would wheel by, an unconscious or semi-comatose patient being taken to or from a theatre of some sort. But it was the medical staff that interested him today. The nurses, passing by one another, always seemed to have somewhere to go to, but managed a quick gossip as they momentarily paused before moving on. The comings and goings appeared like the slow-motion rehearsal of a choreographed dance.

He thought he noticed in the house doctors, especially the young men, something of a swagger as they strode the corridors and wards with their clipboards, or grouped self-importantly around clusters of computer screens in the foyer. It looked like self-importance; but perhaps it was just the bluster of insecure young people whose limited medical knowledge required the bolster of apparent self-confidence. Perhaps they felt they needed to display a proprietorial superiority, the assumption of a secret and guarded knowledge. Everything in the hospital demanded deference to these people. And patients, lest they should ever forget their place in the scheme of things, were kept in complete ignorance about their progress through the system. Time and place and practitioner were unknown variables in an equation of uncertainty. $T + p + P = n \infty$.

A junior nurse led Matthew to a small room off a long corridor where his bloods were taken. A little later she returned to give him an ECG, hmming and nodding as she read the display. After a long interval, a nurse practitioner took details of his medical history, a history that he had related more times than he could remember, a history that probably existed in mildly variant forms on a large number of NHS computers. Another mind-numbing hiatus and then a trip down long corridors to the radiology department for a chest X-ray. A return to the waiting room, the faces of the unknowing attendees growing longer and longer in anxious anticipation, or twitching in exasperation at the lengthy and unexplained delay. Delay. The insolence of office, and the spurns that patient merit of th' unworthy takes...Had Hamlet been an outpatient? Or simply a patient? Matthew would like to think that, if he had been, he would have been sent to Ward 2b. Or not.

Opposite Matthew was a young, overweight woman, the youngest in the room by some years. Her hair was combed tightly away from her forehead in a cross between a pony tail and a top knot, giving her a harsh and aggressive look. Or perhaps it was simply the pain that stretched her face. She looked very unhappy.

A babble in the foyer drew Matthew's attention. A new group of junior doctors was huddled around a computer screen. One of these was a woman dressed stylishly in Muslim clothes. A green printed hijab framed her young face, hiding her hair and wrapping loosely around her neck. A maroon kameez, patterned with subdued decoration, fell to knee-length above her black shalwar. Quite striking, Matthew thought. Beautiful even. Until he noticed that incongruously she was chewing gum. Unattractive, he corrected himself.

The attention of the group switched from the computer screen to the arrival of an older man, tieless but smartly dressed in a pin-striped suit, clearly a consultant of some sort. A cardiologist? Matthew's heart skipped a joyous beat of anticipation. Or did it? Hadn't his heart been skipping beats and adding unauthorised beats ever since his car had been shunted off the road?

No. A neurologist. He summoned the young woman with the pulled-back hair and led her away. Matthew hoped that the man would be able to help her and that she would leave the hospital with a happy face.

At about five thirty Matthew was himself led away to the small room where he had had his ECG. The cardiologist had the stature of a rugby player, or perhaps oarsman, and retained some bloom of youth. He confirmed atrial fibrillation and asked about the frequency of the attacks. Matthew told him in some detail about the only previous attack, about the precise trigger for that and the current attack, and about the occasional flutters and tremors that sometimes awoke him in the early hours of the morning.

'You know your body well!' the doctor commented.

'I do,' smiled Matthew, trying to maintain the mood of false jollity. 'But then I've had it a long time!'

The doctor laughed. He wrote a prescription and said he would see Matthew again in a month's time.

There was a wait of another half an hour before the prescription was ready. The BBC national news bulletin was just coming to an end when he arrived back in the waiting room. Then the local news. It led with the crash that had happened behind Matthew in the moments after he left the road. He was shocked to learn that there had been one fatality and some serious injuries. It seemed that a driver, distracted by an apparent accident in the road ahead, had moved momentarily across the white line, clipping the back of a car coming in the opposite direction. This had pushed the nose of the other car out into its oncoming lane and right into the path of a large haulage lorry. The car had been crushed, killing the driver; his wife and son were now fighting for their lives. There was live film from the scene – flashing lights, cordoned areas, the haulage lorry still in place, a pick-up truck close by – and then the film cut, without introduction, to some *vox pop* interviews.

'He was a lovely, lovely man. It's such a shame. Well, what can one say?' The words of an oldish man with a local accent.

And then another, older man. 'Shocked and sad, really…er…yeh, terrible, terrible news.' No captions, no indication who these interviewees were or what relation they had to the dead man or even to the area.

A third talking head. 'I'm still shaking. I really can't believe it. It's unbelievable.'

Matthew's shock at the news now turned to distaste. What was the point of these interviews? They were false, vacuous even. Distrustful of their viewers' ability to imagine, empathise, sympathise, the news-mongering broadcasters resorted to these shallow prompts to confected feeling. It angered him.

And suddenly, without warning, Matthew was filled with rage. Molten rage spilling everywhere. Rage at the broadcasters, rage at the man in the white van who had bumped him off the road, rage at the ridiculous amount of time he'd had to spend at the hospital. Rage that the medical profession had not saved his father's life.

As a nurse walked by, he leapt up from his chair and screamed at her. 'Nurse, when am I going to get out of this fucking place? This fucking morgue.'

A look of apprehension shadowed her face for a moment at this sudden explosion, but she stopped, walked towards Matthew and, composing her face into a sweet smile, said, 'I'm sorry, sir, we're moving as quickly as we can. I'm sure we'll have you out of here in no time.'

The rage quickly spent, Matthew now was filling with shame. 'Yes, yes, I'm sure…I'm so sorry for my rudeness. So sorry. Please forgive me.'

'It's all right, sir, I know how frustrating it can be.'

Another nurse, who had heard Matthew's outburst, had called Security, and a burly man with the intimidating appearance of a nightclub bouncer was now approaching.

'It's all right, Neil, everything is sorted here. But thanks for coming.'

Matthew sat down again, still mortified at the scene he had created. It was unseemly. And deeply unfair to the nurse, to the whole system perhaps. And completely illogical. Did he really blame the National Health Service for his father's death? His eighty-five-year-old father, who until recently had led an active, healthy life and who had died peacefully at home sitting in his armchair listening to some profoundly moving music?

Matthew felt ridiculous.

Rachel arrived to pick him up just after the medications arrived from the pharmacy. He was free to go. The fast, irregular pulse was still with him, but he had been reassured by the consultant and had stopped worrying.

'Matty, that accident just after we came off the road. It was on the local news.'

'I know, I saw it too.'

'Do you think we were in any way responsible?'

Matthew felt his irritation rising. 'Us? We were bloody bumped off the road! For goodness' sake!'

'I know, but the man on the news said that the one of the drivers involved had been distracted by something ahead, and I wondered if that was us.'

'Maybe. But it's hardly our fault.' He felt the fluttering rise in intensity.

'I know, but I wonder if we should tell the police.'

The confusions of earlier in the day, paranoia perhaps, returned. Who had been driving the white van? Why had it not stopped?

'I think that is good idea, darling. They may be able to trace the driver and reassure us that this was a genuine accident and not some mad hit man of Chapman's.'

'Darling, Chapman wouldn't arrange something like that. He couldn't afford to. It would be too risky.' There was a note of mild impatience in her voice.

'OK, we'll go to the police. Let's just go home for a bite to eat first.'

*

Another waiting room. Another wait. Finally, Matthew was led to an interview room, where he was questioned by a plain-clothes policeman, of what rank he failed to note.

He explained how he had been driving at moderate speed north-east along the Oxford Road, had not seen the white van approaching in his rear-view mirror, had received a glancing blow from the van and had ended up in the field. He told the officer that he had been unaware of the major accident until trying to make his way back on the main road, and unaware of his possible – and peripheral, he emphasised – involvement in the tragic events further behind.

'That has been very helpful, Mr Agnew. We already had a witness statement that tallies with your account and we have, in fact, recovered some CCTV footage from a camera further along the road of what we believe to be the van in question.'

Matthew felt relieved. He had been right to come to the police station. Rachel had been right to suggest it. He could lay to rest his horrible imaginings about the driver of the van, his ridiculous notion that he was a stooge of Chapman's or of Tommy Cooper's. Or even Tommy Cooper himself.

'Unfortunately, sir, we have discovered that the van was carrying false number plates. So we are no further with our enquiry in that respect.' Horrible imaginings sprang like a spectre (or was it scorpions?) once more into his mind. He hardly heard the officer thank him for coming in to corroborate the statement of a key witness.

He rejoined Rachel, who had been waiting for him in the car outside the police station, knowing that another troubled night of bad dreams and half-waking anxieties lay ahead of him.

*

The next day he decided, felt compelled, to locate Sir Peter Gilbert's death certificate. He found that it would be surprisingly easy. He could order a copy through the government's General Register Office. The cost was £9.25 for standard delivery, or £23.40 for Priority delivery, promising next day delivery. Priority was what Matthew wanted, now he had decided to take the plunge.

He filled in the details and went for the more expensive option. He felt guilty and wretched as he entered his credit card details. He had not discussed any of this with Rachel, and he knew what he was doing was wrong. Not right, at any rate. And, as his hand hovered over the mouse to press the Confirm button, up reared the image of Kitty Harper's face, transforming from its genial warmth to a look of frightened concern, perhaps with a hint of hostility. He had promised her, had he not?

Then, as he clicked Confirm, a thrill of excitement ran through him.

He looked at some sample death certificates online to get a sense of what information to expect: personal details such as name, date of birth and address, of course; date and place of death, naturally, and cause of death, date of registration and signature of registrar. Sections 7 and 8 were for details of Informant, which sounded a little sinister, but was no more than the information about the person notifying the Registrar of the death, who had to certify that the details they had given were 'true to the best of my knowledge and belief'.

The cause of death and underlying causes had to be certified by a doctor. Further research by Matthew revealed that the doctor appearing on the Death Certificate was required to fill in a separate form for the Registrar, a Medical Certificate of Cause of Death. A useful document of guidance for doctors was available online, which Matthew downloaded.

Now it was time to wait for the postman.

CHAPTER 16

Matthew is reading the *Times* over breakfast. He is interested to see what the paper makes of the previous night's BBC *Question Time Election Leaders Special*. (No apostrophe. Acceptable? Possibly. No point discussing it with Rachel. She dislikes his pedantry.) There is a long news report about the programme and a waggish piece by the paper's parliamentary sketch writer. The three main leaders have appeared separately, mounting a platform to face questions from a feisty audience. David Cameron has perhaps done just about enough. *Satisfecit*, as his school report might read. Nick Clegg is unrepentant about going into coalition with the Tories. And Ed Miliband. Ed Miliband has sent social media and tabloid sub-editors into paroxysms of slathering merriment by tripping as he dismounts the studio platform. Clumsy fool! Bacon sandwich!

The twittersphere has been abuzz this last week. David Cameron, supposedly a long-standing Aston Villa fan, tells a meeting in Croydon that he wishes that everyone supported West Ham, like him. Oh dear. Claret and sky-blue, both teams. But not really an easy mistake to make. Hashtag heaven.

The day before the *Question Time Leaders Special*, Russell Brand, a comedian of sorts, has released an interview with Ed Miliband on his YouTube channel. In the video, Brand is expansive, self-important. Exhibitionist logorrhoea, steering a teetering course between the Charybdis of empty prolixity and the Scylla of malapropism. Ed is looking a little sheepish in the face of this onslaught, trying to get an adenoidal word in where he can and trying to remain 'on message'. The interview concludes with Brand offering a patronising endorsement of Miliband. He praises Ed for understanding how the people feel. How Brand thinks they feel, perhaps. Another own goal by Miliband. Where's his judgement? Hashtag heaven.

And Milibabes. One of Ed's advisers has suggested that he surround himself with fit young women, young women affecting to find him very sexy. Unlike Bullingdon boy Cameron, who has run to fat a little, or Nick Clegg who is a busted flush. #Milibabes! Hashtag heaven.

In the world of social media, most political debate is reduced either to spiteful and vindictive comment or a mocking celebration of trivial mistakes. The most important moment for Ed Miliband is not when he half-trips dismounting the dais, it is his unequivocal assertion that he will not form a coalition with the Scottish Nationalists. Ed is a serious man, with serious politics. But with poor advisers. And poor judgement, perhaps.

The *Times* thinks that the BBC programme has not been a game-changer. As you were, then. Stasis. In the previous three days, seven opinion polls have been published. Two have indicated that the Tories and Labour are tied, three suggest a 1 or 2% lead for Labour, two suggest an equally small lead for the Conservatives. All these figures are well within the margin of error. One rogue poll gives the Tories a 5% lead. The general message of the polls, then – ignoring the rogue result – is that no party will have an overall majority in a week's time.

David Chapman will no doubt be thinking deeply about the implications of the result. The assumption is that, if the Tories fail once more to win an outright majority, then David Cameron will have to resign. The inside track to replace him, according to conventional wisdom, is occupied by George Osborne. He has been courting friends and allies assiduously for years, so that, cometh the hour, cometh George. However, there is the loose cannon that is Boris Johnson, the beloved buffoon that the public has taken to its heart. Who knows?

But what if that rogue poll suggesting a 5% lead for the Tories is no rogue at all. Chapman will remember that heady night in 1992, when John Major confounded the pollsters' predictions. What if Cameron does win? No changing of the guard needed. That will happen later in the parliament. Cameron has surprised everyone with his announcement in March that he will not be seeking a third term. What analogy had he used? Breakfast cereal. Something like, two Weetabix are good, but three are probably too many. Or was it Shredded Wheat? Matthew couldn't remember.

A party leadership election in 2018 or 2019 was a different proposition for David Chapman, no doubt. People might have lost faith in George Osborne by then, no longer believing in his ability to turn the economy around, sick to death of austerity politics; the loose cannon that was Boris Johnson might have slid across the deck one time too many, and might finally have toppled to the bottom of the Deep. And then. And then, it would be the younger generation of Tory MPs who would come under starter's orders. And David Chapman would be considered a very decent bet.

*

The doorbell. The postman wanting a signature for the stiff envelope he is holding out.

Matthew leaves it in his study before returning to the kitchen.

'Postman?' Rachel asks.

'Yes. Just something for the archive.'

'What?'

'Nothing very much.'

'What?' More insistently.

There is no avoiding it. 'It's Peter Gilbert's Death Certificate.'

A sharp, incredulous, angry response. 'Whaat?… What on earth are you playing at, Matt? You agreed you weren't going to pursue this business. You told your father that, and you told Kitty Harper that. That you were going to leave the matter alone.'

Matthew imagines he is looking somewhat sheepish. 'I know. I'm sorry. It's just that…and I didn't mention this to you, I don't know why, but amongst Dad's papers on his desk were some notes he obviously took after our conversation about Chapman and Gilbert last summer. And he had underlined and asterisked his last point, which seemed to be asking whether I had checked Gilbert's Death Certificate. And of course I hadn't so I ordered a copy from the General Register Office.'

'You're an arsehole, Matt.'

And that was that. He went to his study. The sense of regret he felt at not having taken Rachel into his confidence was very quickly replaced by a sense of excited anticipation as he tore open the envelope.

The excitement intensified as he quickly read the key details of the certificate. Date and place of death: 13/5/91. And the place was…the school? Good heavens, he died at the school. And as far as Matthew could remember, 13 May was the date of the summer term Governors' Meeting. He would need to check that in his notes in the Archive Room. But he was pretty sure of the date. My God, Gilbert died during a Governors' Meeting! Why was that never reported? Why was it not known that he died in the school? Or on the campus.

And now for an even greater surprise. The Informant would normally be a relative of the deceased. In this case one might expect to see something like 'Lady Mary Gilbert, widow of deceased'. But the name is not Lady Gilbert's. It is Dr Tony Marshall! Under Section 7b, Qualification of Informant is written 'Present at death'.

And the Cause of Death:
1   a Cerebral Embolus
     b Atrial fibrillation
     c Arteriosclerosis
2 Essential Hypertension
        Certified by Donald Livesey, MB

*

Looking out of one of the Archive Room windows, Matthew sees a couple of Labradors lolloping along, chasing each other half-heartedly. Some way behind is their owner, enjoying his morning walk along the river. On Matthew's desk is the Chapman File, now a year in the making. He pulls out the notes he had made at the beginning of the autumn term:

13 May
    Govs' Meeting
    -Gilbert in chair; Marshall present
    -fee incr. / HM report (expulsions – West!)

13 May–3 June
    Chapman absent from school

3 June
    A levels start (C. present on exam days)

20 Sept.
    Govs' Meeting
    -replacement of G as Ch of Govs
    -resignation of Marshall (no reason)

    C's pupil record???

Gilbert in chair, Marshall present. Did Gilbert die in the meeting? Why was that not announced at the time? The Headmaster, for example, telling staff the following day at break.

Matthew looked at the documents he had downloaded about the certification of death. The whole registration process was being reformed by the government, a response to the activities in the 1990s of one Dr Harold Shipman, who had been the certifying doctor for all fifteen of his patients he had been convicted of murdering, and of the further 215 he was suspected of killing.

Marshall would not have filled in the Medical Certificate of Cause of Death for the Registrar, the first step in the registration process. The notes of current guidance were clear.

When a patient dies it is the statutory duty of the doctor who has attended in the last illness to issue the MCCD. There is no clear legal definition of 'attended', but it is generally accepted to mean a doctor who has cared for the patient during the illness that led to death and so is familiar with the patient's medical history, investigations and treatment...

In contrast, a doctor who has not been directly involved in the patient's care at any time during the illness from which they died cannot certify under current legislation...

Which would explain why Marshall, witness to the death of Sir Peter Gilbert, was unable to certify the death. Dr Livesey would have been Sir Peter's GP. Matthew checked online to find the practice that Livesey was working for in 1991. It was about thirty miles from Marshall's surgery, but within the same healthcare area, one of the newly set-up NHS Trusts. It was possible, likely even, that the two doctors knew each other. Livesey had long since retired, it seemed; Matthew was disinclined to pursue any further research in that direction.

Matthew's mind is afloat, untethered. It is 13 May 1991.

...The governing body is about to discuss an item that has not appeared on the agenda and which expressly will not be minuted. The Headmaster, Christopher Harper, has been asked to leave the room; because the item about to be discussed concerns his fate.

Sir Peter Gilbert leads the discussion. He is looking flushed and his voice is hoarse and scratchy. 'This is a sad matter,' he begins, a little hesitantly. 'As you know, Harper and I had a disagreement a little while ago over the question of the Head of School. You all know the details of the matter.' Some of the governors have been staring at Sir Peter. Some have had their heads bowed, avoiding any eye contact with him. Dr Anthony Marshall has both hands flat on the table and is moving his thumbs rhythmically backwards and forwards like windscreen wipers. 'I explained my requirement to him clearly, and he refused point blank to follow orders. I had no alternative but to ask for his resignation. Fortunately, he has agreed to go without a fuss. What I would like to do now is formalise the arrangements of that resig—'

A sudden and aggressive rap with the fingers of his right hand and the angry voice of Tony Marshall cuts across Sir Peter. 'This is nonsense. He did not resign, he was sacked. He was sacked because our Chairman of Governors wanted to do a favour for a friend of his, Mr James Chapman, father of the Head of—'

'—to for..formulate the resumpt…the resig…reshig…shig—' The slurring speech peters out as Sir Peter's head falls with a loud thud onto the table.

Tony Marshall is on his feet in an instant. 'Stroke. Someone call an ambulance.' He checks Sir Peter's pulse and rushes for the door. 'I've got a clot-buster in my emergency kit in the car.'

And he is gone. And soon will be gone from the Board of Governors. He will never forgive himself for provoking the stroke that killed Sir Peter. By the time Tony Marshall returns with his medical bag, Sir Peter's heart has stopped beating. And there is nothing Doctor Tony Marshall can do to bring it back to life…

Now Kitty Harper's words come back to Matthew. Her words had challenged the narrative that he had previously pieced together from his investigation. 'A terrible accident,' Kitty had said. It was a phrase that didn't seem to relate to any of the details of the story. But now. Now, they seem to fit. Sir Peter's death, brought on by Tony's Marshall's aggressive intervention at the Governors' Meeting. Progress! He wishes he could tell his father that he is unravelling the mystery, that he could thank his father for suggesting he look at Sir Peter's death certificate.

Matthew drags his mind back to the present. He puts the death certificate in his folder of notes. He has already decided what he will do next.

*

It is Sunday, 3 May. Election Day is only four days away. Matthew is reading in his study. Suddenly he hears a loud, disbelieving shriek of laughter come from Rachel in the sitting room.

'Matty, do come and see this!'

It is the news. A report from Hastings. A report from a Hastings car park, to be precise. 'This is unbelievable!' Rachel says, still laughing. There on the TV screen are Ed Miliband and Lucy Powell, vice-chair of Labour's election campaign, standing in front of a huge stone monument. But it is not a monument. It is a nine-foot-high chunk of limestone engraved with Labour's six key election promises and Ed Miliband's signature. Moses has come down from the mountain. He has brought Holy Writ with him. This monolith, we are told, will stand in the garden of 10 Downing Street when Labour wins the election on Thursday. Promises written in stone. Promises that will endure. That will not be broken. Unlike the quickly perishable promises of the Tory party, the friable pledges of the Liberal Democratic party.

Once more the twittersphere is abuzz. The great slab, the monstrous monolith, has quickly been labelled the Edstone, memorialising what many now see as Ed

Miliband's 'Neil Kinnock moment'. Obituarists of Labour's 1992 election campaign are in general agreement that it was lost at the Sheffield rally, with Kinnock's pseudo rock star 'We're all right', excitedly repeated by him as he leant into the microphone and pumped the air with a fist. Miliband's obsequies are already being intoned by serious commentators in the press. On social media there is a delighted sense of disbelief. You couldn't make it up… *The Thick of It* is back! #edstone! Hashtag heaven!

'You really do wonder who is advising Miliband,' Rachel says. 'It just seems to be misjudgement after misjudgement after misjudgement.'

'Men's judgements are a parcel of their fortunes. Et cetera.'

'I never really did understand what that meant. Explain it to me, Matty.'

'Well…that your judgement, decision-making, goes hand in hand with your circumstances. That, if you are low in fortune, you will probably make misjudgements. It's Enobarbus commenting on Antony's ridiculous challenge to Caesar to resolve their conflict in single combat. Antony has just lost the battle of Actium, having fled after Cleopatra. Enobarbus thinks it is quite absurd that the victorious Caesar would for a moment consider risking all by brawling in single combat with Antony.'

'But Ed's not down in his fortunes. He's level-pegging with Cameron in the polls.'

'Well, yes, but given five years of austerity government, you might have expected Labour to have been making a better fist of it.'

Matthew is now thinking about that great block of stone. What is an archivist to make of it? It is surely a potential problem for the Labour party archivist. Technically it is a piece of ephemera. But not ephemeral. It could last hundreds of years. In a cupboard? Warehouse? Garden? And how would it be catalogued? What would the keywords be? Vanity? Presumption? Commitment? Promissory note? Misjudgement? And how would the item be described? As an artefact that reflected the desperate gimmicks that had become a part of the modern hustings? As an illustration, this carving of manifesto promises in stone, of how little politicians were to be trusted in the early twenty-first century?

*

Matthew's discussion with his American niece at his father's funeral and the finding of his father's note about David Chapman have been interpreted by Matthew as a call to action. He sees his father's query about Sir Peter Gilbert's death certificate as an encouragement to pursue the investigation to the end. This is what he feels. Or thinks he feels. It might, of course, be a deluded notion of self-justification. Whatever it is, there is a limit to how far Matthew will look inward on this matter of motivation. A lack of real self-knowledge perhaps. He needs to believe that he has his father's blessing, which is how he has chosen to see Michael's handwritten note. And his father's blessing trumps the promise he made to Kitty Harper.

He has decided that he will discuss the matter with Ben Macpherson. Ben had been Chapman's academic tutor, overseeing his progress through the sixth form and preparing him for his Oxbridge interview; their relationship at school had been very close and it was very likely that the two had remained in touch with each other. Very likely, also, that Ben knew exactly, or at least better than approximately, what had happened in Chapman's last summer term.

Matthew emailed Ben saying he would like to meet up with him to chat about old times. A couple of days later Angie, Ben's wife, rang Rachel inviting the two of them to lunch the following Monday.

*

7 May. Election Night. The early evening news was predicting a healthy turnout. The leaders are shown, as ever, casting their votes. It is reported that bookmakers' odds are suggesting that the Tories will win the most number of seats, but that there will be no overall majority. The country is bracing itself for a protracted period of horse-trading following the result. Interest will focus on the Scottish Nationalists, who are predicted to make a killing north of the border.

Rachel has suggested that they eat out in the evening and has booked them into the Tickled Trout restaurant, a classy eatery in town. There are a number of good restaurants in town and most do a very healthy trade. It is an affluent part of the country, generously endowed with the well-heeled elderly, the grey pound. While children and grandchildren might be struggling in austerity Britain, this generation is doing very nicely thank you. It has benefited from free university education, cradle to grave healthcare, and constantly spiralling house prices; it enjoyed the liberation of the sexual revolution in the 1960s; and it has retired on very generous final salary pension schemes and triple-locked state pensions. The Tickled Trout is heaving tonight.

Rachel chooses John Dory, with courgette fritti and new potatoes; Matthew is tempted, but opts for a meat dish.

'I finished the James Knowlson biography this morning.' Since retiring Rachel has taken various literary projects upon herself; her latest is to understand better the life and works of Samuel Beckett.

'Ah. Was it good?'

'Interesting. But I suppose biography has all the pitfalls of reliability that history has.'

'Of course. But then it is a kind of history, isn't it?'

When the dishes arrive, Rachel looks delighted with her choice, the large false eye of the fish – St Peter's Thumbprint, it is sometimes called – staring up at her.

'Wow!'

'Here's looking at you, kid!' says Matthew, drawing a chuckle from Rachel.

After the main course, they returned to the discussion of Samuel Beckett. 'I have to say, I'm not mad on the novels,' Matthew confessed. 'But *Waiting for Godot* is very powerful. I always used to encourage pupils to read it or, better still, see it.'

'He is difficult,' said Rachel, who had confessed to Matthew in the past that she wished she had read for an English degree. 'He is difficult, but not as difficult as some of the stuff written about him. I was reading an essay last week on the odontology of Beckett.'

'Rach!' Matthew started giggling.

She looked confused. 'What?'

It was a while before Matthew could say anything. 'I bet that was difficult to get your teeth into.' He guffawed. 'Beckett bites yer bum!'

'I don't understand.'

'Odontolgy is the study of teeth!' He laughed again. 'I think you mean ontology – the study of being!'

'Oh, gosh! Yes!' She clapped a hand to her mouth. 'Silly old me!' Matthew covered her other hand with his and squeezed it affectionately.

Someone was talking about the election. 'I think UKIP

are going to do very well. With those figures in the opinion polls, they should get quite a lot of seats.'

'You can't tell.' The voice of an unseen woman sitting behind Matthew. 'The Liberals often win very few seats compared to their share of the national vote.'

'Yeah, well, I think Nigel has caught the mood of the country. I hope he's going to stuff it up Cameron's jacksie.'

Matthew thought of Leo Beamish's comment that UKIP was like a large turd you couldn't get rid of. In which case, a jacksie – whoever's, but preferably Farage's own – would be an entirely appropriate place for UKIP to be stuffed.

Rachel and Matthew returned once more to the question of Beckett's ontology. 'Of course consciousness is a bugger if you lose a faith that was once strong,' said Matthew. 'The voided space that once contained faith and purpose becomes filled with a sense of the pointlessness of life. Beckett, like Larkin after him and like Hardy before him, was someone who felt his loss of religious faith grievously.'

'Yes. And *Godot*, some people would argue, is an exploration of that painful, faithless universe. Estragon and Vladimir filling their waking time with daydreams, and gossip, and silly games that pass the time painlessly.'

Painlessly. Matthew's atheism pained him. He envied Rachel's residual brand of agnosticism. What he envied more was the equanimity with which she regarded her life and her death. She had explained to him very eloquently in the past that everything in existence on this planet came from the same matter, including the chemistry of consciousness. That there was an ultimate kinship in all created matter.

He had tried to learn from her and had found comfort in looking at nature, where he could see, if not the kinship, the commonality of purpose of living things. The dog that courts the affections of its owner so that it can be fed and walked. The tree, stretching its root systems in search of the best sources of water and minerals. The rambling rose, scrambling for another year, its shark-finned thorns anchoring its climb. The rambling rose pines not for its past, nor frets for its future. Thought-free it seeks the sun, bends towards it. The rambling rose, struggling to be, thought-free. Simple being. Enviable!

*

They walked home arm in arm, enjoying the spring evening, the sense of expansiveness. Foxy was, of course, thrilled to see them and, to celebrate, did a victory lap around the sitting room. Matthew switched on the *News at Ten*. The polls had closed. Time for the Exit poll. A bombshell. It appears that Cameron will win a significant majority of seats and that, with the support of the Democratic Unionist Party, will be able to form a government. The pundits, the pollsters all wrong again. Startlingly wrong.

In the past Matthew and Rachel have stayed up until the early hours watching the results roll in, the declarations, the shocks; and the swinging Swingometers and their modern computerised equivalents, boys' toys for the excited, wildly gesticulating men operating them. Matthew pours a couple of whiskies. What will a Tory win mean? More austerity, cuts as promised; a simple In or Out referendum on the European Union, which will turn out to be a non-event. Apart, perhaps, from seeing the batrachian Nigel Farage return to his pond for good. Promotion for Chapman? Probably.

The early results seem to confirm the predictions of the Exit poll. There is much excitement in the main studio, much excitement amongst the roving reporters. But the Agnews have seen it all before and are not desperately keen to hear the commentaries of the Spirits-of-Elections-Past, the Peter Mandelsons, the Paddy Ashdowns, opine predictably.

At half past one they decide to go to bed.

CHAPTER 17

The Agnews are listening to *Today* on the radio as they have their breakfast. It seems that the Exit poll has given the right steer, but has underestimated the scale of Cameron's victory. He does not need to horse-trade with anyone, and will lead the first Conservative government for eighteen years. Now the cabinet reshuffle will start. And, with the Liberal Democrats routed and the Coalition consigned to history, there are plenty of opportunities for up-and-coming young Tories hoping for preferment. The media are camped outside Number 10 and will remain for some days, noting the faces of former ministers as they enter the building to find out what fate awaits them; and noting these same faces on exit, where they will appear smilingly triumphant or sadly down-hearted; or be smiling weakly in an attempt to disguise their disappointment.

It is the new cabinet faces that Matthew is interested in, but they probably won't appear for a day or two. Will David Chapman be amongst them? Waving cheerfully to the cameras as he enters Number 10 and beaming broadly as he exits? The packs and sects of great ones that ebb and flow by the moon...So, thinks Matthew, we'll live, and pray, and sing, and tell old tales, and laugh at gilded butterflies, and hear poor rogues talk of court news, and we'll talk with them too – who loses and who wins, who's in, who's out.

One who is out, who loses, is Ed Balls, an undoubted star in Labour's firmament; a man who would have been a contender for the leadership of the party, about to be tipped into turmoil once more when Ed Miliband's inevitable resignation is announced, probably later in the day.

On *Today* there is tut-tutting from the political journos. They hadn't seen this coming. No, not their fault, of course. The fault of the pollsters, who have let them down again. The Lib Dems have been routed, that was foreseen; the Scottish Nationalists were rampant, that too was foreseen. Only one seat for UKIP? A bit of a surprise. A Tory administration? A lot of a surprise. Ah, but we see now where we were wrong. We should have foreseen UKIP's leaching of the working-class vote in Labour's heartlands.

*

It is a showery day, but the drive to the Macphersons, who live about ten miles south of the town, is without incident. Matthew has tended to keep a closer eye on his rear-view mirror since being shunted off the road. Every white van, every van in fact, occasions a momentary pause of anticipation.

Matthew explains to Rachel that at some stage of their visit he is going to discuss Chapman with Ben. She turns her head sharply away, emitting a slight hiss, saying nothing. Response enough.

'I've got a pretty good idea of what happened. I just want to confirm this with Ben. And then I can put the whole thing to bed.'

Rachel is rarely sullen, but her silence speaks like thunder.

'Sir Peter Gilbert died in the Governors' Meeting. Both Christopher Harper and Tony Marshall resigned that term. The Chapmans gave the school a large donation. Now Kitty Harper said—'

And now a lightning flash of anger from Rachel. 'Kitty Harper! You absolutely promised the poor woman that you would stop poking around. But here we are, going to the Macphersons to discuss the matter. And no doubt you will spill out your absurd fantasies to them, making yourself look absolutely ridiculous.'

'They're not fantasies. They are hypotheses. Likelihoods even.'

'Likelihoods, my foot! Okay, tell me what happened… what you *think* happened. No, don't. I don't want to hear. I don't want to dignify this silly nonsense.'

'I think Harper asked Chapman to step down as Head of School because he had been violent with a junior boy. I think the parents rang Sir Peter.' Rachel is singing "La la la la" and has covered her ears to block out the sound. 'He told Harper to reverse his decision. Harper refused. Sir Peter sacked him. When Tony Marshall confronted Sir Peter aggressively at the next Governors' Meeting, Sir Peter had a stroke and died. Marshall was so ashamed he resigned.'

Rachel is still singing. Matthew puts his hand on hers, but she snatches it away.

'God, I hate your stubbornness,' she says. 'And your confabulations!'

'Confabulations? Now there's a word!' He laughs gently, dispelling some of the tension.

'But I love you anyway!'

*

It's a pretty little house, cottagey red brick with dormer windows; at the back a flourishing garden that has a small stream running through it. The Macphersons have lived here since Ben's retirement and both have the healthy glow of leisured country dwellers. Ben looks remarkably youthful still. Few ravages of age or body abuse, and his hair is still fair, though it is thinning these days. Greetings are exchanged. Angie explains that she would have liked them to eat outside but the weather has put paid to that, so they have their pre-lunch drinks in the sitting room. She retires to the kitchen to make the final preparations for the meal. Matthew receives the requested weak gin and tonic from Ben and says, 'Well, that was a bit of a turn-up for the books.'

Ben nods. 'Yes and no. The party's own canvassers and pollsters were always very confident. I think in Tory HQ there will be much less surprise that in the country.' Ben is a member of his local Conservative Association. He was no doubt getting the vote out the previous week.

'I suppose,' says Matthew, 'that there is a good chance of David Chapman getting promotion.' Ben gives him a pointed look. Not sharp; he is a very gentle soul. But distinct. Quizzical but without a sense of real puzzlement. A look, perhaps, of 'So you want to talk about Chapman now?' Not that Matthew has told him what he wants to see him about.

'He might well,' says Ben, his face crinkling into a sweet smile. 'I think he has done enough at the Home Office to be given some kind of cabinet responsibility.' Matthew nods. 'By the way, Matt, I was very, very sorry to hear about your father's death. I read a number of his books. Always painstakingly researched and very lucidly written. Real scholarship.'

Before they are led to the dining room, Matthew goes to wax his skis. A foolish circumlocution he has used for many years, despite its lack of currency in any shared repository of lavatorial euphemism. As he is washing his hands he notices, on the wall opposite the toilet bowl, an old school photograph. 1990. Chapman will have been in the lower sixth. At the centre of the image, Christopher Harper, a confident, proprietorial smile upon his face. Further down the row, on different sides, Ben and Matthew. Looking so young! So many familiar faces. And familiar names are popping into his head, but not necessarily attaching themselves to the correct faces. And there, there is David Chapman. That full, open, honest gaze. A man of destiny. And look! There is George West. Not a dreadlock in sight. But a studied untidiness; of hair and shirt and tie!

Over a pleasant lunch they talk some more about Michael Agnew. His long years of widowerhood, his life by the River Thames, his importance as a source of advice for Matthew and his siblings. And they talk about the school. The proliferation of paperless paperwork and policy-making that characterises the regime of the Head, who arrived after Ben's retirement. News is exchanged about mutual friends. They do not have any mutual enemies to discuss; Ben's mildness of manner, his generosity of attitude, has enabled him to go through life without making any real enemies. And there is no further mention of David Chapman.

Matthew's worry about how he is going to broach the subject of his researches, his queries about Chapman, is unnecessary. When the meal is finished, Angie asks Rachel to come to the sitting room for coffee; the men, she says, are going to retire to the snug for some Man's Talk. Whatever that is.

The snug is a small room with a couple of old armchairs, books in little piles everywhere and, sitting on a shelf crammed with more books, beside a truly ancient radio, a bust of Edmund Burke.

The men sit down. 'I know why you want to see me, Matt.' Ben's head is slightly cocked. (An uncanny resemblance to the way Chapman cocked his head when sitting on the dais at Speech Day, thinks Matthew.) He is leaning forward a little. His eyes, full of earnest but gentle intensity, look directly into Matt's. 'I know why you want to see me, and it is high time we talked this thing through.'

Matthew is surprised. And relieved. And then puzzled. How can Ben possibly know what he has come to see him about? Has Rachel told him, or Angie? Has Chapman said something?

'Ah, yes. About my researches into David Chapman and what happened in that final term of his.'

'Precisely.' The same intensity of gaze is in Ben's eyes, but his manner and his tone of voice are urbane. 'Matt, I'm going to tell you exactly what happened. Exactly what happened. I'm going to tell you these things not because I want to, but simply to stop you blundering around.' Matthew is nodding, willing Ben on. 'I am pretty sure that you have put two and two together and made five.' Matthew thinks that he has not come up with any final solution; he is still doing the maths, so to speak. But he says nothing and nods again. 'So I am going to tell you what happened on a particular day in 1991 and I am going to hope that you will then let it all go. Before you get into… deep water.' Deep water. Ominous. Does Ben know about Tommy Cooper?

A final nod from Matthew.

*

The rain clouds had passed by the afternoon, and the drive home was in a brilliant sunshine which was bringing out a rich vibrancy in the spring vegetation. The confidence that Ben had shared with Matthew in the snug was not a topic of conversation. Rachel did not ask. And Matthew was not foolish enough to bring up the topic which had marred the outward journey.

During the day, Cameron's cabinet reshuffle had been progressing. More comings and goings to Number 10. Who's in who's out. David Chapman was in. Promoted to a cabinet position, succeeding a Liberal Democrat who lost his seat in the election. His progress in politics continued apace.

*

As he lay in bed that night, with a mind too active to sink into sleep, Matthew thought again and again about what Ben had told him. Replayed the story over and over, fleshing out the bare bones of Ben's narrative. Flickering images playing in his mind. Images of a terrible accident and foolish, foolish decisions.

...13 May 1991.

The governors arrive one by one in warm spring sunshine. They gather in their customary meeting room on the first floor of the main building. It is a high-ceilinged oval room painted in one of the light blues of traditional Regency decoration. In the middle of the room stands a long oval table, with thick, fluted legs and covered in a blue baize cloth; around it are set fourteen leather-seated, Chippendale style chairs, with a carver seat at the top. Set neatly on the table, evenly spaced, lie fourteen jotter pads, each with a pencil laid across at a forty-five-degree angle; to the top right of each pad, a glass on a leather coaster and, positioned at one and two o'clock to each coaster, two bottles of spring water, one carbonated, one still.

The governors are mostly men, high achievers of some kind or another, and the sounds in the room as they assemble are old-mannish; the gravelly grunts and chuckles that accompany men's small talk.

The Chairman, Sir Peter Gilbert, calls for everyone to take their seats. The first item on the agenda is the Headmaster's Report. Christopher Harper sits at the far end from the Chairman. He reports an unusually high number of expulsions. Concerned looks from the governors. Fee income bound to be hit. Reputational damage. On brighter matters, the two examination years have been shaping up well, and it is reasonable to expect good results in the summer. Some excellent staff appointments have been made over the year. It is expected that all new staff who joined in September will pass their probationary period. And some very good news is that a young, very bright and very sparky Head of Modern Languages has been appointed. On practical matters: refurbishment of the new Prefects' Room, in the main building, will be completed by the end of term. It is all but done now. Finally, the Headmaster would like to thank the governors for their continued and excellent support. And he would like it to be put on record what a truly exceptional Head of School he has had in David Chapman. Harper is delighted to say that he will be joining them for lunch. Some mannish gurgles of 'Jolly good show', or some such.

Sir Peter is beaming at all this good news, his Chaplinesque moustache positively quivering in appreciation; the anxiety over the expulsions is clearly banished. Much of the morning is devoted to receiving dull reports from the likes of the Bursar and the various Chairs of sub-committees. Some of the governors grin and bear it; they like the kudos of being governors and know that the price of such kudos is to sit through mainly boring meetings three times a year. Others enjoy the meetings. They are great supporters of the school and like to feel that they are making a contribution to its success. Dr Tony Marshall is such a governor. He has put two children through the school, has been the San doctor for a spell, has been a governor for many years. When he comes to retire, his absolute dedication, his willingness to do virtually anything for the school's welfare, will be duly noted.

Finally it is time for lunch, which has been laid out in an adjacent room. The Headmaster has insisted that David Chapman, who has arrived with his customary poise to meet the governors, sit next to the Chairman. During the course of the meal Chapman is convinced that, on several occasions, Sir Peter Gilbert has brushed his thigh against his. But poise is poise. One registers nothing on the face, allows no change to one's tone of voice; and moves one's leg away a little, hoping it is beyond range.

Sir Peter is very chatty, eating with relish and drinking freely. He talks about his family, about his military career, about his own school days. And he asks David Chapman about his A levels, now nearly upon him, about his sporting achievements, which are negligible, and about being Head of School. What are the other prefects like? Good eggs? And what about the new Prefects' Room? Sounds splendid. Sir Peter now leans closer to David, speaks in a strangely quiet voice, his fishy breath smelling of the smoked salmon that has been served as a starter. He suggests that perhaps Chapman might take him to have a peek at the new room after lunch and before the afternoon session of the meeting gets underway. Of course, it would be a pleasure, indicates our poised and polite Head of School.

And so the two of them head off after a quickly taken coffee. Chapman has gone via the Porters' Lodge to borrow the key for the room, and has taken Sir Peter back into the main building. The new Prefects' Room lies off a corridor that runs parallel with the Grand Hall. As the door is opened a strong smell of paint greets them. The two men – the old man and the youth – step into the room, the old man closing the door behind them.

There is not a great deal to see. The woodwork has been glossed, the walls lined with paper and painted a slightly darker shade of blue than the walls in the room upstairs where the governors are meeting. Two sofas are pushed up beside one other against a wall, still covered in the thick polythene wrapping paper in which they were delivered. A large oak sideboard stands against another wall. For the moment that is it.

'Not much to see, I'm afraid, sir. But I am sure it will be very attractive once it is fully finished. Once it has all the furniture, and pictures on the walls.'

Sir Peter is sitting on one of the sofas. The polythene wrapping has made a quiet crackling sound as he has sat down and is now squeaking as he moves further back in it. 'This is very comfortable.' He pats a space beside him. 'Come and try it out. See what I mean.' He pats it again.

David is beginning to feel uncomfortable. A discomfort heightened by his desire not to give offence. Reluctantly he sits next to Sir Peter.

'This is nice. Very comfy.' Sir Peter's hand hovers over his own thigh and not far from the boy's. It is a hand that appears to be receiving contradictory orders from the brain of General Sir Peter Gilbert; never a comfortable state of mind in a military man. Uncertainty over – for the time being – the brain issues a command. Sir Peter stands up, and so does David, relieved. A couple of steps are taken towards the door.

And then, a lunge. An unexpected hand reaches towards the upper inner thigh of David Chapman, who thrusts Sir Peter away with both hands. A step back, a trip on an upturned fold in the new carpet, a fall backwards, a dreadful thud as his head hits the hard sideboard's edge. And Sir Peter is upon the floor. There is no sound apart from the thud, no vocalisation, no gurgle, nothing. Sir Peter lies still. Still, that is, apart from a slight quiver in the upper body and the hand of one arm; like the start one sometimes wakes up with when drifting off to sleep after a tiring day. But Sir Peter does not look asleep; his eyes are half open. And if he is asleep there is no sign of him waking up. The lunge. The push. The fall. The stillness.

Chapman is in deep shock, the kind of paralysing shock he has never before experienced. He kneels by Sir Peter, talks to him, inviting a response; coaxes him, pleads with him. Nothing. He feels for a pulse. He can't tell if there is one or not. He has lost his poise, that fabulous poise, that wonderful self-possession. His poise and his self-possession have deserted him. He is breathing heavily, half sobbing. He runs to the Headmaster's office where the Head's secretary, gazing at a computer screen, is sipping a cup of coffee.

As the door opens without a knock she looks up to see an abject, distraught Head of School. 'Gracious, David, what's happened?'

'You must get the Headmaster immediately...I have to talk to him.'

Her normal instinct would be to ask why, what is the problem, but the look of panic on the boy's face is sufficient for her to spring from her seat and run off to fetch Mr Harper, who is quickly brought back, the look of apprehension on his face deepening as he sees the state of David Chapman.

'Headmaster, something terrible has happened. You need to come to the new Prefects' Room.'

When they arrive, the door is open; in his haste

Chapman has forgotten to close it. The Headmaster sees Gilbert's outstretched legs. He rushes in. 'Did he collapse, David?' Harper is on his knees now, feeling for a pulse. And then he is on his mobile phone talking to his secretary, asking her to extricate Tony Marshall from the Governors' Meeting, which is about to resume, and bring him to the new Prefects' Room.

Harper repeats. 'Did he collapse, David? Tell me what happened.'

'Oh, sir—' The tears are beginning to well up in Chapman. 'Sir, he grabbed at me. Tried to touch me. And I pushed him.' He starts sobbing. 'And he tripped on the carpet and...and banged his head.'

Harper is on the phone again. This time to the Sanatorium. He asks for the senior San sister, or a senior nursing assistant if she is unavailable. They are to wait in the Grand Hall where they will find David Chapman, the Head of School, who is to be taken to the San and kept in the isolation room until further notice. Chapman has listened to the call and says he will go and wait in the hall to be picked up.

By the time Harper has finished on the phone, Dr Marshall has arrived. He bends over the body, feels for a neck pulse and shakes his head, mouthing the word 'Gone'. There is a small stain of blood where Gilbert's head is resting on the carpet. 'He must have banged his head when he fell,' says the doctor.

Harper explains what Chapman has just told him. Closer inspection of the body by Marshall confirms that the wound to the head can only have been made by its coming into contact with a hard object with considerable force.

The lunge. The push. The fall. The stillness. And now. Now. This is the moment at which everything could have taken such a different course if different decisions had been made. A series of different decisions. But judgements are a parcel of one's fortunes. Perhaps.

'Right,' says Marshall. 'In that case we'll have to alert the Coroner.' But Marshall's mind is whirring. Coroner. Inquest. Dodgy Chairman of Governors, touching up pupils. Damage to reputations. Sir Peter's. The school's. The trauma of an inquest for David Chapman...'Unless, Christopher—'

And in the next moments, Marshall outlines to Christopher Harper a scenario that will spare the school any damage to its reputation. Will preserve the eminent reputation of General Sir Peter Gilbert. And will protect a promising boy's future from the attentions of an Inquest.

'Here's what I propose, Christopher. That we have this certified as a natural death so that no inquest is necessary. That we present it to the school community as an untimely event that has deprived us of a very loyal servant of the school. That your Head of School is briefed to make no mention of his part in the business. We need to protect the school that you and I love.'

Christopher Harper is a principled man. He was, after all, a Minor Counties cricketer, and is imbued with a sense of fair play. He voices his misgivings to Tony Marshall, suggesting that the whole business is dreadful, it's unfortunate and, yes, people will be hurt, the school may be damaged. But that is the hand they have been dealt, and they must play it the best they can.

'Christopher, I admire your principles...I always have. But I think we need to be expedient here. I think in this instance expediency is more important than principle. People matter more than principles. The school matters.'

Harper is persuaded. Unhappily. And the moment for a change of mind passes very quickly.

228

'We need to keep this just between ourselves. Ourselves and Chapman, of course.'

Harper nods slowly. Miserably. The two men work out a plan of immediate action.

The Headmaster's secretary will ring the Chapman parents and ask them to collect their son from school. She will reassure them that there is no problem. David is feeling a little peaky, and it is best that he has some time at home, with his A levels nearly upon him.

Christopher Harper returns to the Governors' Meeting to give the sad news of Sir Peter's death. There are gasps of shock in the room. Harper says that the meeting is abandoned and that people can leave in their own time. Best not to mention it to anyone until Sir Peter's widow is informed.

Tony Marshall is busy fixing the medical side of things. He calls Sir Peter's surgery, and fortunately is able to get straight through to his GP, Dr Donald Livesey. He tells him that his patient has just died of a stroke. He establishes that Sir Peter had long-standing hypertension, was suffering from arteriosclerosis and had suffered a transient ischemic attack six months earlier. He suggests to Dr Livesey that notifying the Coroner is unnecessary and that the body can be taken straight to the mortuary for certification. The two men are agreed.

When he has finished with the governors, Harper goes to the San. Chapman is resting on a bed, and attempts to stand when the Head enters.

'No, that's fine, David. You stay there.' He sits in an armchair. His voice is gentle and calming. He sympathises with David for the ordeal he has been through, witnessing a death in such a distressing way.

'But, sir, I killed him.'

'No, no, I don't think so. The man was ill. He'd already

had a minor stroke. Who's to say it was the fall that killed him?' David Chapman is to say. He knows. Knows because the sound of Sir Peter's head thudding into the hard edge of the oak sideboard is a sound that will never leave him.

'Will there be an inquest?'

'No, Dr Marshall has spoken to Sir Peter's GP. There's no need for an inquest.'

A look of relief. Not easy to read, because the face of the boy is stretched tight with strain.

Harper tells Chapman that his parents are coming to pick him up shortly. He should gather whatever he needs ready for their arrival and spend the next fortnight at home, out of the school environment.

More relief. More noticeable this time.

*

On the afternoon of 13 May 1991, cars have been coming and going through the school's entrance arch. Not long after lunch a cavalcade of expensive cars exits as the governors take their leave. An hour later, a hearse drives up to the main building to collect the body of General Sir Peter Gilbert and take it away. Much later the Bentley of Mr and Mrs Chapman arrives to collect their son and take him to the isolation and comfort of home.

At the end of the day, Christopher Harper, Headmaster, can be seen walking back to his house, a sad figure, unhappy with his part in the day's events, which he will relate to his sympathetic wife, Kitty, who will try to ease his troubled mind.

*

That, at any rate, is how the narrative played out in Matthew's mind. Shaped here, shaped there, no doubt. Embellished, perhaps, with the odd detail to give the narrative the depth that Ben's story seemed to lack. But it is an account of sorts, an account that coalesces around the bare facts as told to Matthew earlier in the day by Ben Macpherson, historian.

CHAPTER 18

A phone call. Matthew barely awake. Robbery. It is the Headmaster's secretary. A cleaner on her early-morning round has discovered that the Archive Room has been broken into overnight. Matthew leaves his half-eaten breakfast and heads into school. There is a slight chill in the air that will soon be warmed away in the May sunshine. He walks briskly past the great Spanish Chestnut, with hardly a glance. No time to check the progress of this magnificent survivor as it puts forth its delicate buds for what might be its five hundredth spring.

Seventy-one steps up the spiral staircase, taken faster than usual. Matthew is blowing a little when he gets to his room. A carpenter from the school's estates department is there, examining the door. 'A neat job. Professional looking.' No woodwork has been damaged; the lock has been punched through with some kind of tool.

A steady, even tread is ascending the staircase. The Headmaster appears. 'Matthew. Have you checked?'

'I've just arrived.'

There is a harrumph of irritation from Mr Dogget. 'Well, please check now. I am assuming that they have taken the William Smith map.'

Oh gosh, I hadn't thought of that, Matthew thinks. He

retrieves the master key from his pocket and puts it in the lock of the cabinet which contains the treasured map, with its wonderful watercolours. The lock feels secure. Cabinet open. Shelf Three. 'It's there, Headmaster!'

'Thank God!' Matthew wonders if the Headmaster really is thankful. He is something of a philistine and is most unlikely to appreciate the exquisite nature of the artefact. He believes, probably, that the insurance money would be a great deal more useful than the actual possession of the precious map. Doubtless there are policies and plans aplenty that are incubating in his mind, and which a buckshee hundred thousand pounds would bring nicely to a successful hatching.

'I'll do a full check and get back to you immediately, Headmaster,' says Matthew.

'Fine. I'll be in my study. I am assuming that the burglar was after something specific. The estates department have looked at the CCTV footage from last night. There was one person. Dressed in black tracksuit and black balaclava. This room appears to be the only room broken into.'

Oh gosh, Matthew thinks again. A little bit of magic by Tommy Cooper? Is now the time to come clean about his year-long obsession with David Chapman? To explain to the Headmaster that it was the Chapman File that the burglar sought? No, he doesn't know for sure if that is the case. 'Fine. As I say, I'll check and get back to you a.s.a.p.'

Dogget leaves. And so, too, the carpenter, saying he will fit a new lock later in the morning.

Alone, Matthew is now able to make a quick and panicky search of the room. Has Tommy Cooper really made a second visitation to the school? And why? It was only yesterday that Chapman had been appointed to the Cabinet. Only yesterday that Matthew had discussed the matter with Ben Macpherson. Ah. A significant conjunction of events, perhaps.

The lockable drawer of his desk is fractionally open, he notices. Matthew grabs at it. Unlocked. Or more precisely, the lock broken or picked. And the Chapman File gone. But still he can't work out why. The issue was dead in his mind as soon as Ben had delivered his account of Sir Peter's death. Clearly David Chapman had done nothing wrong. There was no scandal attached to him, only a deeply unfortunate incident for which he could not really be held to blame.

Matthew wanted to think more deeply about it all. And he wanted to get away from the school. He did a quick check of the rest of the cabinets, knowing he would find nothing untoward, and then left the room, taking with him the William Smith map; he would ask the Headmaster's secretary to store it in the strong room for the time being.

He knocked on Dogget's door, was invited in. 'It seems nothing has been taken, Headmaster. Very strange. There is not much up there that has any real value. The map, of course. Perhaps the burglar was disturbed.'

'You are absolutely sure that nothing has been taken?'

'Yes…Well, the only piece of furniture that has been tampered with is the lockable drawer in my desk, but there was nothing in that of any value.' Arrrgh. Why mention it? I am going to have to explain about the Chapman File now, thinks Matthew. And then a moment of inspiration. 'Perhaps the burglar thought I kept the keys to the cabinets in that drawer…Or…or a catalogue to the collection which would indicate which cabinet the map was in.'

Implausible. But, 'Yes. Okay. Well, we'll keep the map down here for the time being. And we need to review the security of your room. Do you have a written Security Protocol for the Archive?'

'A what?' Matthew wants to giggle; a welcome moment of levity in a difficult situation.

'A Security Protocol. A written statement. Risk assessment. Policy principles and practicalities.'

'Erm...no.'

'Well, you should. I asked all departments to produce such protocols last year. Let me have something by the end the week.'

'Yes. Indeed.' Matthew didn't really consider himself to be a department as such. Much too peripheral for that. And he certainly didn't believe that every single practice in the school needed to be codified. Or...protocolised! 'I'll be on to it, Toby, as soon as possible.' The less formal 'Toby' a prefix to a request. 'Toby, given that Estates need to do some work on the door and the drawer, do you mind if I go home for the day?'

A half grimace. 'All right. Fine...But be thinking about the Security Protocol.'

*

Matthew was heading east on the bustling M4 motorway, making a visit he had been thinking about since Michael's death. He was concentrating carefully on his driving; Rachel had told him that not only had he become moody and volatile since his father had died, he also seemed distracted and prone to carelessness.

After getting the Headmaster's permission to miss the rest of the day, he had gone home, quickly downloaded a couple of maps from the Internet, made himself a sandwich and a thermos of coffee to take with him, and had set off. For Hyghcliff. Not for Hyghcliff, in fact, because Hyghcliff no longer existed. It had been demolished in the 1980s shortly after Michael Agnew had sold it, and had been heavily developed. Hyghcliff, the site of his childhood home, the theatre of his childhood games, the crucible of his childhood dreams. Matthew had never returned because he had always thought it might be too painful. But now he was ready to revisit, and to find whatever ghosts inhabited that vanished place, hoping that amongst them would be the spirit of his father. Not only was he ready, he was eager, in a strange way; his eagerness a somewhat unsettling amalgam of enthusiastic anticipation and excited dread. Rachel was not with him. She would have been a stout companion, helping him with the difficult moments of nostalgia and grief, but she was away for the day, assisting with a training session at a local solicitors' practice, as she occasionally did. And in some ways, this was a quest better conducted alone.

The theft of the Chapman File was puzzling. It seemed to make no sense. If Chapman had been aware that Matthew was meeting Ben, then Ben would have reported back to him after yesterday's meeting, confirming the satisfactory outcome. Perhaps Kitty Harper had got in touch with Chapman and told him that Matthew was asking awkward questions. Unlikely. And then again…the burglary had taken place only a few hours after Chapman had been elevated to his first cabinet post. Perhaps the motivation for retrieving the file was simply to leave nothing to chance, to tie up loose ends, to make assurance doubly sure.

But why? And then Matthew remembered something Ben had said the previous day. That Christopher Harper could not forgive himself for colluding with Tony Marshall. Harper had told the acting Chair of the Governors the following week that he would resign at the end of the Christmas term. And he had spoken to Tony Marshall, indicating that he expected him to resign also and that if he did not, then he would have to consider whether or not to report his unethical behaviour as a doctor.

And that presumably was the key to Chapman's nervousness. Not that he was guilty of any crime. But that if the press ever got hold of the story, they would have a field day with the revelation that a public school governor, a doctor no less, had failed to notify the coroner of a death that required reporting. That the cause of death had been falsified. Chapman would be part of the story by association. His innocence would count for little in an exposé that would inevitably be slanted with an emphasis on how there is one rule for the rich and privileged and another for the rest of us. Plate sin with gold, and the strong lance of justice hurtless breaks.

Matthew came off the motorway at the Chieveley junction. There were new roads unbuilt thirty years earlier, but soon he was driving east from Newbury through countryside that had a ghostly familiarity.

He recalled the sadness in Ben's eyes when he had told him Chapman's story: the trauma that the boy had suffered in that instinctive push away of Sir Peter Gilbert; the parents' determination that this should not affect his A levels, or his Oxford ambitions or the glittering career that they hoped lay ahead of him as a politician; the gratitude the parents felt towards the school for the way it had handled the incident; the life-changing devastation of Harper in reflecting upon his brief moment of misjudgement; the deep pain that Tony Marshall felt at having to resign his association with a school he had loved with a passion. A moment in time containing an indiscretion by an elderly man; an instinctive response by a young man: with what consequences! Ben was not judgemental in his attitude, either of any of the participants in the unhappy tale, nor of Matthew, whose year-long quest – 'blundering' was the word Ben had used – had caused such unsettlement. Just deeply sad.

The familiar crossroads ahead. On the right there used to be a butcher's shop. Gone. Beyond the newsagents, Byrne's. Still there! Byrne and Sons! But the road that Matthew had walked down a thousand times, cycled down safely as a young child in the 1950s with few cars to worry about, was changed. All the large Victorian houses had been demolished, the land developed. Cul-de-sacs with names the marketing people had dreamt up. Sylvan Close, Beech Crescent, Lime Grove, Maple Court, Redwood Close. Despite the change, there was a hazy familiarity that hung over the road.

Matthew became aware of a dull ache just below his sternum and now he felt it sharpening as though a spiny-fingered hand was snatching at his innards. It was the ache of loss. Of childhood, of his mother. And particularly of his father. The image of his dead father lying, with his soft white hair, upon the platform at the undertakers came to him; a trickle of tear ran from an eye.

After composing himself, he stopped the car and looked at his maps, a contemporary one and a 1960s version. Redwood Close looked the most likely to have been built on Hyghcliff land. He pulled in to the close and parked in a visitors' bay. Small, detached houses, four-bedroomed by the look of them, built in uniform style with fenced patches of garden. Cabined, cribbed, confined, compared to the spacious freedom of his childhood.

But, as he got out of the car and looked up, there it was. Unbelievably. Towering behind one of the houses. The Wellingtonia. *Sequoiadendron giganteum*. The magnificent redwood. Ah! The clue had been in the name of the road: Redwood Close. Less a marketing man's inducement, he had to admit, and more a planning department's acknowledgement of a piece of heritage.

Both his parents had loved the tree. At the time the house was built, it would have been an exotic planting, the first seeds brought over from North America only a few years earlier. His father had told him of the great rush for botanical exotica in the eighteenth and nineteenth centuries, the adventurous trips of people like Alexander von Humboldt and the Lobb brothers. And his mother told him that the ancient Celts believed that trees had spirits. But for young Matthew, with a world of Dinky toys to direct and lose himself in, trees were of little interest. Especially if they couldn't be climbed. The lowest limbs of this giant were too high and in any case they inclined at an angle downwards; no opportunity for exploration. But he did remember the bark of this tree, thick and ridged and red.

An urgent longing to touch the tree drew him to the front door of the house in whose garden it appeared to be. He rang the doorbell. No reply. He rang again. Waited. Nobody in. So he went to the side of the house where there was a six-foot-high wooden door to the garden. Locked or bolted. He stretched on tiptoe and reached over the top, locating a bolt which he slid free.

He was in. A neat patch of lawn, some borders, some shrubs and, in the corner of the garden, with a semi-circular bench placed beneath, the Wellingtonia. He walked towards it, and then looked round again. He wanted to get his bearings, to try to work out where the rockery would have been. Somewhere under the house, he suspected. All those roadways he'd excavated, the rocks his soldiers and tanks had hidden behind. All buried. Gone.

But the tree. The tree, like the Spanish Chestnut at

school, was another remarkable survivor. Not in terms of longevity, which nevertheless was significant, but because it had somehow escaped the developers' chainsaws and bulldozers at a time when planning laws were less strict. No doubt its value as a 'feature' had been its salvation.

He walked over to it, delighting in the rich redness of the bark. It was deeply rutted, and spongy even to the lightest touch. He ran his fingers down the fibrous ridges and fissures, pressing firmly and feeling the gentle give in the tissue. Millennia ago the Sequoia had developed this thick, porous bark as a defence against fire. It could surrender the protective coat to the rampaging flames, slough it off with its heartwood left intact, and grow it back to defend against the next calamitous event. The heat from the burning bark and the brushwood around the tree would open the cones so they could spill their seeds and colonise the scorched surroundings. What a remarkable survivor! Of course, in rural Berkshire, trial by fire was an unlikely hazard; the sharp teeth of a feller's saw were a more real and present danger these days. So now the tree was wrapped around with the new and abstract protection of a TPO. Matthew put his arms as far about the great trunk as he could manage, a gesture of love and of wished-for protection.

He turned to look at the garden again. And noticed, in an upstairs bedroom, that a woman was staring down at him. He gestured to her to open the window. As she put something down on the sill there was a flashing glint. My God, she had a knife.

'Hi. I'm sorry to be intruding. I did ring the doorbell twice but assumed there was nobody in, so I came through the side-gate. It's just…I used to live here, I grew up here as child.'

The woman, grey-haired and nervous looking, said,

'You can't have. We have lived here since the house was built.' There was some aggression in her voice.

'No, not this house, the old house, the big Victorian house.'

She snorted. 'Oh, that ugly old thing. Just as well they knocked it down.'

So the woman would have known Hyghcliff, thinks Matthew. 'Look, can I come in? Can we talk about the old house?'

'No. I've rung the police, they're on their way—'

'What?'

'Told them that there was an intruder in my garden.'

Matthew felt a surge of anger. He wanted to scream at the woman that it was a beautiful house, that it was his garden, that he was not an intruder. But as he filled his lungs for the scream, he felt his father's restraining presence; he sensed how unhappy his father would be if he created a scene. His inhalation became calming rather than the prelude to aggression. 'Well, look, I'll be on my way. I am so sorry to have disturbed you.' He started walking towards the side-gate, hearing the window slam shut. As he closed the gate and walked across the small patch of front lawn a police car drew up. The driver got out, a policeman with a hipster beard and hair close cropped at the sides. A young policewoman, blonde hair tied in a pony tail, emerged from the passenger door.

Matthew walked over to them. 'Are you answering a call from this house?' He gestured to where he had just come from. At that moment the front door opened. 'That's him,' the woman shouted.

The policeman nodded. He gestured with his head, indicating that his colleague should go and speak to the woman, and said to Matthew, 'If you'd wait over here with me, sir.'

Matthew explained that there had been a misunderstanding; he apologised for the fuss he had caused.

'All in good time, sir.'

There was a mumble of the women's voices. The policewoman was taking notes. But soon she was back.

'Right,' said the policeman, nodding again to his colleague.

'So, sir,' she said, 'I gather that you broke into the garden of this house.' She is looking him in the eye. She has quite an attractive face, Matthew thinks, but you would probably need to have a fetish for uniforms to fancy her when she was all kitted up. Heavy rubber-soled boots, multi-pocketed combat trousers, a gilet with many more pockets and loops, shaped for every possible eventuality; and a duty belt with pouches and slots for numerous pieces of kit. She was well equipped to ensure that Matthew was as good as gold: collapsible baton, chemical spray, handcuffs, a radio to call for back-up. And was that a Taser?

But she is not going to be his main interrogator. The policeman asks for his details. When Matthew has given them the policeman asks if there will be anyone at home.

'No, my wife is working today.'

'And are you in employment, sir?'

'Yes.'

'May I ask where?'

When Matthew tells him, he asks his colleague to check. 'Give them a bell, Tracy.'

'Now, look,' says Matthew, 'you don't have to ring them. You can look up the school online and you'll see me on the staff list.' He says this too quickly, possibly with a hint of alarm in his voice.

The policeman ignores him. He stretches out his thumb and little finger and brings his hand to the side of his face. The policewoman nods and brings out her phone.

'This really isn't necessary, officer,' he pleads.

The policewoman has got through to someone. She asks if Matthew Agnew works at the school. She nods towards her colleague.

'Description,' he instructs her.

Matthew then listens while she looks him up and down and speaks into her phone. He is unhappy with her description. The man she is describing is shorter than Matthew, a little plumper, perhaps, and has less hair than he is accustomed to seeing in the mirror.

Someone says something at the other end. The policewoman says thank you and then nods towards her colleague.

'Right, sir, well, that all checks and you don't appear to have any record. Now, could you please tell me what you were doing in this lady's garden?'

'I did try to explain to her, officer. That I grew up here. That her house, this development, has been built on the land that was our family home.'

The policewoman chips in. 'She says you were doing something to her tree.' The direct stare again, but twinkly eyes.

Matthew tries to explain. Explain about the tree. How it was old when he was young, how it represents continuity, the past pushing up against the present. And now he is twittering on about the bark and its fire-resistant qualities, its lack of resin.

The policewoman has begun to look at him in a different way. A look of concern? Of pity? The way she might look at her father perhaps when he said something foolish. 'All right, sir, I think we get the picture. And no harm has been done.'

Her colleague brings it all to a conclusion. 'I think we're done, sir. So…let that be a lesson learnt, sir.' He gives a smug grin. Did it give him pleasure telling a teacher, a former teacher, about learning lessons? Perhaps the man had hated school, hated teachers, and enjoyed every opportunity to get one over them.

They get in their car and drive off. Matthew goes to his car and for some moments just sits there, trying to take in the bizarre events that have just occurred. And then he looks again at the house and tries to work out where the visitors' parking bay is in relation to the old house and garden. He notices a beech tree close to the road that stood by one of the entrances. And all of a sudden he can hear feet crunching the gravel of the semi-circular drive at the front of Hyghcliff. Remembers the sound of his father returning from work, of the milkman calling early in the morning, of visitors coming to the heavy oak front door and ringing the bell.

And randomly, uninvited, another memory comes back to him. Of the time he had brought a friend back to tea one day after school, a boy called Stephen Essen. How strange that he should remember a name that he had not recalled for nearly sixty years! The boy's father had been a butcher who had left Germany just before the war had broken out. Matthew remembered the strange sense of mystery that attached to the outcast Stephen, the mixed senses of fascination and pity that he and the other boys felt towards Essen's Germanic origins. The pair of them had crunched up the drive to find that Matthew's mother had prepared a sumptuous tea for them. He recalled the pride he had felt in his mother as she had met with Stephen's evident approval, and the delight as Stephen's manners had met with her approval.

Sitting here now, he was the outcast, banished from the Eden of his Hyghcliff childhood.

As he started up the engine, he looked towards the house again. There, from an upstairs window, the hostile woman was staring at him, making his sense of exile feel complete.

CHAPTER 19

Monday had been dominated by Ben Macpherson's account of the death of General Sir Peter Gilbert; Tuesday by the theft of the Chapman File, the visit to Hyghcliff and the nonsense with the police. Today Matthew was hoping for some quiet, for a resumption of the ordinary, sometimes mercifully dull business of the archive. He had received some reels of cine footage from the daughter of a recently deceased former pupil. The labels suggested it was of the school, but there was no date. The boy had attended in the second half of the 1930s; with any luck the film would contain some kind of record of those times.

Matthew had sent it away for digitisation and had received a DVD at the end of the previous week. He put the disc in his computer drive and sat poised with a pen and a pad ready to take notes.

A soundless image appeared, grainy and incomplete, spreading across the screen like a sandstorm; in a matter of seconds it had formed itself into clear footage of the school's entrance arch. A steady hand was walking the camera into the school. The river comes into view; on the other side men are scything grass. The next clip is of a fire: the Examination Hall is ablaze. It is the following day now, most of the building has been saved and is shown smouldering. Matthew pauses the DVD and consults the digital collection of the school magazine, quickly confirming that the fire was on 19 October 1937. Excellent! A date for the footage. One must assume that all the clips are from a similar period.

What soon becomes clear is that the film is a chronicle of the academic year 1937/38. There is blurry footage of sport: rugby, hockey and cricket, rowing, gymnastics; and some athletics, a successful attempt at the high jump, with a slow-motion repeat. There is a CCF parade, the cadets looking extremely well drilled. Some of them will be doing the real thing in no time at all. Finally, it is the end of the year and Speech Day. A grainy monochrome, of course, but vivid in its familiarity. Only the way the parents dress, especially the mothers, has changed. The ritual is as ever was and as ever will be. Perhaps. Come the revolution…

The whole film is little more than twenty minutes. It a satisfying addition to the archive and Matthew sets about cataloguing it, including an index of its timings. It is good to be back in the routine!

The phone goes. The Headmaster's Secretary. Will Matthew book in to see the Head before the end of the week? Forty-five minutes. (What?) And, she adds, Mr Dogget suggests that he bring along a 'friend' if he wish. Oh dear. Hence the forty-five minutes. A Disciplinary, by the sound of it. For what? For not having a Security Protocol? Ridiculous.

He books in for eleven o'clock the next day. Then he emails Leo Beamish, asking if he will be his newest bestest friend, explaining that he has been summoned by the Head, and asked to bring a 'friend', so presumably he is in the Dogget house for something or other. Leo quickly emails back to say he will get cover for his lesson and will be there.

*

The Headmaster's study is one of the finest rooms in the school. Double-aspected, one view takes in most of the main teaching areas, allowing an overview of the comings and goings between the different departmental buildings; the other offers a panoramic vista of the grounds: formal lawns, playing fields, the edge of the arboretum. A large desk is positioned in the corner of the room that gives the fullest outlook. The main furnishings form a large U in the middle of the room, two sofas facing each other and two arm chairs at an angle of forty-five degrees to each other and to the ends of the sofas; the open end of the U faces towards an elaborate but unused fireplace. The most spectacular feature of this fine room is its rococo ceiling, with delicately gilded curves and cornices, and a graceful raised design filled in with little landscape paintings in the Louis XV style.

At eleven o'clock Matthew knocks on the door and hears his summons. He enters with Leo Beamish, whose cheerful countenance belies the concern he feels for his friend. However, there is a problem, one which will darken the expression of Leo and will alarm Matthew.

'Ah,' says the Headmaster. 'Leo is your "friend". That can't be, I'm afraid. For reasons that will become clear very shortly. Leo, if you could leave us, please.' He goes, muttering an exhortation of some sort to Matthew; or perhaps cursing the Headmaster. 'And Matthew, if you would like to rearrange this meeting and bring another "friend", I'm happy to postpone.'

'Er...no, let's get on with it.'

Another problem. Sitting in one of the armchairs,

clipboard and pen in hand, is Henry Baines, Deputy Head. So, a witness for the Headmaster. Notes to be taken. Henry is trying to look serious; he is trying, not very hard and with little success, not to look smug.

'Okay, if you would like to take a seat…Henry is here to take notes.'

'Right. Fine.' Wrong. Not fine. Matthew is very unhappy with his presence. He knows that, notes or no notes, Henry will revel in every detail of Matthew's discomfort, will pass up no opportunity to grin superciliously at whatever transgression it is that Dogget has summoned him to hear.

Matthew has sat on one of the sofas and the Headmaster now sits on the other, directly opposite him. 'Right, Matthew,' says Dogget, 'there are three issues I want to…discuss with you. I'll deal with them chronologically.'

Three? 'Three? Oh…right. Fire away.' Matthew is determined to hide any rising sense of unease.

'So, I am going to present you with three areas of your behaviour which I am unhappy with.' He looks to Henry Baines and glances down at his clipboard, a signal to start taking notes. Dogget has his own clipboard from which he will read the arraignment. 'The first point concerns a complaint from Saskia Quinlan.' A complaint from Sass? What? 'She spoke to Sarah Smith at the beginning of last term.' Sarah Smith is the Senior Mistress. Matthew, already uneasy, now feels some irritation rising. 'She told Sarah that you had summoned her to the Archive Room at the end of the Christmas term and had spoken to her about a sexual liaison she had had with a member of staff.'

'So?'

'What do you mean, "so", Matthew? It is completely inappropriate for you to have a young woman alone in your archive room.'

'Young woman? For goodness' sake, she's nearly

thirty. She's not a pupil, she's a teacher. I was her head of department for a couple of years before I became archivist.'

'And it's not appropriate for a woman to be spoken to about her sex life by a man old enough to be her father.'

Matthew remembers that, during the night after he had seen Saskia, he had awoken with an erection, as unusual an occurrence for him these days as waking to a morning's cock-crow. However, he does not believe that he had spoken to her explicitly about her sex life, as Dogget has suggested, and he is surprised that she has made a complaint. And that Dogget is bringing it up five months after the event.

'But...' says Matthew

'But? But what?'

'Well, I don't mean to be pedantic, Headmaster, but isn't that exactly appropriate? Isn't a father – a parent, at any rate – exactly the person to give a child advice on sexual matters? Or is that a responsibility that the modern age has abrogated?'

There are signs of growing irritation in Dogget and an effort at control. 'Matthew, I don't mind your pedantry. I'm used to it. It's your flippancy I don't like. And your chosen blindness to the way things are these days. The way we as teachers are expected to behave.'

'I don't know what you mean. The way we are expected to behave. Have I behaved inappropriately?'

'I have just told you that you have.'

'Well, I disagree. I did nothing inappropriate. Saskia should have told *me* if she thought it was wrong.'

'Nevertheless, this is an incident that should not have taken place...And it will go on your record...Please note that specifically, Henry.'

Henry has been scribbling away noisily. Irritatingly. A full set of notes for the record. Matthew recalls that a well-known game amongst pupils is to stare at the angry wart on the side of his neck. A particular pupil is designated before a lesson begins. He or she needs to stare intently at the wart until Baines starts dabbing it. If there is no blood on his finger or handkerchief, the pupil is deemed to have won the challenge. If blood is visible after the dabbing, the pupil is deemed to have lost his or her challenge, and the forfeit is to groan loudly saying something like, 'Eeeuugh, sir, that's disgusting!' eliciting a 'Be quiet, child, don't be so silly' from Baines.

Matthew stares fixedly at the wart. The Headmaster is continuing to speak; Baines is either taking notes or doodling. Without looking directly at Matthew, Baines seems aware that his ruby-coloured jewel is being inspected. A hand automatically reaches into a pocket for a handkerchief. A quick dab; a quick glance at the handkerchief. A speckle of blood. And now a finger dabs at the wart. A finger inspection, followed by more dabbing with the handkerchief. The creature does not like all this attention. It is now spitting blood. Baines holds the handkerchief to his neck with one hand, with the other takes notes (or doodles) on a clipboard that is now balancing precariously on his knee.

Dogget continues. 'Secondly, Matthew, I was very unhappy to learn, after the break-in to the Archive Room earlier in the week, that you have not seen fit to complete a Security Protocol. It seems to typify to me the way you seem to think that you are above these things. That you don't have to comply with the procedures that other staff have to.'

Matthew thinks that, working in the highest room in the school, he *is* above these things. However, he has the presence of mind not to say so, eschewing for the time being the wordplay that he so loves. 'As I told you on

Tuesday, Headmaster, this was an oversight. I apologised and told you I would get right onto it.'

Henry Baines has been dabbing away at his cursed wart which has broken into open rebellion. He removes the handkerchief from his neck to inspect it; it is now bearing a strong resemblance to the Japanese national flag.

'Oh for God's sake, Henry, do stop fiddling,' explodes Dogget. 'Look, go out and get yourself cleaned up as quickly as you can.'

Henry stands and moves for the door, mumbling an apology. Matthew regards his exit as a very real victory. Or, at any rate, a victory of sorts A victory of warts, perhaps. 'Are we able to proceed without him, Headmaster? I mean, does the…' (He wants to say 'protocol', but bites his tongue) '…does the procedure allow for the meeting to continue without the Deputy Head here to take notes?'

Dogget senses that Matthew is trying to rile him. He pauses and smiles and says, 'We can wait for his return, Matthew. He shouldn't be long.'

'So, off the record, Toby: "If you'll patch a quarrel, / As matter whole you have to make it with, / It must not be with this".'

A quizzical response. With an audible but wordless sound of irritation.

'It's Antony. *Antony and Cleopatra*. Antony telling Octavius Caesar that his complaints are petty.'

'Matthew, are you trying to be provocative?'

'No. No. I just think you are being a little harsh on me.'

Henry Baines soon returns. A lump of cotton wool, already mildly bloodied, has been stuck over the offending wart with sticking plaster. The collar of Henry's shirt has been drenched. 'I'm sorry, Toby. I think it's sorted now.'

'Okay.' He nods Henry to the chair. 'So, Matthew, the third matter I wish to discuss with you concerns a phone call the school received the day before yesterday. I gather you went off campus and got yourself arrested.'

Matthew snorts. 'Arrested? Arrested!'

'Yes. The police rang us to check that the person they had in custody was you.'

'Had in custody?' Matthew laughs out loud, a bitter laugh. 'Right, Toby, this is what happened.' And he explains his visit to the site of his childhood home, his first visit since it was demolished, his longing to touch a special tree that he had grown up with. Technically he had trespassed; he had tried and failed to get the homeowner's permission. He had assumed she was out. She was not. She had called the police.

Baines' hand is whizzing across and down the page of his clipboard as he tries to keep up. Dogget is not interrupting; listening with impassive face.

'She called the police. They asked who I was. I told them. They checked with the school…I was not arrested. They were perfectly happy with my explanation. That was an end of it.'

There is silence for a moment as Dogget collects his thoughts. He glances down at his clipboard and then looks at Matthew, again with an impassive expression. 'Matthew, I know that none of these incidents in themselves are serious matters. But there is a pattern. A pattern to your behaviour which I find worrying.' Worrying? Why? How? 'I think maybe it is all becoming a little too much for you…I have spoken with the Chairman of the Governors and he agrees with me that we should suggest that you step down from your role at the end of term. That it is time for you to take things easy.'

Matthew is shocked. Speechless.

'This is not a sacking. It would be a resignation,' Dogget continues. 'And I'm sure we could make some kind of financial settlement. Nothing big, mind.'

Matthew feels defeated. He has not seen this coming. He wants to get out of the Headmaster's study, his beautiful study, as quickly as he can. 'Headmaster, can I think about this overnight? Talk to Rachel about it before we go any further?'

'Of course, Matthew, of course.'

*

It was a confused Matthew who returned home to an excited welcome from Foxy. He was hoping that Rachel would offer him comfort and consolation. However, the conversation got off to the wrong start and quickly descended into a raging row. Matthew's mistake, perhaps, had been to say that he had been sacked, which was how he saw it, rather than being asked to resign. The niceties of nuance between jumping and being pushed seemed irrelevant in the face of losing a job he had grown to love.

'Sacked?' Rachel had said, incredulous. 'What on earth have you done?' He had discussed his visit to Hyghcliff with her and she had sympathised; this strand of Dogget's dissatisfaction did not come into play. But he had never mentioned his meeting with Saskia and it was Matthew's failure to discuss it with her at the time, and his obviously clumsy way of dealing with a matter he should never have taken on in the first place, that angered her. And perhaps there was a tinge of jealousy, too. She probably knew that her husband had always found Saskia attractive.

So, Rachel's initial surprise had quickly become anger and had moved up another couple of gears when he said that Dogget was unhappy with the failure to produce a Security Protocol.

'And why didn't you? Because you know better?' That was provocatively close (in Matthew's mind) to what Dogget had said.

'No, because I never got round to it. And he would never have known if the Archive Room hadn't been burgled.'

'And why was that? Why was it burgled, Matty?' The nasal 'm' of Matty dripped disdain.

'Because someone wanted to retrieve the research papers I had on David Chapman.'

'Precisely…Because you went on and on with your foolhardy enquiry into something that was none of your business.' She is speaking loudly and aggressively now.

'Of course it was my business. I'm the archivist.'

'*Was* the archivist!'

Ouch. 'That's cheap.'

'I don't care!' She is shouting now. 'You stupid, stupid man. You were told to leave all this alone, but you couldn't. Oh no, you know best…The man on your history tour told you to stop.' Ah, yes, Tommy Cooper. But she is not calling him that. To do so would lighten the tone, would mitigate her anger. 'Your father told you not to go on. Kitty told you to stop. But oh no, not you. You know best!' Rachel's sea-grey eyes are raging. Matthew is feeling queasy. Storm-tossed.

'No, I don't know best,' he says quietly. 'I'm fucking useless. I often feel that. Increasingly so.'

'So why did you pursue this? Why? What were you hoping to achieve?'

'I was curious. It was a challenge.'

'A challenge! I'll tell you why. Because that's you. In control. Wanting to pull the strings. Wanting to think that you, clever you, mighty you, has solved the mystery of David Chapman…has brought down a government minister.'

'It's not like that at all…Look, I've had enough of this. I'm going to take Foxy for a walk.'

'You've had enough of this? *You've* had enough of this! You've just got yourself sacked and you've had enough of this?'

He's picked up the lead and is halfway to the door, Foxy in eager tow.

As he goes he says over his shoulder, 'I haven't been sacked, I've been asked to resign.'

'What?'

*

Matthew and Foxy walk westwards along the river before heading onto a wooded hillside. Purple aquilegia is in bloom and there are carpets of wild garlic. Matthew remembers hacking out into the country on horseback when a child at Hyghcliff; there was a particular banked bridleway through woodland where the smell of springtime wild garlic was overpowering. At that time it was a strange, somewhat unattractive smell; these were the days before garlic had become a stock item in most English kitchens.

The day had started pleasantly, with his viewing once more the film footage of the school in the 1930s. The meeting with the Headmaster had been a shock, and Rachel's withering anger deeply unpleasant and upsetting. But…did the Headmaster have a point? Was Matthew becoming erratic? Was Rachel right to be angry? Had he let her down? And others? As the soft spring air filled his lungs and he took pleasure from seeing Foxy gambolling joyfully ahead, his mind began to settle. He could see how he might be an irritant to Dogget. The man had a tidy mind. He liked things clear-cut. Yes, he had his silly protocols, but they were simply a way of ordering the complex structure of a school in very competitive times. Perhaps it was the moment to hand the archive over to somebody else.

And, yes, he had let Rachel down. He had been headstrong, he had done things without telling her. He had ignored his father's advice and broken his promise to Kitty Harper. Rachel was right to take him to task. He would tell her that when her got home. But was she right to say it was about his wanting control? Wanting to pull the strings? Wanting to exercise his cleverness? He thought not. Is so far as he could understand his motive, this was not it. He remembered his father saying that we are the most unreliable historians of ourselves; one might add to this the observation that self-analysis is not always the truest path to self-knowledge. But insofar as he did understand himself, he felt that the drive to get to the bottom of the Chapman story had been more an exercise of curiosity than anything else; of being dissatisfied with the missing pieces of the narrative; of being driven to piece together something whole, something complete. But then...perhaps at its heart lay the most basic urge of all, towards knowledge, the complete knowledge that allowed one to be in control. To be in control of one's life. As on the ordered rockery at Hyghcliff: a world of Dinky toy traffic directed by Matthew along the carefully bulldozed pathways.

*

On his return, Rachel rushed to the door and threw her arms around him. 'I'm so sorry,' she said. 'I was wrong to get angry, Matty. And I said some horrid things.'

He squeezed her to him. 'No, I think you were right, darling. I was foolish to go on with the Chapman thing.'

While he had been out with Foxy, she had thought about his parting revelation that it had not been an outright sacking but a request to resign; she had decided that this put a different slant upon the business. Her lawyer's mind had worked through Matthew's account of his meeting with Dogget. If the complaint about Saskia had not been relayed to Matthew until five months after the event, then it was questionable; in any case, Saskia should have told him that she intended to make a complaint about him. The failure to produce a Safety Protocol was certainly a disciplinary matter, but in the first instance should have resulted in a written warning rather than constituting an element in a resignation issue. The fact that Matthew had been spoken to by a couple of police officers was neither here nor there. Permission had been granted to go off campus; to call the conversation with the police 'an arrest' was beyond absurd, said Rachel. It sounded, she said, that it was Dogget who was losing the plot rather than Matthew; and she suggested the callousness of the man in not taking the recent death of Matthew's father into account. 'I think, darling, that you have complete freedom of choice in how you proceed. The request for you to submit your resignation can clearly be argued as Constructive Dismissal. If you want to carry on as archivist, you should.'

Matthew kissed her on the forehead. 'The judgement of Solomon!' he said.

They spent the evening on the sofa together, holding hands, cuddling sometimes, feeling very close to each other as they watched television and later listened to music.

That night, Matthew dreamt he was in the Grand Hall. A revue of some kind was being performed and Matthew and Rachel were in the front row of the audience. The Master of Ceremonies, clad in tails and wearing a top hat was...was Toby Dogget! 'Ladies and Gentleman, next up for your complete and delighted entertainment is the prestidigitating Mr David Blaine!'

But it is not David Blaine, it is the protean figure – back for an encore in Matthew's dreamscape – of Tommy Cooper! He calls for a volunteer. From the audience up steps Henry Baines. Matthew boos him enthusiastically! Cooper asks for and pulls from Henry's fleshy finger his signet ring, which has at its centre a huge blood-red stone. Cooper's large hand then pulls a handkerchief from Henry's pocket, a handkerchief that seems to go on and on until it assumes the size of a king-size bedsheet. It is the Japanese national flag! Tommy Cooper drapes it over Toby Dogget, utters a spell that concludes with a curt 'Desist!', whips the sheet away and…Dogget has disappeared! 'Just like that!' says Cooper with a throaty chuckle.

CHAPTER 20

July. The school year has concluded. July, and Matthew Agnew is no longer the school archivist. He and Rachel are in Marlow, staying for the weekend in Michael's flat; they had stayed as his guests on the equivalent weekend the previous year, a sad symmetry. Probate on Michael's estate has come through and the Agnews are sorting out the contents of the flat. Shortly the fate of the flat itself, to be sold or not, will be decided.

Matthew is alone. He is walking along the towpath between Marlow and Cookham; he has a great heaviness in his heart. The visit has been painful, much more painful than anticipated. The flat is full of ghosts. The familiar furnishings emphasise its emptiness. They seem to cry out for Matthew's absent father, who will never again sit in his favourite armchair, which over time has moulded itself to his shape; who will never again climb into the bed that retains still the distinctive smell of the man; who will never again polish with attentive care the marquetry chest that has memorialised his wife for three decades.

It is a big decision, whether to sell the flat, or whether Rachel and Matthew should move into it themselves. Matthew's siblings don't mind. They have no use for it and will be happy to receive their share of the proceeds either from the sale of the flat or of the Agnews' house in the North Wessex Downs. There are attractions to riverside living, for sure, and there is logic, at their age, to downsizing. But the ghosts! The ghosts. And leaving their house by the arboretum would be a painful uprooting.

The previous day Matthew and Rachel had agreed on the destiny of the contents of the flat. Most of the books will go to the History Faculty at Reading University. The desk, a large Edwardian piece in mahogany, will be shipped out to Douglas in Germany. The marquetry chest, with its Meissen monkey band playing their cracked airs, will come into Matthew's care. When he and Rachel had arrived at the flat, he had immediately gone to it and placed his palms gently upon its shining surface in the way he had seen in father do so often, his ritual attempt to feel the presence of his beloved Bridget. And while Matthew wanted to feel her presence, too, it was his father, his deeply missed father, he wished to touch; to sense the hands that had polished the gleaming wood so many times; to offer his confirmation that now he, Matthew, would be the custodian of the treasured piece.

Rachel is back at the flat sorting through Michael's clothes, a task that Matthew feels is beyond him at the moment. She will decide what should be thrown away and what might usefully be given to charity shops. It has been arranged that Mrs Knowles will collect the sorted clothes later in the day and dispose of them appropriately. When she had visited the day before, Matthew had told her that she had been left a small bequest, which had prompted another touching eulogy from her. And he had asked her if there was anything in the flat that she was particularly fond of and would like to keep. Hesitantly, from a hesitancy borne out of a sense of unworthiness rather than uncertainty as to what she wanted, she pointed to a sculpted frog that stood by one of the doors.

'Of course,' says Matthew. 'Do you know, I've never really looked at it closely before.'

'I've always loved it,' she says. 'It's made of serpentine – red Cornish marble. From the Lizard, your father told me. Sculpted by a Penzance man from a piece of the Lizard. A chunk of the Lizard! Can you imagine! Your father bought it in St Ives….So he called it Ivan the Frog!' She gives an affection little laugh and a tear begins to well in an eye. 'Are you sure I can have it, Mr…Matthew?'

'Yes, I would love you to have it. And so would my father.' Matthew is touched to learn of the warmth of his father's relationship with Mrs Knowles. Touched that she knows all about Ivan the Frog while he knows nothing. He has never really looked at it properly before. When he picks it up he is surprised by its weight. It is a lovely creation. It stands about nine inches high, a frog with huge eyes hunched upon a rock that is rough textured and light brown in colour. The frog has been sculpted from the same piece of serpentine and polished finely to reveal a rich pattern of browns and reddish browns, with thin white and black veins running irregularly through it.

He hands it to her. She is ready for the weight of it. No doubt she has dusted it many times. Picked it up and marvelled at this chunk of the Lizard many times. And now it is hers!

Matthew has not brought Foxy with him on his walk. He wants to be solitary so that he can think; keeping an eye on Foxy, especially where the towpath runs close to the railway line, would be a distraction. He is walking through Bourne End Marina, with its rows of pontoons reaching into the river. On the opposite bank lies The Bounty, thronged with summer trade, and Cock Marsh;

beyond its flatness, Winter Hill rises up gently, disfigured these days by a golf course.

Soon it is time to cross the river. To mount the footbridge that has been cantilevered out from the old Bourne End railway bridge. As he crosses he pauses to look down on the river below. The current runs swiftly around the steel piers of the bridge, but bits of detritus get temporarily snagged; an almost disintegrated cigarette packet, a half decomposed piece of reed flapping impotently. A vagabond flag upon the stream. Matthew decides that he will continue his walk to The Ferry, have a bite of lunch and then return to the flat.

*

It is July. David Chapman is still getting his feet under the Cabinet table. Is he impressing David Cameron? Who can tell? It is July, and Matthew Agnew is no longer the school archivist, no longer doing the job he had loved, cherished even. He has resigned. Or was he sacked?

As he walks downstream, Matthew reflects on the sequence of misjudgements that culminated in his final visit to Toby Dogget's study. He relives the panic that David Chapman must have felt when he killed Sir Peter Gilbert. Wonders what induced Sir Peter to make his foolish, tipsy lunge at David. Feels the pain of Christopher Harper as he is bounced into agreeing with the foolish decision, the criminal decision, to disguise the true circumstances of Sir Peter's death. What he cannot begin to understand is why Tony Marshall, Doctor Tony Marshall, took such a risk in allowing the lie to be written upon Sir Peter's Death Certificate. 'Present at Death'. No, Tony Marshall was not present at the death. It was David Chapman and he alone who heard the hard thud of Sir Peter's head that knocked the life out him. Men's judgements a parcel of their fortunes? Were Tony Marshall's fortunes so parlous as to allow such a foolish and dangerous misjudgement? His love of the school, his concern for reputation: admirable. But where was his integrity? Was he tortured with guilt thereafter? Or did a slippery conscience bring quick forgetfulness? And what about Mr and Mrs Chapman? Were they not foolish in making an endowment to the school? So soon after the incident? Would not suspicious minds see something sinister, something bribe-like in the donation, suggesting complicity in the death, or at least in the cover-up?

But the lie, once told, had to be lived. It would have continued to live in its dormant state if Matthew had not chanced upon the stray page of the letter from Tony Marshall to Christopher Harper. And had not been foolish enough to persist in his blundering enquiry. He had ignored his father's advice and written a silly letter to David Chapman. When this had brought the heavy tread of Tommy Cooper into his life, he had persisted. Had ignored Kitty Harper's advice. And not until he had solved the mystery through the telling of the story by Ben Macpherson had he stopped. By then, of course, it was too late. A chain of actions had been set in train. Men's judgements.

Tommy Cooper. Another misjudgement surely. Why had Chapman risked his reputation by calling upon a 'heavy' to frighten a humble school archivist? Men's judgements? Ah, yes. Chapman's fortunes on the up. In need of protection. But the risk.

*

The morning after Dogget had summoned Matthew to his study and told him he wanted him to resign, Matthew had awoken with a light sense of optimism. Rachel, solicitor Rachel, had told him that he need not resign if he didn't want to. And he didn't. He emphatically didn't. He could utter the phrase 'Constructive Dismissal'; it would give the school pause for thought, she had said. And he had awoken with the aura of dream still about him. He had dreamt of a comedy revue in the Grand Hall; Tommy Cooper had magicked away Toby Dogget! He took the dream to be a communiqué from his undervoice. Telling him that he should not fear Dogget. And that he should not resign. He had booked in to see him the following Monday.

The Toby Dogget who welcomed him into his study was in buoyant mood, expansively cheerful with Matthew. He invited him to sit down. No Henry Baines, Matthew noted. A sign of Dogget's confidence in the outcome of the meeting?

'Well, Matthew. You've thought about the little matter we discussed last week? Discussed it with Rachel?'

Matthew nodded. 'Yes, I have.' A look of pleased expectancy from Dogget. 'And we both feel that I should not resign. So, thank you for your kind offer, but I would like to continue as archivist.'

A cloud across the sunny countenance that has been gracing Toby Dogget's face. Surprise. An indignant 'What?' And then a quick recovery to composure and an oily, 'Matthew, are you sure about this?'

Another nod from Matthew.

'Now listen, Matthew, I'm holding all the cards, believe me. So. Do you want to stick or twist?' A definite sharpening of the tone. A hint of threat.

'Rachel has taken me through this, Toby. She tells me that the proper dismissal procedures have not been followed and that if you fire me I could argue Constructive Dismissal.'

What sounds like a growl seems to escape from Dogget. An irreverent thought fleets through Matthew's mind. He wants to tell Dogget that he knows a man, a big bruiser of a man, who can magic him away. So he had better watch his step!

'Matthew, I had wanted to avoid this – for all kinds of reasons, which you will probably understand – but you are forcing my hand. I would like you to resign, and am happy to argue for some kind of financial settlement, small. But if you don't resign, I shall fire you. I have had a complaint that you have been harassing David Chapman, no less.' Matthew is silent. Shocked. Wondering who has made the complaint. Ben Macpherson? Kitty Harper? Presumably not Chapman himself. Dogget breaks the brief silence. 'If you want me to go into chapter and verse I will, but I am going to give you one last chance to take the sensible course.'

*

Matthew is approaching Cookham Bridge, The Ferry just beyond. He had of course taken the sensible option. Of course? He had taken the sensible option. Because to have taken the other option might have pitted him against unknown forces. Did Dogget know the truth about Sir Peter? About Christopher Harper? Was he now a guardian of the lie? The Lie. Matthew was tired; the fight, the curiosity had gone. He has been depressed for a while now. The grieving for his father has intensified the melancholia that has crept up on him, enveloping him with a sense of the inadequacy – pointlessness, perhaps – of his teaching career. And now, the loss of his archive role. What left? Give me your arm, old toad; help me down Cemetery Road. But no old toad to assist; he had been cruelly snatched away.

At the end of term he had paid one last visit to the Archive Room. As he collected his belongings, scooped them into a bag, he took a last look at the river below and at the dead alder tree on the opposite bank on which a basking cormorant sometimes perched. The blanched, bone-like branches were birdless today. They looked more like a *momento mori* than the roosting perch of a living creature.

*

The barman serving Matthew at The Ferry is cheerful and chatty. A student, probably, doing holiday work. He recommends the steak and kidney pie and pours a glass of cheap Rioja. Matthew finds a small table that looks out onto the river, with its busy flow of boats and happy people, and waits for his pie.

Somebody observing the solitary figure would note that he is not one of the happy people. They would see a middle-aged man (elderly?) with an expression of pensive sadness on his face.

Matthew is thinking about the events of the last year. There had been a moment when it had seemed that he was dealing with a story containing the old-fashioned elements of tragedy. A brilliant young man, successful, with even greater laurels beckoning. A brilliant young man, ambitious, power-hungry and successful, brought down through a small error; a misjudgement made in a moment of turmoil. A brilliant young man who in a moment of weakness has listened to his co-conspirators and taken the wrong course of action. A brilliant young man who carries a secret, the exposure of which will destroy him. A brilliant man, no longer young, who in a moment of hubris, hires a scoundrel to deal with his nemesis. Career in tatters.

But this is not the story at all. In the story that Matthew is retelling, there are no kings or princes, no heroes of high tragedy, no villains. He has come to understand the way it perhaps was always going to end. No great exposure. The defeat of the little man. A loser. It has not after all been the story of David Chapman, whose sort, in the end, with their power and their privilege, always win. It has been the story of Matthew Agnew. And what kind of story? Melodrama? No. Not enough action or suspense to bate the breath. Matthew Agnew is, in the parlance of cricket, a batsman who has scored nothing; and if St Peter, at the Pearly Gates, were to resort to a cliché beloved of cricket commentators, he would no doubt say that Matthew had not troubled the scorers. Not enough good, not enough bad. An ordinary life. The life of the little man. Willie Loman, Michael Henchard, J. Alfred Prufrock. Willie Loman, dreamer of dreams, seeker of success and significance, choosing a senseless death that will not achieve his unachievable dream.

*

Matthew is heading back to Marlow. Once more he is standing on the Bourne End footbridge, looking down upon the river. His love of wordplay has not deserted him despite his gloomy thoughts. He notes with satisfaction the name Bourne End. The End of Bourne. He is thinking of a famous line of Bob Dylan's, 'He not busy being born is busy dying'. Ha! The end of born.

How tempting to slip in. To drift away. He'd written a novel thirty years earlier; for three decades it had lain in a box file in his study. Unread. Untouched. But he still remembered its last sentence, a sentence that much of the latter part of the narrative had been moving inexorably towards: 'Never had the river looked so inviting'.

To slip in. Now? He could find a suitable piece of the riverbank and slip away, but soon would be bobbing along in full view of the people aboard cruisers, of walkers on the towpath. He would be ignominiously hauled out, grappled with a boathook perhaps. He would have to invent, for his rescuers, some mishap that had tumbled him into the water; or to admit that he had decided to do away with himself. Better, much better to slip out in the darkness, hoping not to be spotted by an all-night fisherman or a midnight reveller. To cease upon the midnight with no pain.

He takes the stairs down from the cantilevered pedestrian bridge and walks to the edge of the water. Here in his mind he rewrites the end of the novel he had written thirty years earlier.

> He moved to the riverside of the bridge. A late-night cruiser was making its way upstream, a nearly full moon reflecting a silvery path for it to follow through the water. As it passed, its wash created a small eddy. In a moment, the river closed around it and it was as if it had never been. He looked down beneath the bridge. In the half-light he could see a discarded cigarette packet floating on a lazy current. The river would sweep it downstream, through locks, over weirs, and by degrees it would decay. Snagged on a pier of the bridge was a decomposing piece of reed flapping impotently. A vagabond flag upon the stream. Sweet Thames, run softly, till the end of my song.
>
> The moon gleamed on the smooth, silvery surface of the water. Never had the river looked so inviting.

But wait. Willy Loman was wrong. His sons were ordinary, no better, no worse. His wife was better than ordinary.

He was so wrong. And so was Matthew. The increasingly intense moments of gloomy self-doubt, of deep dejection from which he suffered were self-indulgent. He'd had a privileged life in a privileged corner of the world. He wasn't the best teacher that ever lived, he wasn't the greatest leader of men. He was ordinary. And his partner, his pilgrim through life, was better than ordinary. She was more than half of the whole that was their relationship. She brought blessing to his life. And as he walked along the towpath, he knew she would be waiting for him in his father's flat.

A man had just pushed a small rowing boat out from a landing. Two young children in life jackets sat in the stern, clinging on tightly to the bench while the father manoeuvred the craft out into the river. The prow had nosed downstream, and he was pulling strongly on one oar to turn the boat about.

'And so we beat on, boats against the current'…As the quotation came to mind, Matthew reflected that so much of his experience of life, of his world view even, had been mediated through literature. At one remove from direct experience. So what was the thing itself? The essence of things was surely not to be found in mere words.

He looked again at the craft. The father brought it parallel with the riverbank and started to row powerfully upstream, the boat bobbing like a nodding horse at each sweep of the oars until a steady rhythm was achieved. And now the children relaxed their grip on the bench and squawked in gleeful pleasure as the boat picked up speed.

A quickening of pace as Matthew headed upstream himself, keeping more or less abreast with the happy boatload. He walked towards where his own happiness awaited him. Where his world would be set to rights.

He had reached a terminus of sorts, for sure. But it was not the end.

Acknowledgements

With thanks to Special Rider Music for the
quotation from It's Alright, Ma (I'm Only
Bleeding) by Bob Dylan
Copyright © 1965 by Warner Bros. Inc.;
renewed 1993 by Special Rider Music

With thanks to Faber and Faber Ltd. for
permission to quote from
Waiting for Godot by Samuel Beckett
The Whitsun Weddings by Philip Larkin.

Also by the same author

"*Deadly Diplomacy gripped me from page one and made me want to carry on reading until all was revealed ... the insider knowledge for the storyline means that a genuine insight into the world of international diplomacy suffuses the whole book ... highly recommended.*" (www.crimesquad.com)

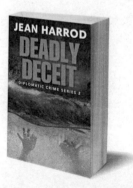

"*Jean has followed the first law of writing. Write about what you know. Jean Harrod is the Agatha Christie of the contemporary diplomatic world.*" (Alastair Goodlad, former Minister of State for Foreign Affairs)

"*Jean Harrod writes with an authoritative hand ... very readable.*" (www.lovereading.co.uk)